D1387290

NILE BABY

Elleke Boehmer

ayebia

An Adinkra symbol meaning
Ntesie maternasie
A symbol of knowledge and wisdom

Copyright © 2008 Ayebia Clarke Publishing Limited
Copyright © 2008 *Nile Baby* by Elleke Boehmer

This edition first published by
Ayebia Clarke Publishing Limited, 2008.
7 Syringa Walk
Banbury
OX16 1FR
Oxfordshire
UK

Co-published in Ghana with the Centre for Intellectual Renewal
No. 25 Olympic Road, Kokomlemle,
P. O. Box CT 3903,
Cantonments,
Accra, Ghana,
www.cir.com

Distributed outside Africa, Europe and the United Kingdom exclusively by
Lynne Rienner Publishers, Inc.
1800 30th St., Ste. 314
Boulder, CO 80301
USA
www.rienner.com

All rights reserved. No part of this publication may be reproduced in whole or
in part, except for the quotation of brief passages in reviews, without prior
written permission from Ayebia Clarke Publishers.

British Library Cataloguing-in-Publication Data
A catalogue record of this book is available from the British Library.

Cover design by Amanda Carroll at Millipedia
Original painting by Robert Craig ©

Typeset by FiSH Books, Enfield, Middlesex.
Printed and bound in Great Britain by CPI Cox & Wyman, Reading, RG1 8EX.

The publisher wishes to acknowledge the support of
Arts Council England SE Funding.

ISBN 978-0-9555079-3-9

Available from www.ayebia.co.uk or email info@ayebia.co.uk
Distributed in Africa, Europe & the UK by TURNAROUND at
www.turnaround-uk.com

The dead trail with the living still
Beyond amends.

David Constantine, 'At the Time'.

The Soul: My place of hiding is opened,
My place of hiding is disclosed.
Light illuminates my dark ditch.
I have hidden myself with you, stars that never cease to burn.
My face is revealed, my heart sits upon its throne.
I am here and am not banished.

The Egyptian Book of the Dead.

The Beginning

I know this for sure. When Alice Brass Khan saw the baby flop out of the glass jar that day, she saw in its eyes, nose, and mouth the shape of her own face. There they were; she spotted them that very minute, her own high African cheekbones.

* * *

The sunlight radiating through the branches of the weeping willow tree made a pattern of silver stars. In the middle of this galaxy stood Alice Brass Khan, my friend the Science Boffin, looking tall and disgusted. The drooping branches and the radiating light split her into strips of shining colour as if she were some person in a legend: a prophet, a healer from a different realm of life.

That was Alice with her bird-bright eyes, she was always more easily looked at in bits, in strips. The same as on the day we first spoke.

From the off, from the word go on that day we first spoke, she looked straight through me, like she knew everything about me.

Which she couldn't have done because it was only our second term at Woodpark Secondary and we'd arrived here from different primary schools at opposite ends of the city.

Which she might have done—looked straight into me, Quiet Arnie, I mean—because just the same as me she didn't fit in here, she wasn't a neat match. She saw like I saw that

Woodpark Secondary crawled with people who were taller, fitter, faster, louder and cooler than we were, *by far*. And not half as interested in the folded, wormy insides of things, be they alive or dead.

Things like the cold, wet body lump lying here at our feet with its crumpled grey forehead and squashed-in nose. And those tufts of strange, coarse *grown-up* hair sprouting at the back of its head.

That first time we spoke—it was the middle of winter, a sunny day, the second Friday lunch-break after Christmas—was also the first time I helped carry out her plans.

I crept up that day on her and her friend Yaz Yarnton, Alice swinging inside the stripy green octopus of the willow tree the same as now, Yaz sitting cross-legged burying her sandwich crusts under dead willow leaves. I came along softly like a cat-burglar behind curtains but I could tell she'd noticed me by how she shifted the direction of her swinging and looked at me out of the dark corner of her left eye.

At the very same minute we spotted the crime. It was Justine Kitchen in her shiny pink puffa jacket. Good-at-everything-and-admired-by-everyone Justine was taking a pencil-case off one of the little kids, Rahat maybe, or Saif, the kid jumping up and down like a poodle yelping on its hind legs.

At the very same minute we broke sprinting out of our cave of willow branches. I snatched the pencil-case and put it back in the little kid's hand. Alice grabbed the outstretched arm, pushed back the pink puffa, and gave the wrist a Chinese burn so sore Justine's eyes filled right up with tears.

That was Alice. No one so much as committed something unfair, including calling her Science Freak, Brown Boffin, Frankenstein and the other cruel names kids called her, without reaping the consequences.

2

Another minute and we were back inside the willow tree catching our breath and grinning at one another. And then I knew—like she knew but without saying a word—that the person standing there in front of them was a friend-in-arms.

By then Yaz with a bored face on had picked herself up off the ground and wandered in the direction of the bike sheds, the place where the girls who talked strictly about girl things always gathered.

That first day was the day we discovered that Alice's way home was pretty much the same as mine; down School Road with the smelly ditch on the right, and into narrow Selvon Street. Then my street, Stratford Street, where the two-up yellow-brick terraces looked exactly like the houses in her street, Albion, three streets down and to the left, at a right angle to Stratford.

That first day was the day we also discovered that by walking slowly and in time and dawdling at corners we could cover the whole range of our most interesting topics: like the thinness of the best skimming stones, and where to buy the sharpest penknives, and what kind of sticks are softest for whittling (willow is good). Also, the problem of growing up, or, better, how to avoid it for as long as possible (by ignoring it, mainly by skimming stones). As we got used to one another we now and then mentioned our sad and untidy families, but this was in short bursts and then on to the next thing. The topics we always returned to were knives, sticks and stones including the ammonite and the salt crystal we stole off her classroom's nature table and, best of all, the inner workings of living things (like the dog's eye I found for her after several weeks' searching).

Alice had it in her to be a True Young Scientist, at least that was what our biology teacher Mr Brocklebank said, and as long as I could tag by her side I was happy to help her make her discoveries. He said she had the steady hands and cool heart of a scientist, and, above all, the sharp eye of the pioneer investigator, the one who goes in front. To encourage her he lent her books—*The Human Anatomy Picture Book*, Paige's *Essential Physiology*, *The Pocket Atlas of the Moving Body*—but I lent her a hand, and watched how her lips moved like water around the difficult words: *Diverticulated*, *Mitochondrion, Squamous* and *Epithelium*.

For whole long weeks Alice and I were a team-of-two, operating in tandem, with Yaz Yarnton and everyone else well out of the picture. To me Alice was Energy and Ideas and Amazingness and all I wanted was to stick to her. I wanted to be her channel, her antenna, whatever it took to give shape to her schemes. I was the kid at school who hardly spoke, who didn't draw attention. Sticking close to Alice I felt different from myself somehow, woken-up and wide-awake, both at once.

Which is why today was so strange. It was strange even counting the day last month with the dog's eye. Today, I thought to myself, squinting up at her standing against the light, feeling the grey specimen pressing its wetness into my leg, today was the very first time some *thing*, *some body*, had properly come between us. Today Alice inside her nest of willow branches looked like she had seen a ghost. A ghost she knew well.

Chapter 1
Alice and Arnie

Alice Brass Khan watches the head poke into the open air, then drag its body after its shrivelled chest and grasshopper legs. She wiggles the Kerr jar to work it free. Formalin pours over her fingers. The body flumps to the ground, curled on its side. Fallen leaves and sand stick to a wet, pasty cheek that's not really cheek, just surface, rubber surface, like a key-ring doll.

The thing, a tiny person, is now facing her. She can see a flattish nose, a small, bunched chin. The face, if you'd call that crush of nose, eyes and cheek *face,* is human *and* not human, both at the same time. It frowns darkly at her.

She sits back on her haunches, leans against the rough bark of the weeping willow tree. She wipes her hands on her trousers.

'Oh damn, Alice. Damn-damn-damn! What do we do now?'

'*Shut up*, Arnie Binns.'

'We can't get it back in now, *ever.*'

Alice aims a sharp kick at her friend's shin. He lurches back. Scuffed dirt powders the small creature's head.

'Now you've gone and done it,' he mutters. 'What'll you do now? It's messed now, it's dirty. You can't put it back in.'

He huddles into his oversized fleece.

'You're no help, are you Barmy Arnie? 'Course we can put it back in. It came out of the jar, it can go back in. But first I want a closer look.'

'I'm not touching it whatever you say. No way.'

'No one was asking you to. I was always going to be the one to touch it.'

Alice stretches out her skinny, brown arm but can't make the contact. Her hand hovers over the body. She pulls the hand back, she sticks it out again. A new idea hits her. She tests the breeze on a wetted finger. Outside its usual watery environment, the thing, the *body*, could dry out fast.

She hears Quiet Arnie murmur, 'So what're you waiting for?'

Her fingers rush at it. The surface of the baby—or she should say *foetus*, she's read up on foetuses in the library's *The Body: An Amazing Tour*—the foetus surface is moist and oddly hard. It's awful. *Awful*. It doesn't *give* to her prod.

She rubs at a grain of sand that has stuck to the wasted dolly arm. The skin wrinkles as if it might strip back like a shirtsleeve, even peel right off. The grain of sand doesn't budge.

She hears Arnie sniff. She guesses he's probably crying.

'Time to get a move on,' she says. She won't look at him. She might want to slap him if she did. 'So what happened to everything you were saying about wanting a go? Helping me get the jar *no problem*? Even this morning. Let's rescue the *little creature*, you said.'

She rummages inside her schoolbag for her special black velvet pouch and shakes from the drawstring opening a silvery-bright razor blade, the last in a plastic tray of four. Gillette Mach 1. *Guaranteed Surgical Sharpness*. She had removed the tray of blades from Mum's ex-boyfriend B-J's overnight bag one early morning some months back. All this time the blade has lain in readiness in the pouch beside the other knives, waiting for just this moment.

'Eech!' Alice yelps as if winded.

6

Arnie has thrown himself down in front of her. 'Don't, Alice. Don't cut, not yet.' He is bunched into a ball and his arms are tented around the jar of yellowed formalin and the small, dead body lying in its patch of wet sand.

He rubs his teary face inexpertly against a shrugged-forward shoulder.

'What are we here for then, Quiet Arnie? Our plan was to take a closer look.'

'At least let's look at the *outside* of it a bit longer.'

'We've got till only five, when football practice ends.'

His forehead to the ground, his head upside down, Arnie Binns is suddenly eyeball to eyeball with the creature's face. The scratchy smell of the formalin catches the back of his throat. He gives a soggy sneeze. He sees that the thing has a neck, a kind of a mouth, nose, even tiny crumpled ears, all the bits that he has, too. He puts his fingers to his own face to make sure of this—this amazing *like*ness. The pinched join between his nose and mouth, the bony bulge of his forehead—are exactly the same.

He'd never have expected it. The wrung-out, meant-to-be-unborn dead thing is built exactly like they are him, Alice, anyone else.

'Its eyes are wide open, did you see?'

'They would be, Stupid.'

Alice is busy telling herself, '*body* not *baby*. *Body, body*. Not *human*, not *face*. *Body*.'

'Eyelids grow in later,' she says. Has she read this, or is she making it up? She can't decide. '*The Human Anatomy* Mr Brocklebank lent me has photos, colour photos. But this one must be older than five months, so maybe its eyelids were about to grow in. Or maybe it died with its eyes open and they've, like, frozen. The calf foetus that sits on the shelf near it is younger, I'd say, younger for a calf, and its eyes are open.'

'You mean that before we're born, the first thing is that we're awake? Later on we learn to close our eyes and sleep?'

'I don't know, Arnie. You *really* are wasting time. Move over. I want to get started.'

She poises the blade between index finger and thumb.

'You're sick, Alice.'

'If I'm sick you're sick too. You've been in on this all the way.'

'Maybe you're right,' Arnie ducks his chin. 'Maybe I'm sick too.'

His shaved head laid on the ground beside the foetus reminds Alice of something uncomfortable. A silky globed thing, blue-veined, glossy...the sight queases her stomach. The other week when they were at work in her back garden examining the beautiful dog's eye, she saw it then, his ball; yes, that was it, and it gave the same feeling, her stomach turning right over. How it squeezed out between his leg and his short shorts, the stretched skin shining in the sunlight like some *growth*.

She has to look away.

Overhead she sees the milky-bright sky spin through the willow leaves. On the main playing field beside the school are the moving shapes of the footballers. It's a Thursday afternoon and, if they chose to, she and Arnie might be hanging out there watching the practice. But she and Arnie don't choose to. They don't *do* football. They don't *do* sport. She does Science, especially dissection. She does The Body: The Complete and Amazing Tour. And Arnie does whatever she does and gets in the way like now, his shiny skull lying in her path.

A few minutes more and she could take this sharp razor and nick that shininess ever so slightly, draw the thinnest line, a warning only, nothing so as to hurt.

Arnie is whispering, 'Thought it'd be like a small monster or gnome, a baby orc. But it looks more like us than like a monster. It's like a human, sort of, a baby human.'

Alice fixes on the foetus's bluish unseeing eyes just over the hillock of Arnie's cheek. Its deep-sea fish-eyes that never saw much if anything of the airy world.

'It *is* a baby human, Barmy Arnie, what else? You must've looked like that once. I looked like that once. Where do you think we grow from otherwise? A shark pod maybe? A mongoose?'

'You know what I mean.' Arnie lifts his head a few inches. He blinks at the sight of the blade aloft. A squelching wheeze enters his breathing, as though he has suddenly developed a cold. He says, 'Please don't let's rush, Alice. Don't let's waste our chances. Look, the thing is perfect, so perfect. It could have become a person, think of that.'

'Could've become a person but didn't. It died. It was got rid of, left in some kidney bowl in the hospital, dumped by the side of the road.'

Puffing her lips she places the blade on the black velvet pouch and folds her arms.

'Dumped and then popped in a glass jar and put on a shelf,' she persists. 'They obviously weren't too squeamish about bottling humans back in those days. I mean half-humans. Mr Brocklebank says the lab storeroom was built as part of the early school buildings around the World War I. The specimen collection will be from that time. Just the same as then, I think we shouldn't be squeamish. Life didn't work out for this thing. It became a specimen instead.'

But her hunger to handle the creature won't go away, blade or no blade. She *must* touch it. This time she chooses a length of dry willow twig and, stretching over the top of Arnie's head, rolls the thing onto its sharply spined back. It won't stay put. No matter how hard she prods, it keeps flopping over, thickening its coating of sand and leaves. Eventually she shoves it up against the four-pint Kerr self-sealing jar it came in, crouched on its side, grubbing in the dirt. Upright would be too human. The arms clenched to its chest are totally too human.

And the five globules of fingers on each of the miniature boxing-glove hands, them too. And the ghostly but staring eyes. And how, when she pushes, the arms *claw* at the willow stick like a human thing.

She follows the corded string—*umbilicus*, she reminds herself—that uncoils from the middle of the thing's stomach as if a snake had burrowed clean into the body. What it has of privates is tucked away between its spindle shanks. She prods the stick some more but the folds and creases of the rubbery skin don't give way. With Arnie looming she doesn't exactly want to *dig in*.

She gives one last push to make sure it'll stay put, propped against its wall of glass, and it's like something cold knocks into her, something jolts her. Sliding her eyes up from the chest where her stick still pokes to the—the almost face, she sees as clear as clear can be that the thing could be a kid like her, almost like her, Alice. *Her*, that is, not just any kid but a kid like her, not wholly from here, England, but African, half African. Yes, she could make-believe the thing was nearly African, demi-semi-African. Look at its sharp nostrils and tall, wide forehead and cheekbones, like her own face in the bathroom mirror, brushing her teeth in the morning. She could be staring into a face she belonged to.

Maybe. Or maybe *not*.

Maybe not. She rocks back on her heels. That grey skin covering the cheeks, the forehead, is so deeply wrinkled she's probably seeing things. Mad to think the specimen could be joined to her somehow *and* to Africa. How could it? It was a scary ghost that walked through her brain just then and tripped her up. The thing down there is spooking her. Arnie with his cheek in the dirt eyeballing the thing is definitely spooking her. The major obstacle to today's project, it turns out, is her helper. His creepy scalp still sits in front of her face. His stupid wuss tears still shine on his cheeks. He's the one who's happy being close to the thing, poring over it like some desert explorer studying a newly unwrapped mummy.

Stupid Barmy Arnie Binns is still properly in the way.

She's suddenly become aware of how fleshy he is, all body-body-body, thick with flesh; flesh, gristle and bone and shiny skin, taking up room. He's a fleshy, weaselly animal blocking her view of their prize. She looks down at the thin ledge of dark hair growing across his top lip, and his narrow, skewed chin, a spade with a twist in it. How pitifully he can tuck that chin into his chest and beg. Some days when he comes over on the playground and wheedles—What can we do today, Alice, what can we open up and look at, what can we cut?—She wants to push him over and squash him like an ant.

Today was set to be a cutting day but now Alice is not so sure. Arnie has sat up and tucked the foetus against his crossed legs. To touch it he uses his fleece sleeves folded into mitten shapes around his fingers. The foetus body is not much longer than his foot. He is stroking it, almost. His hands are cupped over it, kind of making its shape in the air.

She stands up and stretches. She needs a break. She walks a short way off and wraps herself in willow branches. Dry willow leaves descend in drifts. By holding onto the branches with stretched-out arms she can sway in an arc while keeping her feet on the ground. She can twang from side to side like a rubber strap. It's fun to do. It makes her think of the Bandar-log, the monkeys in *The Jungle Book* and their special world up in the trees.

From where she's standing Arnie's hands, thank God, screen the baby-thing from view. Just this minute she doesn't want the sight of it in her face. The thing with its funny, wonky foetus mouth and tiny, pointy nostrils. And its eyes, those especially, its unblinking, empty eyes.

A silence encircles Alice Brass Khan and Quiet Arnie under the weeping willow tree. The creature lying between them with its staring eyes insists on this silence. It is not after all a baby warbling up and down the octaves. It doesn't raise its hands to the light and watch the movement of its fingers. It is a pale thing, an earthworm-pale almost baby that has never made a sound.

The creature has a horizontal, inch-and-a-half-long incision across its middle, under where its ribs would be, or are. Alice made this cut. She made it a minute or so ago with her bright razor blade. She already wishes that she hadn't made it; stooped down and grasped the razor tight, reached around Arnie's arms and made the cut, all in one quick flash. It didn't feel good to make the cut, however small it is. It didn't feel very good at all.

A minute or so ago she brought her blade close to the roof of the creature's belly. She balanced and levelled the blade like a javelin thrower about to deliver the strike of her career. She knew she should give herself time. The cut was made, the cut suddenly happened, even before she realised how close to the body her blade was.

It didn't feel good. When the creature's squashed but dignified face stayed so rigid, when its confused frown did not deepen or fade; its eyes never once flinched.

Though, if it *had* flinched, how bad wouldn't that have felt?

She has looked at the face so long she is sure as can be. The thing in some odd way reminds her of herself.

The foetus's opened flesh makes a mouth shape, slightly pouting. It doesn't bleed. That's the strangest thing. Inside the cut is a knot of noodle-coloured string. Vermicelli guts. The string is littered with tiny black speckles as if the creature was digesting when it died, or is rotting away.

Alice feels a prickly heat under her eyes, the same she gets from eating too much chocolate.

She is aware of her right hand still holding the razor, her palm pressed over the drawstring pouch of blades and knives lying on the ground. She feels how the knives' familiar, reassuring hafts open and separate the small bones at the base of her fingers. She is proud of her knife collection: the Santos pocket penknife; the Victorinox solo knife, the sheathed but blunt Stanley knife taken from B-J's discarded toolbox, the short metal nail file and the razor blades, the Gillette the newest and the shiniest. Mr Brocklebank has said that for small dissections a razor will do nicely in place of a scalpel. But Mr Brocklebank probably wasn't thinking of do-it-yourself jobs in the swampy area at the back of the playing field, here in the den by the weeping willow tree. He probably wasn't thinking of the Year 7 kids getting stuck into specimens from his very own lab.

She pushes the pouch to one side and picks up her willow stick, prods Arnie with it. He looks up and she hands it to him. She mimes widening, pulling.

She wants him to prise the incision open? He shakes his head.

'You wanted to help, didn't you?' she says, 'Be part of the team? You wanted to *do* something. To it.'

His shaking head becomes a blur.

Out of the corner of her eye she catches by accident the creature's creased and level stare. This foetus face gazing up at her is so small and detailed, so *exact* in its plain, everyday details—eyes, cheeks, pointy chin, those dented nostrils like her own—that she feels stupid, scolded and stupid. A coward and a bully could have done no worse than she has done.

A foetus in a jar of formalin is a specimen. A spade is a spade. This is what Alice knows. An abandoned newborn baby is a naked, doll-like object wrapped in a bit of a newspaper. She must keep telling herself this. It is a thing left on a doorstep that is stained with chewing gum and urine. What kind of a life is that? What kind of beginning? Far better then to end up as a foetus in a jar; or, better yet, dissolve into a shot of pills. Better to be unborn than miserable, isn't that so? She knows about Morning-After pills, the ones that bring off babies. Her big sister Laura has an unused pack in her knickers drawer. Several times Alice has handled the pack, read the instructions on the back, picked at the bit of sellotape sealing it closed.

A spade is a spade. A foetus in a jar, however bulky, is a specimen. But something has shaken her, something about this weird, growing silence surrounding them is rattling her. If it weren't for Arnie sitting there staring, bug-eyed as the creature itself, she might like to lie down on the ground and cry, drop her black velvet pouch and all her blades in the streambed there at the corner of the school fence, and go home to have a good, long cry.

Instead she wipes her razor blade on her sock.

* * *

At that instant, pushing away Alice's willow twig, I understood. At that instant it dawned on me that this baby who had flopped so unbothered out of its jar onto the ground in front of us was a miracle thing, like a visit from an angel.

That was the main difference between Alice and me. If Alice could see the wood for the trees, I liked to see only trees. If for her the world was all matter, for me there was

14

magic—magic and mystery everywhere; in clouds that take the shape of dragon's wings, in unexplained cold spots in old houses, in uncanny coincidences. I puzzled about water dousing and strangers' eyes meeting in recognition across crowded rooms, about the dead appearing to the living and all mysterious apparitions. I believed in Elves, silver-skinned Elves. I knew that shooting stars were signs from other planets. I was sure that I'd one day be lucky enough to see the auras that I'd found pictures of in books, rays bursting from people's heads like living crowns. I felt that Alice's halo was purple, spiky and very intense.

Even this body here might have an aura, I thought, the thinnest of auras still clinging from the time when it was a living thing.

'Arnie loves Alice, Arnie loves Alice,' our classmates often teased, '*A love-heart A.*' Alice's answer was to knock in their knees from behind with her fists, the same as when they called her Brown Boffin. But for me this claim was true in a way. What I loved about Alice was the glittering plans I could see forming in her eyes. How her face turned gleamy when she was thinking, like now, leaning against the willow trunk with her eyes shut. How her big-knuckled hands were always in motion, testing the textures and temperatures of things and tapping the knives in her pocket.

I so loved her plans that I'd had no idea, I couldn't have thought, how today's project would turn out this ugly and messed-up.

When she'd put the blade to the creature's flesh it was like a stitch, a bad one, in my ribs. I'd never felt a shame like this before, like a sickness, a physical pain. How could we have ended up hurting something so neat and small? So young yet so old, so perfectly made? Definitely we hadn't meant to, and yet that's what had happened and I'd done nothing to prevent it. At the last minute I'd not lifted a finger. I'd helped do harm and now—would harm now follow us? How far would we have to run to escape?

I forced myself to look down at the crumpled grey body lying on the ground between us. *A picture of who it might have been,* something I'd caught one of mum's beauty studio clients once saying, crying into the scented pillow in the treatment room.

Why did we have to go and dirty the creature's small face with sand?

I thought of a World War I mother looking like the Scottish widow in the ad but with her big cape bloodstained. I imagined this lady stooping to pick up the little corpse that had just this minute dropped from her body and tenderly placing it in a jar, stroking its head before screwing on the lid, bottling it like jam.

Unless I spoke I'd choke on the silence.

'Alice, couldn't you have said a prayer, a few words, before you did that? Cut it? "Some surgeons do," my mum says. Say a prayer. To make sure the person's soul doesn't escape through the opening.'

'Flipping heck, you still here, Arnie? I thought you'd've got lost by now. What do you know about what I did or didn't say? I could've been madly praying all that time I was swinging off the branches, waiting to cut. All that time you were in my way.'

'But you weren't praying. I watched you.'

'Look, what's eating you? In case you weren't listening, this foetus here died a long time ago. 1914, 1918, remember? It hasn't got a bloody soul to lose.'

'Not now it hasn't.'

'Not ever. It never had a soul.'

'The soul could've stayed drifting around it. Bits of it hanging about, from when it was waiting to be born. There they were, the bits, hovering down the years, dazed and confused, and just then you chased them away, the last bits. You zapped its soul. You made this hole here. You'll never close it now. We'll never be able to sew the soul back on.'

'*Arnie*!' Alice was yelling, obviously not caring who could hear. 'Just shut it! Lay off me. I feel bad enough as it is, OK? I really do feel bad. There are plenty of reasons for feeling bad. So shut-up. Shut-up, shut-up! Or get lost.'

Her lips snarling at me, her eyes staring so hard I couldn't hold her gaze, I looked down again at the cut in the thing's middle. I saw that nothing was happening to that dark space. It was an open-mouthed, clay-grey cut she had carved, neither expanding nor closing. It wouldn't go away, that was for sure. Together we had committed a deed we couldn't undo.

'I can't get lost.' Speaking to the foetus. 'Remember? The football people would notice we'd been hanging around down here on our own.'

'If I say get lost you get lost.'

She brought her face up close to mine, the heels of her hands resting on the ground, the razor blade still in her fingers, pointing upwards. Then the blade seemed to slip in my direction. It seemed to move of its own accord to where my arms were folded on my legs. It touched the tip of one of my fingers. It shouldn't have been touching me but it was. There was nothing between the cutting edge and the pink whorls of my fingertip than the narrowest line of shadow. Dark red shadow reflecting off the blood in my fingers.

Not since the day we worked on the dog's eye had we had a stand-off like this, and that day was one-of-a-kind, the icky eye bits lying scrambled on the melamine bread-board. At heart Alice knew like I knew that conflict between us was unwinnable. Her will drove into my vague dreams and got nowhere. I might look all give but it was only to a point. Beyond that point she could not crack me. Silently I now whispered this to myself. You can*not* break me, Alice, you will *not* cut me.

* * *

Holding her silver blade to Arnie Binn's finger, Alice is caught by a memory of herself and Laura when they were little: the two of them making x-ray patterns under their duvets by shining Mum's big torch through their hands and making them glow like Chinese lanterns; Laura saying, 'Whatever colour we are, dark brown like me, light brown like you, we're all of us red inside.'

It would be so easy, Alice knows, for the blade to edge itself cleanly, experimentally, into the outer layer of Arnie's skin, to the point where it grows redder, darker and redder. For the blade to make a small but definite graze: a single droplet of scarlet blood welling.

And then Arnie is snatching back his finger, his face looking bloated and feverish. For a moment he teeters off-balance. Then as he braces himself his elbow strikes the Kerr jar standing beside him. It wobbles, topples. Alice, blade in hand, catches hold of it, but not before a gush of the remaining formalin has hit him on the leg.

He grabs his cheeks as if he's been slapped.

'It touched me, Alice. It was like—it touched me. The thing touched me.'

Alice ignores the sympathetic shiver that runs down her spine.

'The thing *didn't* touch you though, Arnie. You knocked the jar.'

They're in this together, she reminds herself, they need each other, two brains working as one.

That's it. She rests her blade on the drawstring pouch.

'But it's been sitting in that jar for *ages*. The formalin's been *all over* it. It was *so* cold.'

I know I know, she nods, waits for his gasping to calm down. But now his wide eyes are stretching even wider open, and she, too, wakes up to it. The space of silence in which they've been sitting has suddenly expanded. The quiet is everywhere. The playing field is deserted. The football players long ago packed up and headed home. The spectators and other stragglers have disappeared. By now the school gates will be locked.

They will have to find their own way out, and the foetus with them.

Alice can't remember if her original idea was to take the jar back to the lab storeroom and slide it onto its high shelf just as if it had never been tampered with. Match the jar's bottom to the dust-free circle marked on the wood. Maybe she never quite thought through this stage of her scheme. The prize she wanted filled her brain and left no extra space.

What's clear now is that an attempt to return the body today would be crazy. The lab will be locked up, even the cleaners will have gone home. And the thing's outer surface—skin—is already leathering from exposure. Before making plans to return it she will have to get hold of the formalin Mr Brocklebank keeps for frog dissections. She will have to refill the jar.

As for the cut, she knows she will have to pay for that cut. The cut she has made purses darkly open.

Arnie follows her train of thought, so it seems. He breathes in hard, making his nose noises, and brings both his hands towards the creature, ever so gingerly. It has touched him through its formalin; he will have to touch it back. He takes another breath and lifts it, begins to slide it back into the Kerr jar. Easier said than done. Some of its knobbly bits have to be angled and squeezed to fit through the jar's mouth. The cord thing is surprisingly stiff, almost a spike. He has to push.

Alice watches a moment, then joins in. With her right palm she forces down a jut of elbow, then ankle, knee. Her hands are bare and Arnie's hands are bare but they are past caring about contact. She tries even so to avoid the touch of the cat's-paw fingers.

The skull goes in last and must be pressed down with Arnie's hand this time. The skull pops back up, round like an apple. He forces it down once more.

But in spite of their best efforts the thing looks uncomfortable in its half-empty jar, slumped against the glass, the skin plastered to the dry, inner surfaces, puckering. To replace the spilt formalin they fill the jar from the football ground water-fountain. Then Arnie screws the copper lid on tight. Alice can tell it takes a lot for him to do this but they don't stop to speak.

They make their way to the back corner of the slatted school fence, to where the boggy stream bed in the waste ground behind the playing field runs along the wooden slats on its way to the river. There's a loose slat here they've noticed before, in case it might one day, like today, come in handy. Using Alice's Victorinox handle as a lever they yank at the slat and create a space wide enough for Arnie to slither through, belly to the ground, cheek by jowl with the stream. Alice passes the Kerr jar through to him, then follows on her back, so she can brace her knee against the slat. She works her feet free of the fence but can't lift her head. The spiky edge of the chicken wire that covers the stream bed along the length of the fence has caught her hair in a snarl. Arnie puts down the jar to help her. He has to twist her head from side to side to get her free.

They cross the swampy area beyond the stream by balancing on the overturned supermarket trolley lying partly submerged in the sludgy green mud.

By now the light is fading. The afternoon is over. Hundreds of invisible, cawing birds are roosting in the chestnut trees down by the river. The tops of the trees, visible over the roofs of the nearby houses, make a froth of bright new leaves and moving birds.

And so a new test begins: how to lay to rest their prize, their antique but unborn dead.

They begin to prowl the neighbourhood of the school. They know they must find a safe place to deposit the small body, even if just for the night, but their movements are aimless. It could take a day and more to tidy away this problem, thinks Alice. Squeezing the thing back into its jar could be easy compared to this. They can't leave the foetus exposed, is Arnie's feeling, not on a wet night like tonight. It would be terrible to put it out in the cold, dark, open air.

As in new housing developments all over England, Woodpark, their neighbourhood, the southern residential extension of the city, is located on a length of flood plain. Its pie-sized shape is created by the curve of the Chartwell River on its northern side, and, to the south, by the angle formed between the railway line and the main road leading out of town to Reading and the southern coast. Once, before the smart, new town houses were built, this wet, flat area of the city was simply called the Plain.

The name Woodpark, Alice scoffed when she first heard it, must be straight out of Enid Blyton. There are no woods anywhere close to Woodpark, nor even, come to think of it, bar the chestnuts by the river, any mature trees at all.

Arnie and Alice now make their way down School Road, along the smelly ditch, past the community centre with its barred, high-up windows, and into Selvon Street. At the Londis on the corner of Selvon Street and the main road out of town they turn on their heels, strike out left, and at the end of Latvia Wharf they meet the river. They keep bouncing off these neighbourhood borders. Each time they change direction they exchange the jar between

them and pull their fleeces and coats tight around it. Neither wants to be in long-term possession.

Stratford Street, Woodpark's long axial road, forms a cul-de-sac at its southern end. A play park for toddlers fronts the raised curve of the railway line. Alongside the play park, separated from it by a stream, is the Council Recreation Ground with its obstacle course and concrete skateboard rink and, against the railway line, a strip of reedbed where, on most weekends, used condoms like white squiggles criss-cross the ground.

Trailing down Stratford Street for a second time the two arrive at the gate to the Recreation Ground and glance at one another. Alice points her chin in the general direction of the reeds.

'Where we brought the ammonite?'

The ammonite was stolen from the nature table in her classroom and split here on the Recreation Ground using her metal nail file. Like the salt crystal and the human kidney stone, the second and third pieces of loot from the nature table, the ammonite, when sliced, fell for an instant into two clean halves, then collapsed into dust. It laid bare none of the mysteries they had hoped for, not a single inner whorl or mazy passageway. It took hundreds of millions of years to form but when it fragmented it left no more than a pile of rough dust behind.

'Not in here, no.' Arnie grasps the jar closer to his chest, deeper inside his fleece.

'The reedy area makes a good hiding place,' Alice hesitates.

Too cold, he indicates with a shudder, too damp.

She nods and takes over the jar. They walk on.

A steady but drenching rain begins with a wind behind it. They keep their heads bent, their coats beating like mainsails. For the third or fourth time they find themselves on the road out of town, the evening traffic grinding by, stirring up the puddles and spouting water into their trainers. They pass the Cote Dazur chip shop, the Angling Emporium, the City Council Waste and Recycling Centre. At the Fox and Flagstaff pub their feet slow down.

Past here they're not sure of the area, especially in this rain. Who might they bump into? What off-duty policemen, teachers walking dogs? Where might they run and hide if they had to bolt? Alice has zipped her coat over the specimen jar but it makes an awkward bulge.

They have no choice but to turn yet again, retrace their steps. The pub, the bus stop just beyond the pub, the Recycling Centre. The Recycling Centre. They have passed it several times already, each time without a second glance. It's not the right place for their World War I scrap with its scrunched-up face. But the daylight has almost completely melted away. Arnie is shivering badly, worse than Alice has seen anyone shiver and shake before. The notice on the gate says the place closes at seven. They have a moment, a tiny opportunity.

They walk through the tall gates. The Recycling Centre is an orderly waste ground stacked with broken-down kitchen goods and out-of-date machines with screens. Apart from the two of them pressing on down an avenue of abandoned televisions, there is no one about.

They find a spot shielded by a blackberry thicket, behind a tall wall of fridges. Blinded by the rain Alice passes the jar to Arnie. She begins to hack at the ground with a stone, then with the lid of a vegetable crisper from one of the fridges, then a clattering ice-tray. She remembers their work on the human kidney stone, how it broke up into resinous blobs under the blows of her file. A preserved foetus probably requires just the shallowest of graves, she thinks, but the ground though wet is hard as stone. She can't seem to make even a scraping in the ground.

Arnie stands by with his arms folded around the jar.

In disgust Alice throws the ice-tray into the blackberry bushes. They walk on. Behind the fridge wall they encounter a skip piled high with pruned tree branches and hedge clippings. Alice takes the jar off Arnie and gestures with it. They might unscrew the jar lid and jolt the thing out, chuting it into that large, spiky nest? Pitch the jar after and hear it crash?

He fiercely grabs their burden back off her, clutches it to his chest. As if they could! After what they've already done to it—fly-tip the creature like a bit of scrap! Suddenly he knows he can't go through with it; not here, today, dump the body in this place where stale rubbish-bin smells smear the air. They dragged it off its safe high shelf. They took charge of it and then they turned on it, hurt it, dirtied its face. How, in this recycling wasteland, could they now leave it behind?

Alice gives up the jar without a fight. Never before has she felt such force in Arnie's fingers.

Nothing for it. The place is closing, a siren somewhere in the direction of the main gates is wailing *wee-wah, wee-wah*, a sound of broken crying. They must go home, think again, take the jar along. It's Arnie who'll take it. 'I'll look after it, no problem,' he says mumbling. 'There's one less person to hide from at home than for you.'

But that's not the real reason, he can tell, though he can't say it out loud. The real reason is that the small body has laid hold of him. The scrumpled face has marked him somehow. The way it has survived all today, as if with courage, with spirit. For years and years it sat on its high shelf, quietly roosting. And then it descended. It came and tapped him on the hand and stepped into his life. And its ordinariness—its puzzled frown, its clutching hands and folded ears and cheekbones like Alice's—its overwhelming ordinariness has gripped his heart.

24

Chapter 2
Alice

Fed up as she suddenly feels, Alice swallows the sneaking suspicion that this is because Arnie has taken home their prize. When they said goodbye at his front door she was happy to see the back of the specimen. Happy to see the back of the specimen *and* her friend, Arnie shivering madly, clutching the cold jar to his chest.

But she can feel something's bothering her, something's threatening to frustrate her. That's how things work. She makes a decision—yes, it's definitely the right choice, exactly right—then, minutes later, she's reverting, regretting it. She's wondering how she could've been such an idiot. What a crazy way to go on. Especially when that specimen almost, kind of, she was sure for that moment, looked, well, like African family, like somebody she belonged to.

She threads her way down Stratford and then into Albion Street, winding around whiffy black rubbish bags put out for tomorrow morning's collection. She stops with her eye fixed on the rain-blurred middle distance.

By rights she should have claimed the Kerr jar for herself, the jar and the embryo corpse inside it. She could've sat up late and studied it, couldn't she, under Laura's halogen desk lamp? Looked at how the birth cord meets the body. How that huge head fits together with that puny, skinny neck. She could've got something in return for the tears and the trauma. By rights she should have insisted and elbowed Arnie out of the way. Didn't she discover the thing in the first place? Wasn't the cunning plan to get hold of it *her* cunning plan?

Still, if she's honest with herself, it was a relief when Arnie took it over just then. Walking on she kicks a black bag to add weight to the thought. The bag splits across the bottom, spilling out a clod of leftover rice.

She must keep telling herself this, she decides. It wouldn't be scary to be saddled with it but it was OK to let it go. She wasn't too petrified at any point, she's pretty sure, not even when she used the blade. It was being burdened with that young-but-old dead thing, dead but human-like thing—that felt funny. Funny as in bloody horrible, in fact.

Barmy Arnie, on the other hand, trust him to warm to it as if it were some sick pet.

Alice parts wet branches of overgrown lavender to make a pathway to her front door, No 7. The rain's receding and mist rises from the small front garden. The lavender breathes out its reassuring smell.

Well, she tells herself, Arnie's welcome to the thing for the night, whatever he's planning to do with it. Cuddle it like a teddy maybe. Wrap it in an air-tex blanket and tuck it under his duvet. Two heads on the pillow, cute as two buttons.

Tomorrow, soon as they're allowed into the school buildings, they'll have to find their way back into the old lab storeroom and replace the jar on its shelf, no matter what. Use the cover of some early-bird classroom tidying and try to overlook the stick-like cord. Turn the thing's wound to the wall. She'll have to call Arnie once she's settled in and had some toast and jam: break the bad news.

Come to think of it, she wouldn't be surprised if he'd already happened upon the same idea, though reluctantly. And if he already knew *she* had the idea. Some days the two of them tune into a communication channel that, she likes to imagine, links their houses underground. She'll knock at Arnie's door at the instant he phones her. She'll open her mouth and he'll speak the word she was about to say. It's nothing mystical of course, though he probably thinks so. They spend a huge amount of time together so the connection grows from there.

But even their connection might not help Arnie come to terms with the bad news today. This evening he looked very sombre carrying his burden, very sunk into himself. She'll have to push him hard to drive home the message. Brace yourself, Arnie, we'll be peeling ourselves away from your genie in its jar.

She stands with her hand on the doorknob, the Chubb key snugged into the lock, her thoughts moving ahead. It's her habit, mental stocktaking in her own porch. She likes to have the whole home routine planned in advance, every evening, so there are no surprises, no bad surprises. Her mother and sister are past masters at producing huge parcels of bad surprises, gift-wrapped in awkward shiny paper, with ugly bows on top.

The first time Alice caught herself here, hand on doorknob, key in lock, lavender in the air, was the day B-J left, Mum's boyfriend but one, before over-friendly Frankie, who himself departed not too long ago. The day B-J left, her big sister Laura entered one of her long-term silent sulks, two whole weeks that time, where she refused to hear anything said at home, though everyday she talked to her boyfriend Phoenix for hours on the phone.

B-J, real name Benjamin John Holmes, was—probably still is—a tree-surgeon with a year-round tan, massively in demand amongst the property owners with large gardens who live along the river. He was around since Alice was three, that is, for as long as she can remember. Every year he was the one who took her to the Christmas panto. He

27

makes sure, he made sure, to show up at school sports days and meetings of the Neighbourhood Watch.

But eventually B-J grew tired, so he said, of being 'the single gravitational field' holding together the three females of the family: their mother Jilly Brass, depressed freelance editor on permanent sick-leave; seventeen-year-old Laura, 'I may look shortsighted but my dreams are focussed'; and Alice herself, her tight curls, copper skin, and will-power making the photographic opposite to Laura's wavy hair, coffee colours and full-time, all-purpose shilly-shally.

Alice suspects that more than anything else B-J grew tired of Mum's constant fatigue, her dizziness, migraines, numb and painful legs, and the hundred other complaints that to this day keep her to the house, bar occasional shopping trips and visits to the local beautician, who is Arnie's mother Evie. At first he began restlessly and repeatedly to check the time on his watch, as if he was a man with a mission. And then he yawned. Between time checks he yawned. He yawned his way through several weeks. He yawned in your face even when he spoke to you. Finally he left with the words *Take Care* thrown carelessly over his shoulder.

Ever since Alice makes efforts to be the family's replacement gravitational field. She's the single person who on a daily basis talks to Laura as well as to Mum.

Like a new parent approaching a sleeping baby she stands poised at the front door. Quickly she's ticking off which party will be most annoyed with the other tonight: Mum probably. Who she's not likely to see for the duration of the evening: Laura, usually. Who in a frenzy of comfort eating at lunchtime will have consumed the ready-cook meal she has earmarked for their tea: could be either/or.

She turns the Chubb in the lock.

On bored afternoons with Arnie, when she whittles sticks and tests the sharpness of her collection of blades and he looks on, they sometimes discuss, in spite of themselves, their lopsided families. They try to avoid the topic; there's a lot of other stuff to talk about, but still it comes up like a bad penny regarding their single, stand-all-alone mums, regarding Alice's tidily beautiful, vaguely dyslexic, dramatically emotional sister.

From these conversations Alice likes to work up self-help slogans that explain their lives. In Arnie's case the top priority is *Everything clean*. Though his mother's job is to groom the whole neighbourhood she's incredibly untidy and messy. She can't put a thing away, can barely shimmy a shirt onto a hanger or wash a tea mug, while he likes every single thing in its place. He dusts chairs with his sleeve before sitting down. He rinses the kettle with white vinegar once a week, the bath every other day. On Sunday nights he irons his clothes for the week as well as Evie's six white tunics, one for each working day. Arnie hates a rind, anything with a coating or too thick a skin.

For herself Alice thinks that it's *Everyone happy* that explains the universe. Or, *Everyone happy enough*. On balance this is a taller order than Arnie's. If one day she succeeds in getting both Laura and Mum to smile simultaneously she'll be so ecstatic she'll cry.

She pushes open the door.

The house is quiet. Most evenings Alice will hear in the hallway the sound of Laura's purple half-moon radio filtering through the coffered ceiling from her bedroom. The radio's on most of the time, even when Laura's asleep, even when she's in the bathroom where they have for good measure a jellyfish-shaped waterproof radio suckered to the wall.

Tonight the silence up there means Laura's probably out and, if that's so, most likely at Phoenix's. Her boyfriend

Phoenix has lately decided that he prefers to minimise the time he spends under the same roof as long-term disappointed, whingeing Jilly, though he can't eliminate it altogether. Laura's taking a break before the Sixth Form in order to confront her learning difficulties, a.k.a. her confidence vacuum and related ups-and-downs, so Jilly's house has to be a place to hang out.

Alice spreads her wet coat over the hallway radiator and moves in the direction of the kitchen, toast, strawberry jam, then checks herself. In the shadows of the dining room she sees her mother. Yes, it is Mum sitting hunched at the table, which is a surprise since the family generally avoids this chilly north-facing room.

'Jeepers, Alice, where've you been?' Jilly Brass jumps as her daughter slips an arm across her shoulders. 'I've been daydreaming here so long I almost forgot where I was.'

As she speaks Jilly's fingers rummage fretfully through the makeup bag planted on the table in front of her.

'Darling,' she says, 'next time you go shopping, pop into the pharmacy and buy me new lipstick. Look, see, I've nearly run out. Makeup bag's in carnage. Take the reference number, go to the Rimmel stand and ask for a replacement. Make sure they don't think you're buying this belly-dancer scarlet for yourself.'

'I could take the lipstick and match up the colour.'

'No, rather not. There's a bit leftover. I'd be afraid you might lose it. If they're out of my kind of red, I'd be lost.'

'School's busy this week, Mum, science stuff. Write the reference number on the shopping list. I'll try over the weekend, soon as I can.'

Jilly wrinkles her nose. 'You certainly have been up to something at school, pet. You smell terrible, of some medical thing. You're keeping it aboveboard, I hope, not harming small, furry creatures.'

Her mum can have no idea what she's been working at, but even so Alice knows she will immediately begin to blush. Within moments, sure enough, ripples of heat are beating up over her cheeks. This is how her own skin betrays her. Lightly she manages, 'Of course, Mum,' while turning with careful smoothness in the direction of the kitchen. 'Is Laura out?'

The kitchen is in an even more dishevelled state than usual. Shredded baby spinach leaves lie confettied on every surface, the floor included. Dishes overflow from the sink.

'No idea. Not heard anything from her room for hours. She cheeked me earlier when I complained about the smelly steak she was grilling for lunch. So I shouted; so she flounced off. I do wish your sister would stop consuming those disgusting slabs of flesh that take up all our freezer space. Before she vanished she made some remark that I could do with a no-grain diet too. "No grain, no pain," she yelled, waving a bush of spinach in the air. I was, quote, *blubbery all over* for a woman of my age. And when I said something regarding Phoenix, some small innocent remark, can't remember, probably that he was around a good deal and always sleeping, sleepy or sleeping, she threw back the usual, concerning what did I know about the straight and narrow? Look how you two came into the world from different dads, uninvited. Different dads! I mean it's such an old story and so untrue.' Jilly's voice droops exhausted. 'She's in her room or at Phoenix's, I don't know. Hasn't been seen since.'

To Alice her mum's lines are as familiar as the patterns in her own palms; today sharply etched, she notices, from handling that foetus's formalin-soaked body. She begins to clatter her way through the unwashed utensils and frying pan in the sink. She shovels fatty meat cut-offs left on a chopping board into the bin.

In the background she hears Jilly's distressed murmurs as she tests kohl-pencil stubs on a notepad. 'Shocking, really shocking, and so insulting, too'.

Alice's kitchen noises supply a daily accompanying rattle to her mum's remarks on stand-offs with Laura, remarks that always follow the same course and carry the same content. Phoenix's somnabulent crimes of indolence. Laura's fecklessness, the murky and ambiguous circumstances surrounding the girls' birth-father and Laura's problem with these. That's to say, with the fact of whether Farouq Khan, Alice's natural father, an amiable taxi-driver who left for his native Sudan about ten years back when she was two, is also Laura's dad.

Farouq's blown-up photo stares from virtually every wall of every room in their house. There's the handsome black-and-white portrait study with thick eyebrows and moustache over the sitting-room mantelpiece. There are the laminated copies of the same portrait arranged in a chequered pattern in the bathroom. And the blurry, bluish 1980s colour prints in the bedrooms, except for Laura's. But still Laura persists in marching the stairs and pacing her bedroom, loudly demanding her *Real Dad's* name. In amidst her overall vagueness this is the one thing that has her fixed and definite.

'Who was he, mum? I *really* need to know. He looks *nothing* like that bloke there on the wall, and that's for sure.'

It has been Jilly's consistent claim that her two daughters *sprang from the seed* of that bloke there on the wall. She used to be mad about Farouq Khan, she says and says again; she *adored* him. He was romantic, dark and handsome, his moustache was luscious, his eyes warm chocolate. She says they met in the days when Madonna sported puppy fat and there was a Berlin Wall and a straight-down-the-line Cold War rather than the shambolic mess in the world today. They wanted heaps of babies together but in the end he couldn't bear it any longer here in drizzly old England and decided to return home. So, she says, they elected to share a *remote togetherness*. Ordinary cohabitation was not for them.

To be frank, Jilly freely admits, cohabitation was something they were never particularly good at. Even when he lived in this country Farouq was a fly-by-night, in and out, here and gone again. Between the time of Laura's birth and then Alice's, he flitted back to North Africa for a couple of years.

'And that's when my father, Farouq's predecessor, disappeared for good, basically,' is Laura's mutter as she stomps a pathway into her bedroom carpet. 'Off to have more kids with his African wife.'

The truth is that Laura's birth certificate agrees with the bare facts of Jilly's story. As for Farouq Khan himself, he isn't a reliable correspondent, or in fact any kind of correspondent at all. He doesn't verify the claim one way or another. Alice believes Jilly and the birth certificate, but Laura sticks to her doubts.

Thinking *Everyone happy*, Alice points out that Laura has the same round eyes as Farouq. 'Look, it's the exact same Paddington Bear stare.'

Laura says photographs lie, and thank God she doesn't have those eyebrows.

Alice remarks that the two of them have similar tones of African colour, no mistake, harmonising North African hues. She lays her arm alongside her sister's. See their brown-olive skin, hers just slightly lighter, Laura's just slightly darker, and their identical dark eyes.

Laura retorts that this means nothing. 'You colour-blind, Alice? Just because our skin's off-white doesn't mean it's the same brown. Don't take it badly but mine's way darker than yours.'

And look at their hair, she adds, tossing hers, Alice's is a good deal curlier. Her own father might just as well have been some fly-by-night, here-and-gone-again Jamaican, Moroccan, or bloke from Chad with semi-straight curls. In her youth Jilly obviously had a taste for exotic men.

The bottom line, Laura says, is that her childhood memories of Farouq from the time when she was little, even from the time he finally left, shouldn't be a blank slate, but are.

Archly she asks Jilly to point out the toys Farouq once gave her. A father, especially an absent father, would send his child presents, wouldn't he? Or maybe pictures: photos of the Nile in flood-time, of the muddy waters rising and falling and washing donkey carts, dead egrets, cooking pots and rafts of water hyacinth out to the Delta and the sea, the same as in her *National Geographic Yearbook*? She'd like to see pictures of the great African river in flood, Farouq standing in the midst of all its kaleidoscopic clutter.

'He's a Developing World man,' Jilly scowls furiously. Where'd he get the money to buy you things? Where'd he get the camera to take the pictures? Remember *Feed the World*, your favourite carol when you were at primary school? Remember, *Do They Know it's Christmas Time at All*?

'He'd earn money from his taxi-driving maybe?' Laura fires back, desperate to hear a different story. Her set opinion is that she was conceived during a one-night stand Jilly shared with a passing stranger. If Jilly only came clean about this she'd feel happier. And why not come clean? How is this alternative story more shameful than the Farouq fantasy? She believes the story of her life misses an opening, a first moment, first beat; it feels undercut and askew. If she were asked to tell a new friend about herself, she wouldn't know where to begin.

Alice now mounts the stairs with a plate of jammy toast and a glass of raspberry smoothie. Laura can be relied on to get hold of small luxuries like lo-fat yoghurt and fruit smoothies when, like this week, like very often, or in fact most of the time, she's on a diet. Food shopping, she says, suppresses her appetite because it tickles her fancies.

Jilly's usual trilling refrain trails after Alice as she climbs. It's the one on which she ends her daily ranting. Her voice grows louder and more high-pitched the further Alice recedes from view.

'You girls're *too much*,' she finishes up. Alice sees her raking through her big mop of Marianne Faithfull hair and shaking her upturned handbag over the rubbish bin. 'Too cheeky, too wilful, too much to cope with. *Too, too much*. I've done my best for you. Too bad your father— yes, *your* father, you *two's* father, possessive plural—can't come out of the desert around old Khartoum to do his share. Too damn bad.'

Past Laura's bedroom door Alice thuds her footsteps loudly, clatters the plate and glass. She loses Jilly's voice. She owes her sister a signal in case she's in there with comatose Phoenix. Laura has a Sheraton hotel *Do Not Disturb* sign hanging off her door handle, a B-J donation from a Save More Trees conference. The sign keeps Jilly at bay but isn't a reliable indicator of who's behind the door. Or What they're Up To.

At school Yaz Yarnton cross-questions Alice with hungry fascination about the Hot Sex that her sister and her boyfriend must definitely be Up To. '*Definitely*. You've seen the pills in her drawers, haven't you? Phoe is really fit. I know what I'd be doing if I was seventeen and in her place.'

In reply Alice rolls her eyes and puffs her lips to convey fathomless, infinite, uncontrollable boredom. In the last few months, since the incident with pink-puffa Justine

Kitchen, since she got friendly with Arnie, she experiences an urgent need during these conversations with Yaz to slip away. Go find her friend Quiet Arnie skulking somewhere inside the branches of the weeping willow tree. She couldn't care less what Phoenix and Laura get Up To behind this door, whether on the bed or the floor or up against the chest of drawers, some of the Sex Sites Yaz has suggested. Or, correction, she does care, but in this special way: she cares not to care. She doesn't care to imagine her sister's ordinary, familiar, *sisterly* body involved in what Yaz, opening her eyes wide, calls Sex Acts, especially not Sex Acts with putty-legged Phoenix. It makes her want to gag.

Alice's narrow room is at the back of the house, squashed in cosily alongside the drying cupboard. She draws her curtains, notices how thickly the grey after-rain mist is draped across the trees in the garden. She settles cross-legged on the rug beside her bed with her snack.

Quiet fills the room. This strange absence of Laura's radio murmur: into the stillness rises a picture of their Thing as she last saw it, stiff in its jar, carried in Arnie's arms. Better that way, she thinks surprising herself, better safe in Arnie's hands. Its weirdly familiar face: good not to have abandoned it among the electrical goods at the Recycling Centre after all. Under a hedge in the misty-damp darkness, left behind like a broken kettle.

She pulls down two of her favourite books from the shelf above her bed, Grassick's *Human Anatomy Picture Book*, her first long-loan from Mr Brocklebank, then *Astronomy in Colour*, bought with last birthday's money.

The Human Anatomy straightaway falls open to one of the pages she most often visits: *The Eye in Close-Up*. Beside the silver-brown curve of the cornea and the iris and the purplish red stalk of the optical nerve she lays the second book, opened to its pages on Mars. The ruddy planet lies cheek by jowl with the veined circle of the eye. With her finger she traces out the two big rounds.

According to Mr Brocklebank, scientists have discovered that the planet Mars is full of water, just like an eye. Imagine that. Its sub-surface skin is loaded with the stuff of life, basically frozen dust.

It was only the other week that she and Arnie dissected their shiny dog's eye: bluish, black and white, no red to it at all. Compared to the eye everything they had done before was plunder, even counting today, just pillage and plunder.

Alice leans back against her toasty radiator. Energy bills in their household are Jilly's responsibility, which means that even in the springtime the heating is on and no-one suffers cold. She pulls the *Anatomy* on to her lap and snuggles the backs of her legs into the pile of the bedside rug. Her eyes feel heavy, her head muffled by the room's dry heat. Circle shapes, ellipses and rounds, planets and pupils and the dented tops of foetal skulls, begin to spin and spiral behind her closed eyelids. The planet Mars in the book has an oval mark or crater at its lower left you can make believe looks like a pupil. You can imagine it winking at you, a blood-red eye.

* * *

The beautiful, bluish-black dog's eye, an Alsatian's eye probably, Alice daydreams back.

They tackled the dog's eye a couple of months or so from the cold day they first walked home together, she remembers. Already there were daffodils everywhere in the garden. Like their work on the ammonite in the Recreation Ground, and also the shattered salt crystal and the fragmented kidney stone, the dissection was part of the business of sharpening her *investigative eye* that Mr Brocklebank said he so admired.

Under pain of twenty Chinese burns to his arm she told Arnie *never* to mention their failed experiments to a soul.

The afternoon following the kidney stone's collapse she had turned her curiosity to the zoology laboratory with its dusty storeroom lying at the century-old heart of the school. By now she was beginning to long for something with proper insides to dissect; 'diverticular enclosures' *Essential Physiology* put it, a body with 'constituent parts' to excavate and explore. Biology was a new subject this term and Mr Brocklebank had already heaped praise on the neatness of her first dissection, of the gut of the frog. Nodding thoughtfully at her offer of help—tidying, dusting, putting away, anything—he had said he was happy to arrange for her to lend a hand when he set up Sixth-Form dissection projects. He had introduced her to the guardian of the storeroom, the yellowed skeleton Henry hanging on his iron frame, his joint hinges rusty, his cracked left eye-socket giving him a mischievous winking look.

And now here, on this springtime afternoon, up on the highest shelf in the old lab storeroom, she spotted the interesting collection of wide-mouthed preserve jars, the neatness of the row of jars contrasting with the clutter on the shelves further down.

She made a mental note to bring a torch from home, to shine a light on those jars bulking so whitely through their coats of ancient dust.

But it was Arnie, like it or not, who made the break-through and discovered the Alsatian's eye. It was Arnie who located the local veterinary hospital, a converted house on the western end of the city's long High Street, and who, after a week of laying siege to the place, reported that the vets' cleaners were their unknowing helpers, their guides to finding proper material to cut. The cleaners, chuckling together in a guttural language, dropped into the bins beside the back door important bits of extra rubbish, things like scraps, lumps of steak and kidney.

She would never forget the sight. She remembered it whenever she studied her favourite, but always flatly 2-D, illustrations in her science books: the naked eye winking up at them from a soggy mess of surrounding rubbish. You couldn't mistake it. It was the real thing, a real specimen. An eye, wide-open and surprised, its top edge decorated with its eyelash, a bristly frond. A large-sized dog's eye, in Alice's opinion, twinkling when the streetlight caught its wetness.

She didn't think twice. It was an early spring gift. She reached down with both hands. Her fingers made contact with an extreme smoothness.

'Please let me hold it, please.' Arnie was wheedling into the back of her skull all the way home. 'I'm owed a go.'

But he didn't get to touch the eye until it lay in pieces the next afternoon in her rain-soaked back garden. The problem was that she couldn't get enough of fingering it; of rolling it on her worktop, a melamine breadboard propped on a brick in the grass; of feeling the eye deliciously dry and cool under her fingers.

Even as she drew out of her trousers' pocket one of her greatest treasures, her grandad's 1930s cut-throat razor, thin, tapered, still surprisingly sharp, she kept her palm cupped over the eye's round smoothness.

'So?' she scowled when Arnie shifted uneasily at the sight of the blade. 'Got to start somewhere.'

The cut-throat razor was the very first blade in her collection, dating from the time of B-J and discovered by chance one day in Jilly's bathroom cabinet when looking for tweezers to extract a splinter. The cut-throat razor was the only one of her blades she didn't as a rule carry with her. It lived wrapped in a soft cloth in her bedside drawer and Jilly seemed never to notice it had vanished.

Without a moment's hesitation, as though she had practised years, she sliced the blade straight into the eye's cornea following the line of the iris.

'Best to go quickly, so you don't screw up. I saw a cataract operation on late night telly once. They went in fast.'

The pressure of her fingers on the edge of the eye released a clear semi-liquid jelly: *the aqueous humour.* She pressed again and the *vitreous humour* squeezed up from behind.

Next, she cut around the iris and removed it, a funny, extensible umbrella without a centre. She spread it across the tip of her finger. Arnie reached for her hand but she elbowed him away, transferring the thing gently to the melamine.

'*Yes,*' she said as she eased the clear globe of the lens out of its silky-dark retinal bed.

The lens was a translucent marble, a glass pebble, no longer an animal thing. She held it up to the light, she remembers. She looked at it for ages. It was a tiny, shimmering planet: Venus, not Mars.

She would store it in her bedside drawer, she thought then, along with her other treasures: the matchbox full of ammonite dust, a globule of their kidney stone, her cut-throat razor itself.

'We've got to get us another one, Alice Brass,' said Arnie hiccuping. 'I want a chance with it. I scored that eye for us.'

A tear was running down his lip and along the skew-whiff angle of his chin and exploding on the wet grass.

'Don't spoil it,' she gave his ribs a push. She held the lens steady on her free palm. 'Bet you've never seen anything so beautiful.'

Arnie shrugged and then, without warning, placed his hand over the long razor lying on the board, his fingers squidging the ashen eye bits. For him the action was decisive, very firm.

She grabbed his wrist. 'Be careful, Barmy Arnie, it's sharp. I practised with it for weeks on Laura's lettuce leaves, slicing along their veins.'

His skin was turning dark-red, his eyes heavy, almost sleepy. Alice gripped his wrist tighter. They were wrestlers in reverse, pulling against one another though kneeling face to face, the muscles in his skinny arms taut with effort. It was now that she saw the testicle straining out of the leg of his shorts, lightly veined in blue.

Hard to believe that it wouldn't emit a clear jelly just like the eye if cut.

She shifted her grip and he fell away from her. She grabbed hold of the blade but somehow dropped the lens. The lens disappeared into the wet grass, in amongst the daffodils. Frantically she patted the ground round about.

'Get out, Arnie,' she hissed. He had spoilt the loveliness of what they were doing and right this minute she hated him. 'Don't come round to our house again unless I say so.'

In place of the clean, perfect lens was this mess she'd have to hose away before Jilly spotted it.

But Arnie was already tracing a path in the direction of the back gate. He cast a single look over his shoulder, his expression gloomy and impenetrable.

Later she wrapped the razor-blade in its soft cloth and slid it behind her wardrobe, up against the bedroom wall. Arnie knew that her bedside drawer was her hiding place. If ever he came searching he wouldn't think to look here. She'd have to dream up an enormous task, she decided, pushing the blade along as far as it would go; an enormous task to give him a chance to make up properly for what he'd done. There'd have to be an important challenge, she thought, a bigger and more perfect prize, more perfect even than an eye.

* * *

Who is to say when life kicks off? Grassick's *Human Anatomy Picture Book* begins by addressing its readers, as if with an eyebrow raised in conspiracy. *Who sets the clock ticking? The blobby cell mass? Or is it the heart itself? All we know is humanness is not created in an instant.*

The eye is the window of the body, says *Human Anatomy*. With the dog's eye, Alice thinks to herself, browsing sleepily, she opened the pane of the window. With the dog's eye she crossed the line of what they call endogenous skin.

But it's beyond this barrier that the real thing lies, she knows; it's beyond here that the pulse of life sits beating.

From the day after the dog's eye incident she began to bring a torch to school in her book bag. Every afternoon, she remembers, she let the milky-murky shapes on their high lab shelf dance under her beam, the large shape at the end of the row especially.

The shape that's the most familiar and yet most haunting of all was weaving in the circle of her torchlight like a kelpie.

One day Mr Brocklebank found her trailing a cloth over a storeroom shelf, her torch hastily stuffed into her apron pocket. 'Been there ages,' he said in answer to her upraised stare. 'A local GP's bequest in 1916, the year the school was founded, halfway through World War I. Our own and extremely rare collection of preserved mammalian embryos, bovine, canine, primate, all in order of evolutionary complexity.'

When she continued to stare he took the cloth from her hands. 'Can't exhibit it openly nowadays,' he shook his head. 'People're no longer used to dead things sitting about.'

Then he opened the lab door with an uncompromising turn of his wrist and stood back to let her pass.

On this late April Thursday, earlier this afternoon, Brocklebank had a dental appointment and asked her to tidy and lock up on her own. Knowing this, she had lain in wait for several days. Yesterday afternoon she had positioned the wheeled storeroom ladder in readiness at the far end of the shadowy row. This afternoon she let Arnie in through the fire-exit to help with the job.

Gingerly she climbed the ladder and measured her stretch. She steadied herself a minute, her left shoulder supported against the wall, then made a heave. Her hands were cupped around the jar. She inched it towards the edge of the shelf, rubbed at the thick dust covering the glass, the embossed cursive letters *Kerr*. Her breath buzzed in her lungs. There behind the glass, as she'd expected, inside the skylight she had carved, was a pale grey, five-toed globular foot.

Below Arnie held his arms up to her. She can see him now, as if etched in her mind's eye. He grabbed the jar tightly as she handed it down; he clutched it to his chest. Already his hands were grey with dust. She felt a tension in her forehead that was almost unbearable. For a minute or so she had to grip the top shelf to prevent herself from falling. It was as if something inside her head wanted to break out, burst free.

* * *

The *Anatomy* lies heavily in Alice's lap. The planet Mars melts into the Human Eye, retreats into itself, melts again, like a mini-film on cell-division rewinding, playing, rewinding. Her neck is in a crick and her forehead aches. The skin on her back feels roasted by the radiator.

She stretches her arms, rolls her shoulders, then listens out. An hour or so must have passed. She must have dozed. Her raspberry smoothie has grown a skin. By now Jilly will have gone to bed. Laura could have crept home.

The quiet house has developed a different quality, a kind of undertow. Gradually she becomes aware of a *hic-hic-hic* sound somewhere, here upstairs, down the passage like a radiator clicking. Or is it something more human? She eases the *Anatomy* on to the rug and moves to the door. The sound deepens into a woebegone noise, a moaning and muffled gulping. It's issuing, more loudly now, from the direction of Laura's room.

She's at her sister's door without thinking twice. Only when her knuckles have made contact with the wood does she remember how still the room was earlier, how she gave the usual warning sounds and there was no reply. Has Laura been in there all along, crying quietly, wanting to be on her own, her duvet covering her mouth?

Laura's Hormones Gone Mad, is Jilly's signature tune. A Hopeless Case. Can't do a thing about her. Alice isn't so sure. Laura has never cried as steadily and brokenly as this.

She puts her head around the door. Her sister is facedown on the bed, her long hair pulled about, her eyes swollen. Looks like something more powerful than teenage emotion has her locked in its vice.

'What's the matter, Laura? You OK?'

There's no reply, though the sobs diminish.

Alice checks the room for signs of disruption but everything is in its place: the purple radio beside the bed; the poster of Johnny Depp from *Sleepy Hollow* on the wall, beside that a newspaper blow-up of Nelson Mandela exiting prison, raising his clenched fist high. Second to Johnny Depp, Nelson Mandela is Laura's Favourite Living Person. Around the computer screen are the usual blu-tacked quotations from Sarah Jessica Parker, Alice Walker and *The Little Book of Quiet* printed in neat handwriting on a pink card. And the white MFI bookcase with its arrangement of Christmas day photographs taken over the years by B-J according to a now dead-and-buried tradition. Jilly and Laura with their long eyes and Julia Roberts noses.

'Make you think of a Citroen car, those faces,' B-J used to say. 'Lippy and lateral and difficult to run.'

The pattern of faces isn't quite there in her own case, Alice registers for the two-hundredth time in her life, turning from the bookcase. In every photo frame she looks crumpled, just out of bed. In fact almost exactly like Phoenix in the school photograph Laura seems to be clutching to her chest. Phoenix's eyes are stained dark with oversleep.

Alice puts her hand on Laura's scattered hair.

'You OK, Laura? What's the matter?'

More snuffling and swallowing.

'Is it Mum? Was she angry with you? The stuff about Mr Khan?'

The name Mr Khan is their private joke. It's a code to signal how little they credit Jilly's dreamy stories, however real or unreal father Farouq himself may be. 'And when, Alice, did you last see Mr Khan?' 'Driving his kh-har in Khartoum of course.' 'Oh, Laura, Laura, I just can't cope with Mr Khan. Can you?'

A sudden sharp sniff from the bed. 'I don't know what's wrong. Really I don't. Whatever you do, don't say a word to anyone. Especially Mum. *Especially* Phoe.'

'As if I would.'

Laura crushes Phoenix's photo into her stomach.

'I have a bad ache. Here. Just here.'

She's gripping herself so tightly her knuckles stand out blue.

Alice settles herself on the bed in the crook of her sister's legs. She waits a while in silence and gradually Laura's story begins to trickle out, in gulping stops and starts.

'She's not been great all day,' Laura says sniffing, 'not all week actually.' She feels queasy and dog-tired, no idea why. And she's bloated and squishy all over, swollen up like a frog and hating it. It *definitely* can't be period trouble, all that's fine. It's a different kind of queasy, horrible, choking, which comes when she least expects it. She feels she wants to be ill and then can't be ill, goes dizzy instead. Gags like a maniac but her throat stays dry. Her throat's just about raw from the gagging.

She turns to the wall and puts Phoenix's photo beside her on the pillow. She begins to rub her arms as if she's freezing cold.

'I called this help-line yesterday,' she tells Phoenix's photo. 'I chickened out of seeing the doctor. I went, sat around and got tense, then picked up the help-line number in the waiting room. They talked about this sickness teenage girls can get. Looks like I've got all the symptoms.'

'And you believed them?' Alice can't help snorting. 'What do you know about this help-line? They're probably a call centre somewhere in Thailand or the Sudan. You were probably talking to a dam-builder or computer student or someone like that, desperate to earn some extra cash talking rubbish to a foreigner.'

She's shocked at how blank and defenceless Laura's face turns.

'*Don't*. You sound like Mum. The help-line person was a grown-up lady, actually, and she gave an explanation. That was something, something I needed. See, Alice, I'm scared, dead scared. I'm scared it's something, like, a lot worse. I don't know, environmental. Poisons in the water, all the carcinogens we live with. I worry there's something evil cooking up inside me. Is there some tumour? Have my tubes been squeezed or something?'

Alice wishes she hadn't said tubes. Especially *squeezed* tubes. *Something's cooking up inside her*. It makes an obvious situation too obvious, so much so that Laura herself is staring it in the face and not seeing it. Laura was always one for walking into lampposts.

What possessed her, Alice, to mess about so long with that jar today? she asks herself. It's given her ideas, or, more like it, one big, uneasy idea. Could that be why, today of all days, she had to lift that ghostly jar down from its shelf? It was fate after all, fate guiding her hand. She's been picking up without realising it that there's something the matter with Laura, something awful to do with unwanted growths, half-baked, wrinkled things—the kind of things that fetch up in storage jars.

She shoots an x-ray glance across her sister's middle. She notices how under the cover of the duvet folds she's weirdly pulling and pressing at her body, as if checking for some budding possibility.

'Alice, lay off the glowering. Look, it's not like I'm going to die from stomach sickness or anything like that, you needn't worry. I'm sure it's this teenage thing. *Quinsy*, the help-line lady said, something like that, stress-related, kind of teenage ME. I need rid of the bloating and queasiness, that is all.'

She subjects her stomach to another furious kneading.

'I'm trying not to worry, Laura, but I don't trust your help-line. I think we should think of a different solution.'

Alice hears how her upbeat voice starts out fake, then grows serious. As she gets up from the bed she suppresses the impulse to grab Phoenix's photo from its pride of place on Laura's pillow and chuck it away. Silly trouble-maker. Then she stops in her tracks. Hang on a minute, there's something in that. *Chuck it away.* She looks again at Laura's pinched and pressed middle. There's something in that thought that might hit the spot.

She bites back the sigh of relief rising to her lips.

It might be, yes, the likeliest way out.

She throws a hug around her sister's neck, making sure to avoid her lower half. Laura looks up puzzled at the force in her arms.

'You stay warm now,' Alice says. 'We'll definitely think of something, we'll come through this like we do. I'll check my biology books, they're always useful. Grassick's one, and *The Pocket Atlas of the Moving Body*. And there's something else, a surprise, a secret that will help us see better what's going on. But it means I have to pop out to Arnie's for a minute—won't be long. You can rest in the meantime. I'll get you a couple of paracetamols from the bathroom. Don't cry anymore, Laura. I'm sure we're going to be OK.'

Her sister turns awkwardly to face the door. As she lifts her head from her pillow the attempted smile in the corners of her mouth shrinks into a wince.

Chapter 3

Arnie

Bunched in a ball on my bed, me and him side by side,
legs folded tight at the knee just the same as him, and
the bedside light catching the moony glow of his head.

From next door in *Evie Deluxe*, the beauty therapy
studio Mum operated out of our house, I could hear her
instructions overshadowing a client's softer, up-and-down
voice, telling her she would look better this way; no, *this*
way. When clients came in the evenings, between 7.00 and
9.00 p.m., I could hear all manner of voices and stories
through the thin partition wall. But things were on my
mind this evening so I didn't tune in as usual, what with
him squashed inside his glass cradle like an overgrown fish
and the steely smell of formalin trumpeting his presence to
the world.

Got to do something for him without delay, him with
his baby hands. Can't have Mum sniffing his smell from
the landing.

I hear the swishing of the women's feet going
downstairs and the Yale clunking open. Open, shut.

'Arnie, hallo? You there?'

'In my room.' Announced casually, like on any ordinary
day.

But I popped him ever so gently under the bed, beside a
box of Lego pieces. Good thing I swept out the dust
bunnies only last weekend.

Mum came to stand on the landing. I could sense her
Snow White mouth pursed close to the closed door, her

lips jutted forwards to give that feeling of whispering cosily.

'One more lady this evening, pet. Mrs Silver, eyebrows job. You'll be all right?'

'I'm fine, Mum.'

'What do you think? Shall we do something quick for tea? Quick and tasty, a fry-up? We've got eggs.'

'Sounds good,' I said, 'I'll wait.'

Slim, smiley, her eye velcroed onto the bright side of life, my mum could be called a Perfect Mum except that she wasn't really my mother, not my biological mother. My real mum Sheila died when I was a tiny baby: *complications arising from childbirth*. At the time I was probably bigger than him though, this little fellow here, is my gentle but lumpish fish.

When I was two, Dad married Evie, that is Mum, who couldn't have children, so she adopted me as her own, a much-wished-for cuckoo to fill her empty nest, she said. I've always been glad she was happy to adopt me, that someone so easy to get along with wanted me that much. Maybe even too much, as jealous Dad all too soon began to feel.

My Dad Danny was a cool dad. I mean truly, really, literally cool, as in temperature-cool. Dad's work was to fill Coke, Evian and Lucozade drinks dispensers and collect the coins. His hands always felt cool and clammy because, so he said, he handled so much refrigerated metal. He'd be away days, driving his red-and-white van all over the country, stopping off to stash cans at garden centres, petrol stations, community and sports halls, basically anywhere you can think of where can machines stand.

It will sound strange but at the end of last summer, at the beginning of the new school year, he left to set up house in the north with a new lady because he said Evie didn't love him enough, she and I didn't miss him at first. For a good while we didn't miss him, till I began to wonder about what to do when the toaster broke, and who to kick a ball with on the Recreation Ground, and Evie sitting by herself night after night just watching the telly.

The way things were now I wouldn't mind a visit from my dad, or, better, being invited to his new house and meeting his new lady. What was special was that she was from Africa, the west coast of Africa, inside the Bulge, and very tall, so Dad told Mum on the phone. He thought she might need to be prepared.

'Prepared for what I can't think,' Mum said, her mouth unusually small and sour. 'It's hardly like we're about to invite them over.'

The new lady, Mum said Dad said, began her life in England as a student nurse and was now a Refugee. She was Angry about Oil and so her government didn't want her any more. Her village stood in a massive river delta where the mud ran black with oil from the wells sunk by international oil companies mad for profit. That Mud was Inseamed with Petrodollars, she said, but the People were Poor as Dirt.

They'd put her on a 'Banned List' for asking awkward questions.

I told Alice all this, about the tall lady from West Africa, thinking she'd be interested, but she surprised me with a casual shrug. 'So?' she said and held up four fingers. 'The west of Africa is this many thousand miles from my Dad's neck of the woods. Or jungle.'

At Christmas Dad sent me a Save the Children card, signed only by him, and at Easter time a chocolate egg in a padded envelope that arrived broken. The envelope showed his address on the back. The address made me think that it would be nice if he could give me a proper call, to say, 'Arnie, how about dropping by some time?' Or, 'Son, I've bought a spare bed just for you.'

Even if in his heart he didn't really mean it.

Mum was an almost Perfect Mum because she managed every single day, rain or shine, to look freshly brushed and scrubbed, even when she felt off-colour or sad. In fact even on the day Dad left she washed her hair and put in highlights. To the women and the few men who came to her for *Evie Deluxe* treatments she gave free moral support on top of the grooming and waxing. I knew this of course because of listening through the wall.

The only thing about Evie I would say was that I didn't get to be with her as often as I'd have liked. Her clients lying on the other side of the bedroom wall on the raised treatment table, Dad's DIY handiwork, got to talk to her a whole lot more than me. Mum had to work six full days a week which meant that though we were under the same roof we didn't actually *see* one another very often or spend time together. And there was no point complaining. As she repeated several times a week, she had to work these long hours because Danny didn't send us enough money to live.

Then again—sunny-side up, she'd say—I was allowed, because she worked at home, to knock on the beauty-room door and call my message through if ever I needed her. Can I go to see Alice? Shall I get us bowls of muesli/boiled eggs/toasted cheese for our tea?

Tonight was unusual in that respect. I was generally the one to fix the tea.

Sitting there on my bed, our pale, deep-ocean fish sheltering beside the Lego box, I heard the salon door close behind Mum and Mrs Silver. A sharp click. Even if I missed hearing clients on the stairs, I knew Mum was in there with someone because the door's shutting sounded crisper.

Right now, I decided, *straightaway*. The feeling was urgent. Bundle my fleece around the jar, my nubbly, browny-white fleece, *brushed Egyptian cotton*, fresh from the washed laundry pile, and Get Him Out Of Here. Downstairs and out of the house but bundled warmly.

I groped for him, wrapped him and crept downstairs, through the kitchen and out into the garden, holding him like he was crystal, diamonds, feathers, all at once making sure he didn't slip through the folds of fleece. I wanted badly to protect him. It wasn't safe for him inside, not as safe as I'd thought. Number one, his smell was a dead giveaway, strong and sneeze-making. Giveaway two was how loudly, at the very smallest movement, the liquid in his jar sloshed around his bits.

The back garden was as dark as a pocket and the sky overhead misty, dusty-orange with streetlight glow. Standing perfectly still, with the glass jar held still and its liquid still, I had the feeling we were about to begin some important ceremony, some offering to the gods in pagan times.

Then I reminded myself in Alice's voice that this feeling had to do with nothing more than an undersized baby corpse: an ancient and very dead baby.

'But a baby that had once been a living thing,' my own voice couldn't help replying. If we were in its place, wouldn't we want to be shown some kindness?

Then again, Alice's voice came back: 'We weren't dead, so how could we think ourselves into the place of the baby?'

In our small, neat garden, I soon discovered, there weren't too many corners to hide a large Kerr storage jar, big enough for about, say, 2 or 3 kilos of flour. Mum grew her annuals in pots arranged down the right-hand side of the lawn in a regular zigzag pattern. She kept the grass and bushes lining the pathway down the middle as closely trimmed as her ladies. There was nothing overhanging anywhere and very few shadows.

I placed him first on the cool bricks of the pathway, under the splayed branches of one of the larger bushes. I peeled away the fleece to make his bulk look littler. But then, standing back, I still could see him clearly, a pale blob like some yoghurt plant; or, no, a tiny foetus elephant, smooth, pearly, its head hunched forwards, its trunk tucked up, its feet already chunky.

Seeing him cowering under those branches gave me gooseflesh so I took him back and wrapped him again.

Next I tried the shed at the bottom of the garden. The shed stood inside the convenient shadow of the old spare-parts warehouse over the garden wall. I had cleaned out the shed not long ago and knew there was nothing in there but general dryness, a few rakes and spades stacked in a corner. I put him in the centre of the shed floor, faraway from all shadowy and looming objects, just as if he was a living creature who might be scared of the dark.

But no sooner did I begin to close the door on him than I lost it. For his sake I lost it. A thick, bulging and unbudging blackness reigned in that shed. It was too dark and lonely. Think how many nights he had survived on his lab shelf before Alice and I had taken him. Among all the preserved embryos he had, she was sure, been the only human. He'd sat through all those nights for all those years in isolation, totally out on a limb. His endurance was 100 per cent.

I opened the shed door to let in the misty light, then sat down on the raised wooden step and tried to think. On account probably of his having been moved about, my blobby hunch-backed creature slumped back a centimetre or so inside his jar and glugged, definitely glugged. At about the same instant a half moon surfaced from behind the blowing mist. It made it look like he was breathing, sucking breath in and out. My mouth turned to sandpaper.

Imagine the dragging sounds he would make if he escaped the enclosing glass, I couldn't help thinking.

Imagine him pushing his mushed face and moony skull over the rim of the jar and flopping to the floor, dragging his skinny belly after lying on his back like an insect, legs in the air, his wound exposed, his mouth chomping with the effort. Think how he would eyeball the shed with his pale eye-bulges, goggle at the grey rectangle of the door and my face in the middle of it.

It was weird, mind you, how a thing with such dead eyes still seemed to fix me with its glare. Even when I wasn't looking directly at it, I sensed this frozen gape. And then suddenly I saw. He gave this frozen gape, I realised, because he *was* frightened. He had once been badly frightened—in fact petrified. With this shocked grimace he had stared his death in the face.

An even bigger reason to show him kindness, so I wrote an invisible note to Alice. Let's give him the best deal possible. Help him round off his second life, his shelf life, as comfortably as we can.

But I couldn't think just at this minute what that best deal might be.

The neighbour's ginger cat trotted slantwise through the garden. He was on business of his own and paid us no notice. A good sign. Our thing, my fish, I reminded myself, wasn't an elephant-calf or a ghost or a mini-monster or anything that might disturb a cat. It was basically a leftover, an antique, past-sell-by-date specimen that should have been tidied away years ago.

For a second then I did wonder about getting rid of it, in one fell swoop. Do what we meant to do hours before. Chuck the bottle over the wall and into the warehouse yard; hear it shatter and go plop, or more like splat, splodge.

But the thought made me sick to my stomach. And I registered trouble. I saw the headline. *Suspicious Baby Corpse Found in Deserted Yard.* Within days all England would know about it. People lapped these things up. In the magazines Mum kept in the hallway for her waiting ladies there once was a big story about a Horror Hospital. Through the partition wall I'd heard them talk about it: a hospital room secretly stacked with fridges full of baby bits and bobs in jars. *Kept for research purposes*, the doctors said.

I picked up our creature once again, rubbed the glass with the nubbly fleece to give a little warmth. Then I returned him to the spot under the big bush, except this time right up against its central knot of branches. The shifting shadows in there more or less camouflaged his paleness.

The doorbell was clinking as I stepped back into the kitchen.

Mum had said Mrs Silver was her last client of the day so this couldn't be anyone to do with the salon. And wasn't a visitor. Evie and I didn't have surprise visitors. And it couldn't be Alice either. She had her way of sliding her Sports Slice card along the snib of the Yale and creeping in unannounced.

But it *was* Alice. It was Alice, red-faced and out-of-breath, her skin steaming, her whole self on the warpath.

She hit me in the arm as a greeting. Her whisper was venomous and urgent.

'Got to talk to you in private. *Now.*'

The worst thing—we'd been discovered. Police, scientists from the local university, social services, you name it, were hard on our heels, come to grab him back.

But Alice had thought of something even worse than the worst thing. Alice always anticipated. She fired fierce words into my ear as we made our way upstairs. I could feel her cheeks glowing against my face.

'Listen up, Laura's pregnant. I'm sure as I can be.'

In an instant I sensed the threat we faced. I felt it like a thud into my ribs. I meant not the threat that Alice and I

56

faced, but me and it. Me and him, especially him. I could feel that Alice was about to drag our creature into the very middle of her crisis.

'Laura's lying in bed holding her guts,' Alice was saying. 'She's bloated like a dead horse. I talked to her and she says she's desperate. Jilly's no help at all, never would be, and Phoenix's useless. Thing is, Laura doesn't think she's pregnant'—Alice's voice sank to murmur—'in fact she's thinking far worse, of cancer, poison, that kind of thing. Troubles that can't be reversed. So it's up to us to help. This thing *can* be reversed. We've got to show her a way through.'

Of course, I nodded, of course.

'I'm thinking we could show her the specimen. Only that. Give her a bit of a jolt. She must see what she's got into, what she's got to deal with. Right now she's turning her face from it all. She needs to shock herself awake, plan out what to do. The body will do it for her.'

Then, as I knew she would, Alice moved on rapidly to what she had come for. She brought her forehead close to mine.

'So where's it gone? The specimen? The jar? We need it now and badly. If I show it to Laura I know she'll keep our secret. It'll be our secret for her secret. And then, first thing tomorrow morning, I'll take it back to the lab. We'll all want rid of it by then. I'll smuggle it in under my coat. The ladder'll still be where we left it. I'll sit the jar back in its place and turn the cut to the storeroom wall. At least this is one experiment we've done that might have a good result. So, Arnie, where is it? We haven't got all night.'

But here for once she had put a foot wrong. For once I wasn't about to roll over and give way to her ideas. Her face was sparkling, amazing, crazy. Her eyes glittered with her incredible, genius solution. I was totally in awe of her.

I'd walk around the world for her, twice over. But that wasn't the same as agreeing with her plan.

So I played for time. I sat down slowly and deliberately on the bed, choosing the exact same place as before. I folded my feet under me, I studied my hands. I watched her out of the corner of my eye.

Tonight Quiet Arnie would have to work as quietly as a ghost.

'The doctor?' I said carefully. 'Don't they have something to say?'

'Laura hasn't been to the doctor. I mean, she tried to go but got scared. Maybe she doesn't want the news to leak back to Jilly. Maybe she'll go to the doctor when we've given my idea a chance?'

She broke off suddenly and tossed her chin at me.

'So, Arnie, where've you hidden it?'

At that moment I saw a whole set of things map out in clear lines and edges. I saw there was a hunt on and I saw who was quarry. I saw for the first time that Alice could be vicious. I despised her, almost: my friend, jumping to her decisions, pushing me around, wielding her implements of death, too graphic by half, aiming to shock her poor sister out of her wits with a biological freak show.

But I also saw that I had a new collaborator, though passive. And I saw that I might put my head to his quiet head, and think in silent chorus how to survive.

I said, 'You know, Alice, that what you're planning isn't right? Scaring Laura about what's the matter. Making her think she's growing this nightmare monster thing when it might be something completely different. It might be fine. You're forcing her in this single direction. Embryos anyway—they don't want to die. Look at the face on our one.'

'Shut up, Arnie. Who talked about dying? We know nothing about the story of our one. There's no comparison between it and what's going on with Laura. All I want is to give her a wake-up call, to say, Laura, this is reality, this is what your problem could expand into. You wouldn't in any case be able to see the thing that's inside my sister with the naked eye, or not yet.'

She spat the word *eye* with supreme scorn.

'When this thing is sorted,' she went on, 'I'd be happy to spend time on the Questions of Life and Death. But not now. Right now I need to get hold of the jar. And you need to go and haul it out of its hiding-place.'

'I'm thinking of that thing about souls,' I said still idling, back-pedalling, slowing the minutes down. 'There was something Evie once read me from the *Reader's Digest*. Unborn people, I mean the spirits of unborn people, they choose the bodies they want to live in. They hang about in the universe waiting for their time to be born and then they choose their bodies. Do you want to cut off one of these souls before it has even had time to land?'

'*Arnie*! I don't believe I'm standing here with Laura waiting sick at home and you're spouting rubbish. I don't believe it. I don't believe you believe it.'

'I don't know what I believe. I enjoyed what Evie read. It was a good story. I'd never thought of that before, being unborn.' Making it up as I went along, unspooling like a broken cassette, 'I imagine unborns are spirits floating in amongst the asteroids, drifting like dandelion seeds as they line up for their birth.'

Alice grabbed me hard. In two seconds she gave me two dead arms. Her eyes shone dully, like boiled onions. She looked exactly like she did when she made to stick her blade into me on the playing field earlier today but this time I felt no fear, not even the tiniest jab of fear. My scheme was coming into focus as I talked. Something inside me lifted off, spread its wings wide and was airborne.

I couldn't exactly fit thoughts to the feeling, though it had to do with more than freeing myself from Alice's plan. It had to do with life, *Life*. The thing in the jar wasn't just a thing. I knew this like I knew I had a beating heart. The two of us had carried it, rescued it. It had become something of our own, close to us. It belonged to us now. It was real, though dead, a little human after all. It looked something like us, like a small brother or sister might have looked before birth. I could even say the child Evie and Danny had never had together and now never would. Of course it wasn't *really* a brother, a baby, I knew this. But it *was* a one-time living thing, a once-alive creature taking refuge in this house that was usually so empty of children and so full of clients.

'God, you're a wuss, Arnie!' Alice was saying. 'I worried about relying on you and look where it's got me. You're delaying me badly now. Can we please *hurry up*? Can't you see, it's a stroke of luck we have that specimen? Get that into your head, it's a stroke of luck. As for spirits, foetuses aren't fully alive until they're born, OK? A foetus, especially a little one, is a parasite like nits. Better out than in.'

But there was such a look of dark confusion in her face my throat closed. As I made my next move my breath rocked in my chest. I was down on the ground again and creeping blindfold. Never before had I had a secret from Alice.

'Thing is,' I hoped she'd not notice how stiffly I spoke, 'about an hour ago I stashed the specimen jar in Cannon's warehouse over the garden wall. I had to. You could smell the formalin everywhere in the house. You know, the World War I vintage. It's a difficult route back in there, across the pile of scrap in the warehouse yard. We won't be able to fetch it before Evie goes to bed. If we go together now she'll ask why.'

Sweat was in my armpits and my face burning.

Alice was straightaway suspicious. Her eyes flashed questions. Why hadn't I mentioned the warehouse at the start? How come I had sat on this information so long?

'I'll go for him on my own,' she blurted.

'No, Alice, no, please! You don't know the way. What if you knock something, make a noise, even hurt yourself?'

'I wouldn't hurt myself.'

'Hurt your hands, I mean. The hands that have to carry the important specimen back into the lab.'

She refused to flinch at this. For long minutes her eyes bored into me unblinking and her fingers still squeezed my arms. Her lips moved as if she was trying to bring scattered words together but she kept quiet. What my own face was doing I couldn't tell.

The click of the salon door jolted us out of our stupor. We stepped back from each other. Alice scrubbed her hands across her head.

We heard Mrs Silver leaving and small sounds of Mum sighing and squeaking the floorboards in the hallway and giving a cough.

'Hallo, Arnie? Alice with you?'

She'd have spotted the extra pair of trainers.

'Yes, Evie,' Alice called out clearly, calm as a statue. She was already halfway down the stairs. 'Actually I'm just heading off. I came over to check on some homework with Arnie but'—she threw me a baleful backward glance and thrust her feet into her shoes—'he's still busy with the book I wanted, this special project. He said he'll walk it over to my house a bit later tonight.'

'You children take care. And give my regards to your mum, Alice. Tell her we'll catch up tomorrow for sure.'

The front door Yale lock snapped shut. If Alice gave a reply I didn't catch it.

* * *

Fried eggs and bacon were my favourite meal but I hardly tasted the tea Evie cooked that evening, my thoughts were chasing each other so fast. I slurped up my egg in two gulps. It was a thing I usually did but tonight I hardly tasted it. I had to make a getaway, I figured this was definite. Get him as far away from Alice's grabbing hands and murderous mad mission as possible. Locate a hiding place somewhere safe and quiet and unlikely and wait for things to cool down. With Alice you could rely on things eventually cooling down. She stopped so crazily aiming for what she wanted and, suddenly, without warning, came to earth.

As for a strategy, I had first of all to find a good strong bag to carry him in, like a rucksack, or, better, some shopping bag where I could balance the jar and keep an eye on him. There was Mum's willow-pattern Past Times totebag, for example, ordinary-looking and well-laminated, hanging on its coat-hook in the hallway. I might borrow it a few days. It would do the job.

About a place to bolt to I wasn't sure. Dan's mum Daphne lived not too far away, in Aylesbury, but she was very old and frail. And there was a second place where I might go, though I'd not been there before, and wasn't exactly wanted. Dad's big, red face was there, and his growly voice, but I couldn't picture it just yet. It made a blob of fog in my head.

The evening itself progressed according to plan, which was good. After tea I cleared the table and Mum washed up. She was chatty but tired, and her remarks as she held utensils under the hot tap kept drifting off into silence. 'Mrs Silver, she does go on about things...' 'You'll help me out later won't you, Arnie, the usual Thursday...?'

I stacked the morning's washed plates in the dresser. I wiped the counters and cooker and let my quiet schemes race on.

Money: I definitely needed money. There was forty pounds in the brown envelope in my cupboard, birthday money, and dinner-money change in my pocket: forty-two pounds fifty. Enough to be getting on with until I got to my destination, my fuzzy, blob-of-fog destination. Till Dad's clammy-cold hands could be persuaded to hand out some more.

I was operating on auto-pilot by the time it came to Evie's regular, pre-weekend, de-hairing treatment. Usually I wasn't too keen about helping her out. I wouldn't say no but I wasn't keen. The wax was burning hot for one thing. For another you can have enough of bare, goose-flesh skin.

But today nothing touched me. I went through the motions and my schemes sped on.

Off on a big adventure with my unusual teddy.

I'd extract the Kerr jar from the bushes after Evie's bedtime, I reckoned. Wrap the jar tightly in the Egyptian cotton fleece; use it to pad him out, the little fellow; hold him upright in the Past Times bag. Remember my toothbrush, the money envelope, a clean pair of socks. My red platypus beanie baby for good luck. Leave behind all non-essentials. The one thing I missed was a road map. We didn't own one. But National Express Coaches had signs up, didn't they, to show their destination?

I swirled the wooden spatula round Evie's pot of wax on its special hot plate, watched the gloopy spiral dissolve back into evenness, stirred again. She had on her usual Thursday night sleeveless top. She raised her arm and crooked her elbow to lay bare the pit.

'You know the score. Slap it on. I'll scream if it hurts.'

She stretched her elbow to the ceiling.

'Why do it if it hurts?' I said.

It wasn't the first time I'd said this.

'I don't know, darling. The hurt doesn't last? Maybe I feel better afterwards? And that's more than can be said for some kinds of hurt. Anyhow, smooth is cool nowadays, I'm afraid. Perfect is the name of the body game. It keeps me in business.'

I thought about hurt, Evie hurting. I reminded myself to leave a note.

Away for the weekend. School coach trip. Crack-of-dawn departure. So sorry but forgot to tell you.
Love.

Tomorrow was Friday. If things worked out with even 50 per cent success it would be Saturday before she panicked. And by then I'd have called. I'd have hoped to have called.

I smeared on the wax like buttering a sandwich.

I'd write the note last thing before leaving. I was checking off items on an imaginary To Do List. Leave the paper on the top stair where she'd be sure to see it. Fridays were busy days for her. Everything should be fine unless for some reason she bumped into Alice. But this was unlikely. Glowering Alice intimidated Evie. Alice and family, she said, were *plain awkward*. Jilly Brass though a regular client was *in the parent department, impossible*.

'You been swimming today, Arnie my pet?'

'No, why?'

I stepped back too quickly.

'Looks like it. Your wrinkled fingers. There's something like chlorine on your skin.'

She stretched up her nose. I lurched back a second time, spatula in hand, droplets of hot wax spraying.

'Arnie! Watch what you're doing.' She rubbed her neck furiously.

'Sorry. It was an accident. Sorry, sorry.'

'You've *got* to be more careful. Weren't your teachers saying how you're more focused nowadays, darling, more centred? Show me how it's done.'

The buttering continued in silence. The fridge gave out its usual painful sighs. I glanced at the kitchen clock. Just past ten. An hour or so till her bedtime. Four or five hours before our leave-taking if I worked quickly, if his gurgling self co-operated. National Express coaches departed all through the night, didn't they? I'd seen the posters at the coach station.

Evie sat like a statue, her armpit stiffly plastered in wax. Then with her left hand she laid muslin strips on to her skin and, grimacing hard, ripped at the tiny hairs with gusto.

'There, smooth as a bubble, just like I like it.' Her smile back in place. 'Pity it doesn't last. How bodies keep sprouting. But that's my job. Smoothing and sloughing over and over again.'

She only ever waxed one pit at a time. To do two at a go, she'd say, was to be a sucker for punishment.

I walked over to the television and turned on the video, the week's taped episode of *Casualty*, her favourite. *Casualty* was generally on while she was working so I recorded it for her.

Straightaway there was a badly injured man being manhandled into an ambulance. With her hand tucked into her freshly treated armpit Mum came over and sat beside me. We watched this kind of stuff together. It was how we spent time. It reminded us that it was better to watch side-by-side sitting on the settee than upstairs in our bedrooms on our own. It was better to be feeling squeamish together, I mean, than alone. The day of the Twin Towers we sat here on the settee counting the bodies out loud, the people falling down the buildings, falling so fast they left their lives trailing far behind them. 'Eighty-one, eighty-two. No, we've already seen that clip. Eighty-two, eighty-two.'

But today things were different. Today my head was a rumpus with all I had to do: a bag to pack; a note to write;

a body to save. And meanwhile his funny moon-head craned out for me there in the shadows of the garden.

I thought about how Alice once told me she liked to build pictures of the world without us in it. Thinking of impossible worlds, she called it, as if we had never lived. 'We're all of us the fossils of the future,' she said, 'we're bones and ash in waiting.'

Well, maybe so, I said to myself, but not just yet. Live bodies go on sprouting, they go on making skin. Look at all the work Evie had tidying up her clients. Which meant that where there's life there's something to be getting on with. There are things to belong to and journeys to make. There's a long path to walk before morning.

* * *

For the few hours I lay in bed that night I hardly slept. Again and again I lurched out of a thin, watery daze imagining I could hear voices—the voices of Evie's clients that, every day and evening, came seeping through the partition wall between my room and the studio. Everyone who came to *Evie Deluxe* seemed to like to talk babies. They talked men and they talked babies, but I wasn't interested in the stories about men.

It was the stories about babies that I imagined all night I was hearing, stories that shaped themselves around the half-life of our foetus, its life before birth.

There was the silvery-voiced lady's story: the lady who always said she felt so empty, so hollow, echoey and empty, she couldn't imagine what it would be like to be a whole person again, when one bit of her was lying in the graveyard sanctuary where they placed the stillbirths and the pre-term deaths, the miniscule urns of ashes. How her baby had died inside her when it was quite small.

'And still he wasn't in a hurry to be parted from me. They had to induce. For a while then I had the belly but felt nothing. It had all *gone cold*.'

And there was the story of the twins who had lain warm and intact in their amniotic sacs, 'pictures of who they might have been'. The story belonged to the steely-haired woman whose skin hung loose on her body, who came twice a week for Evie's hour-long back massages. Tonight I could hear again just as if she were speaking directly to me how she'd been *visited* by two sets of twins, her word, and not a single one born alive. When the babies came out they were still warm, she said, perfect and warm, but they never opened their eyes; they never knew their own birth. And, as if her gaze might spark from them a flicker of recognition, she had stared at them till they were taken away. She was cursed, she whimpered, cursed by life.

And there was the young woman, twenty, twenty-one, not many years older than Alice's sister Laura, with a false tan and big doe-eyes. Her sing-song story clung to my memory most tightly. Every week I used to listen out for when she left and secretly watch her walk away up Stratford Street trailing her bag in her hand.

For the first time in years her life was fantastic, she had explained to Evie in a whisper one day. I'd crushed my ear to the wall. After the car accident, she'd said, they rebuilt her face. She had a new face, a new job and a new man. Her first serious man. And then a second accident happened. She found she was carrying a baby and she wasn't ready, not ready at all. Her voice had growled with distress. She wasn't ready and her boyfriend wasn't ready. She knew she'd resent this child always if she had it. *Always*. She had visions of dropping babies from high windows, of tapping small skulls against the headboard of her bed.

So her name was written on a list and the list was put into action. The baby was taken out. That is to say, *slurped*. I'd clearly heard her say it. I could hear her say it now.

'*Slurped*, Evie, like a hairball or a cyst. Could anything be hoovered out like that and not break into a hundred pieces?'

Chapter 4
Alice

Alice sits on Laura's bed, her sister's stone-heavy head sunk in her lap.

Laura didn't ask to have her here, it's true. She had raised her head just a fraction when Alice pushed open the door. Sleepily she had shoved over to make room, grimacing at the coldness of Alice's skin, then tucked her arms reluctantly around her sister's legs. She had murmured something into the pillow, an inaudible but uninviting word; *sister* or *silly*.

But Alice wants to keep watch. It's a kind of vigil for Laura, for all of them. The window out to the street is open, a cool breeze streams in. Nelson Mandela in the newspaper poster on the wall catches the glow of the bedside light and beams out at the world. Johnny Depp is in shadow. She has her *Human Anatomy Picture Book* beside her, to help straighten out her thoughts. Her wrists, she notices, ache from how she gripped Arnie's arms just then. She hopes this won't create difficulties with getting the specimen jar back tomorrow, lifting it up to its high shelf.

Arnie has planted his seeds of doubt in her after all.

On the bedside table next to the purple radio lies her pouch of knives; here as a mascot, because she likes to look at it, imagine the blades lying hidden inside the black velvet, quiet and powerful.

It took a while for Laura to sink back into slow-breathing sleep. It took even longer for Alice's panting to ease after the sprint home. Now at last there's a bubble of quiet to think inside. She rests the back of her head against the wall. She keeps her ears open. Arnie'll be along soon enough with their Special Piece of Homework. Through the open window she'll be able to hear him call.

Sliding a hand from under Laura's head she manages to spread open on the sheets *Human Anatomy*'s full-colour illustration of the womb: a pregnant uterus in its first trimester to be exact. Inside a shell of yellow skin nestles a pod of pale-pink baby encased in lumps of red, purple and blue. The illustrators have drawn the thing way too big and way, way too pink.

With small shifts and tugs of her hips and her sister's shoulders Alice positions Laura's spread-eagled body at such an angle that she seems to grow out from her own crossed legs, foreshortened. Then she turns *Human Anatomy* upside down. This way she can imagine the situation virtually in 3-D. She can align the diagram to the dimensions of her sister's groin. *Groin*, a grown-up-sounding word. She can imagine this unlikely cluster of organs *here*, embedded over in that flesh *there*.

She wipes her sweaty palms on her trousers.

She knows it's mad, in fact completely bonkers, off her head, but sitting like this she could almost imagine carrying out an investigation on Laura by herself—a solo job. That is, if there really was a chunk of unwanted cells in there, a tiny salamander, an eel without even a heart, she could imagine probing towards it using no more than her diagrams and this real-life model and her own special nous.

Navigate with care, keeping well to the middle. Remember to go *down* as well as *in*.

Nudge around the cervix that in all the pictures awkwardly protrudes.

Find something to stand in for a stainless steel speculum, a nifty instrument she's read about in the specialist physiology books stacked in piles in the air-conditioned backroom of the High Street bookshop. Her own knives, obviously, are far too sharp.

She could make an attempt, no problem. Think how she struck into that dog's eye like a true marksman, without putting a finger wrong.

It all goes to show how the best-in-the-world prop for tonight's project will be the multi-coloured pod of the specimen foetus. It will give an exact demo. It'll shock Laura into facing up to things for sure.

Once Laura's awake she'll position the jar on a book right here where she's now sitting. Tighten the lid, maybe reinforce the seal with clingfilm, place the specimen upside down, bottom in the air, so it'll mimic exactly what's happening inside her sister.

Look Laura; this is what's going on inside you; it mirrors your situation to a *t*.

She wriggles her legs to keep the blood moving and Laura sighs in her sleep.

Thinking *specimen* and *situation* jogs a feeling in Alice that Arnie's long in coming. Not like him to delay, especially when she's the one handing out instructions. Maybe Evie was late to bed, she thinks, or the warehouse was in darkness. Maybe he's groping around in there even at this moment, barking his shins on invisible planks. Whatever has happened, she hopes he's keeping that jar steady—steady and safe.

She squints over at the quotations on the pink card Laura has stuck around her computer screen. There's a new one, bigger than the rest, plastered on with a fat blob of blu-tack. She can't read it easily from here though Laura's writing is painstakingly neat and square. From here it looks like poetry that doesn't make proper sense.

Suffer me not to be driven back at the gates of the dead, she slowly deciphers.

May I come forward in peace on quiet feet.
May I not be turned back.
From henceforth may I behold the face of the Sun and
the countenance of the Moon.
May my heart sit upon its throne.
The Egyptian Book of the Dead

She frowns just the same as if Laura were awake and sitting up in front of her. The words make her feel depressed. Why bother with poncy, gloomy, foot-shuffling stuff like that? To the extent of printing it out in your best handwriting, too?

* * *

Around midnight Alice falls into a thin, restless sleep, her neck awkwardly angled along Laura's low headboard, her legs numb with the weight of her sister's head.

'Don't close your eyes,' she tells herself at the same minute as her eyes begin to close, and the glow of the bedside light frays into pieces.

She tells herself she'll wake as soon as Arnie calls up from the street.

As soon as she hears his call, she'll let him in and make him jammy toast and explain everything calmly and in detail. That the *Human Anatomy* diagram is an oversized map, the foetus a 3-D model. 'You could even think of it as a sign from your precious Unborn,' she'll tell him, 'a pointer to us here in the realm of the living.'

Save Laura: here's how.

When he sees it all laid out, there's no way he won't be convinced.

But he doesn't call up and he doesn't come. At five o'clock the misty draft nudging in through the open window wakes her. She transfers her sister's head to the pillow and slips off the bed. She rubs her legs to get rid of the pins-and-needles. She walks over to the window. A yellow-grey dawn sky hangs low over the houses opposite. The damp air smells metallic, as if there was a chemical factory somewhere nearby leaking pollutants. Pollutants and poisons: Laura's diagnosis of why she's poorly.

Alice leans out of the window. There is no one about, no passing car or bike. The four-year-old twins who live across the road, Amina and Isla, habitual early-risers, haven't yet risen. Their pink curtains are drawn. The milk float hasn't yet made its deliveries. And no glass jar containing a grey-white blob has been left in the porch. There's no note that she can see; no explanation for this absence.

It's a bum deal. Arnie, it looks like, has let her down.

For a second she feels she could spit in disgust, let a fat mucus gob fly out of the window and on to the street below, but she doesn't have the energy for spitting. A heavy disappointment is dragging at her chest, a massy, gluey slump of disappointment. Her friend promised to come but instead has peeled off on his own; that's now obvious. He has dumped her idea, basically, and hijacked their prize. And she hadn't expected it of him. She had cooked up a good plan, a neat, clever and *kind* plan, and he usually liked her plans. She told him like she always did that she didn't mean harm, but this time he hadn't bought it. What she wanted was to bring her sister to her senses and for that Arnie has shrugged her off.

That same sister, Alice can tell, has several hours left to sleep. She's lying on her side, her face shoved deep into her pillow, her breathing slow. She's definitely not wrenched apart by pain, or not at this moment anyway. In profile her lower half doesn't look abnormally bloated, a little swollen maybe, not unusually so. All in all she appears incredibly *untouched* and restful for a person in her *condition*.

Though Alice has read up everywhere on organs and disease, the bodies she knows about are bodies in states of stillness, bodies in diagrams. With respect to *live* bodies her knowledge comes from myth, from what Jilly the hypochondriac swallows whole in *Woman's Own* and recaps over breakfast instead of eating. Lurid reports involving gigantic growths and tumescent hernias; twenty-four-hour writhing, superhuman agonies, wounds like caves.

To Alice a body in distress should be noisy whereas Laura is amazingly immobile and unconvincing.

She tiptoes downstairs and checks the hallway and then again the porch for a sign of Arnie. Nothing. No post-it, no coded message, no arrow diagram in sticks and stones signalling anything.

'So is this what he meant by that talk about the warehouse and the garden wall?' Alice puzzles. He never meant to give back the specimen jar, not at any point? '*No, Alice, no,*' he whined, 'I stashed it over in Cannon's warehouse.' When had he ever said no to her before? He meant to keep the jar from her from the very beginning. That was the secret behind his burning face.

Jilly's mobile phone is on the hallway shelf. On school days Jilly lets Alice use it. She switches it on now, covering the speaker slit with her thumb to muffle its start-up tone. There's a text from Yaz about meeting after school, nothing more. It's no use calling Arnie's house. He'll have made a getaway, she feels sure. He'll have covered his tracks and laid down decoys. And their foetus-in-jar, their sitting-duck, will have gone along with him.

Suddenly Alice feels the gust of energy that was pushing her forwards go *phut* out of her sails. She sits on the first step of the stairs; rests her head in her hands. Her clever strategy dims to grey fuzz like the image on a broken television. Think, *think*, THINK, she must think what to do, but her brain feels blocked up and tired.

By now Arnie could be in hiding somewhere down on the riverbank or even out of town, with their Special Homework tucked under his arm. The thought prickles her. What was she on about when she threatened him like that? Squeezing his arms, comparing embryos to nits? *Of course* he'd leg it, and fast disappear into some hole God knows where. Quiet, easily hurt Arnie. Why didn't she *think*? Look at how peacefully Laura's sleeping. Look how flat and small, pretty much her shape is. What was all the rage and panic?

Desperate as things seem she must try to find him. She must transfer herself into his thoughts and imagine what he might be plotting. She must stay mindful of the secret outlawry of their bond. He'll be heading away from Woodpark by now, she's certain. Why stick around when there are bodies to save. *Souls* to save?

She hears a soft creaking upstairs, of a body turning in bed, and feels an uncomfortable heat rise to her temples. There's still Laura's *condition* . . . but for now it'll have to be put on hold. Impossible to deal with two pressing matters at once. If Laura can sleep like a very heavy log then she can also wait in line for her treatment. Where there's no specimen to display, they can't in any case set the treatment in motion.

As for Alice herself, her main job now is to avoid raising an alarm. She'll have to go to school today and pretend nothing has happened. Help sweep the lab at break-time while avoiding the storeroom as if it were some quarantine area. Avoid even a single glance at the telltale gap on the top shelf. And remember to present an excuse for absence to Arnie's class teacher on his behalf.

One thing's for definite. Faffing about with specimen jars in Arnie's company has created *way* more trouble than it was worth.

She pads upstairs to comb her hair and brush her teeth. She tiptoes into her sister's room and retrieves *Human Anatomy* and her pouch of knives. Laura's mouth is wide open, sloppy and noiseless. In the full-length mirror opposite the bed Alice notices she's still wearing yesterday's clothes. She steps up to her reflection. Her green combats are muddy around the bottoms but otherwise fine. The long-sleeved t-shirt is barely creased.

On her way out she stoops to check at closer range the new quotation stuck on Laura's computer. Could be important, a nudge concerning what's *really* going on with her. But it's as she suspected, just stagey stuff; the kind of thing Laura's into: dark, sickly poetry about Meaning and Death. *Suffer me not to be driven back sighing at the clanging iron gates of the dead, etc, etc.*

She leaves her knives in their velvet pouch on the bedside table in her room. Can't risk drawing attention today of all days by having them clinking about in her pocket. She grabs a long-life teacake from the kitchen bread-bin.

In the hallway she runs into Jilly, sleepy-eyed in a padded, mauve dressing-gown.

'You're off early, sweetheart. Did you manage to get yourself some breakfast?'

Alice gestures with the teacake.

'You could have changed your socks. You'd those stripy ones on yesterday.'

Alice shrugs. Nothing to be done about it now. Her mouth is full of chewed teacake.

Still her mother blocks her way, surveying her narrowly.

'I don't know, my darling,' she blurts, and her eyes fill with tears. 'Sometimes it comes home to me, I'm not a very good mother to you and your sister in fact, am I? If we're honest with ourselves, Laura's forever grumpy and rude. You run wild and stay up till dawn. I heard you creeping about last night; couldn't sleep as a result. With

Farouq gone so long I'm your mother and father rolled into one. A kind of super-parent, or meant to be. And see, I don't even succeed at being a decent mum.'

'You're fine, Mum,' Alice swallows hard. 'There's no problem. We're fine. Teenagers are moody. Laura's a teenager. Before we know it I could turn moody, too.'

'But even if you weren't moody, even if you were perfect kids, impossibly perfect mega-kids, the fact is I'm not best adapted. How many are? Amongst lifeboat crews there are those who can't swim, did you know? Lifeboat rescuers save lives but they themselves drown in the water. That's the kind of thing I mean. Some mums aren't born with the skills. We're just not suited.'

Alice attempts to sidle past the padded dressing-gown but Jilly makes an unexpected move. Her arms jerk forwards and grab. She folds her daughter to her mauve chest while at the same instant giving her a strange and desperate little shove. Her fingers dig into Alice's back.

Then, as quickly as it came, the pressure is turned off. She places a kiss on Alice's crown and pats her hair goodbye. The whole encounter is spasmodic, awry. Alice yanks hard at the front door and almost stumbles out onto the path. With relief she feels the open air on her cheeks and the lavender bushes grazing her calves.

Jilly produces a small wave, twiddling two fingers in the air.

Overhead is a sound from Laura's room, faint though swelling, like low moaning. But Alice, walking a fierce bee-line through the garden gate and up Albion Street, does not hear it. Jilly, imagining Laura fast asleep, hears the sound but puts it down to the noise of young children in some neighbouring house: Isla and Amina, the hyper-lively twins across the road.

She drifts into the bright, south-facing front room and switches on the computer at the table. For the hundredth time this year she goes to the web-site of Friends Reunited. But she doesn't log in; she doesn't have a password. She can't bear the thought of visiting daily and Farouq never being in touch. And he wouldn't be in touch, would he? How could he, driving taxis all day in dusty Khartoum and earning a pittance? In downtown Khartoum the internet cafes are few and far between, she imagines. She imagines a single tiny kiosk in ice-cream colours and a white person in trendy specs collecting money at a rickety till beside the door.

Logging on every day and finding no response, she couldn't bear the dull ache she'd feel in her chest; in the very core of her, a far deeper ache than the irrational feeling of rejection she gets just by looking at the Friends Reunited web-site logo. Still she pretends to visit, to remind herself that one morning soon, she really-and-truly will do it. Register herself and throw out a line to Farouq. His deep, melty eyes.

She wanders over to Alice's housekeeping moneybox perched in its usual place in the middle of the mantelpiece, under the soulful gaze of Farouq Khan's photo. The moneybox is where the family petty cash is stored. Alice has Jilly and Laura under strict orders not to tamper with any part of the box, not to fiddle with the stopper in the bottom, not to shake out coins for treats from the corner shop. But this morning Jilly knows that to cheer up she'll have to break the rule. She's a rubbish Mum; she'll risk Alice's cross-patch face. Par for the course. She needs a bit of chocolate. There's nothing like chocolate to lift one's spirits when the girls leave her blue.

A whole new £2 coin conveniently tumbles out at the first shake of the box. Jilly pulls on a jacket, pastel pink, flatters her pale spring skin-tones, and lets herself out of the house. The corner shop is close by, at the corner of Selvon Street and the main road. After popping in there, she thinks, she may stroll further. She may stroll to the river and find a bench. She could spend a pleasant hour in the mild grey light watching the ducks, nipping off pieces of her bar of chocolate and savouring each morsel with meticulous slowness.

Chapter 5

Arnie

Bunched in a ball on the riverbank not far from my school I lay with my hunched-backed fish in his willow-pattern Past Times shopping bag stretching cool against my leg. The purple night giving way to a bright grey morning and the shadows looking as solid and smooth as the objects throwing them.

We lay hidden behind a wall of reeds trying to get some sleep, my legs folded up just the same as his; a muzzy smell like dog's breath coming off the foam-blotched, brown water.

Coaches to the north-west, it turned out, left town early, at around five in the morning; coaches to the north-east were later. For two hours or so I'd hung around the coach station in the darkness. I'd sat perched on a fold-up seat, my head tucked inside my hoodie, but with the London commuter crowd growing by the minute, I'd begun to worry. Our neighbour-but-one in Stratford Street, Phil, a computer programmer with a broad, white face, took an early bus into London every morning. I didn't want him to surprise me. I didn't want to surprise him. Not him, nor anyone else.

Here on our familiar Chartwell River I could spend my hours in hiding undisturbed. Lying by the reeds close to the water's edge I could cover my creature with my body. This place was a safe, long river-bend downstream from where Alice and I came sometimes to sit, especially on weekends, to whittle sticks and skim stones and pass the time.

Alice, radar-brain at full throttle, would by now be hard on my tracks.

But even with the reed cover it was a challenge to find some peace on this stretch of the river. If I'd had more courage, I'd have shifted further downstream again.

First along the tow path came two policemen, full of smiles and conversation. One was off to the Bahamas with his new girlfriend. He told his partner she might be *The One.* They stopped nearby to peep at a set of photos in a wallet and so, I guessed, managed to overlook me squeezed up against my reeds, hardly letting myself breathe. They also missed the teenage boy and girl who came wandering in their wake, giggling. Later, when I left the river, I saw the pair of them lying under a May bush not far off with a syringe hanging from the bloke's sleeping hand. He was bare-chested and his shirt lay clumped under his back.

After the policemen and the boy-and-girl couple a police helicopter buzzed into view and positioned itself overhead, directly above the council houses on the bank opposite. The helicopter didn't stick around long, but it was the scariest visitor. I was sure I could feel the stir and sweep of the whirling blades on my skin, and the roaring of the engine rocking my skull. I pressed myself deeper into the reeds then, till the reaching arms of a blackberry bush on the other side of the reed barrier scratched my cheek and my fish-baby gurgled in his bag.

Unless I was lucky, careful and lucky, he could at any unguarded moment give us clean away.

Dogs came by too; their bouncy, wriggling backs, always with invisible owners calling sharply. I wondered about being sniffed out. My creature had no smell of his own, did he, because of the formalin? But what did I know? A lot of his original liquid had spilled. Alice's stupid cut in his belly could go bad. Any minute now he might begin to stink the stink of rotting and death. The stink of the half-chewed rat next-door's ginger cat once left in our garden.

Finally I thought I saw through the reeds Alice's mum Jilly Brass walking past, though it could have been any middle-sized woman in a pink jacket eating chocolate. I even thought I heard Alice herself calling, but it was probably only a high-pitched dog-walker. After hearing her voice I lay for another half-hour, till nearly nine, nine-thirty, the sky darkening; trying with every muscle in my body to resist the urge to creep out, show myself like some Stig-of-the-Dump.

Good idea, yes, let's give up this mad, dead-baby project.

Then I remembered the fixed light in Alice's eyes. I remembered what her hands had done to my arms and how she planned to shock poor, sick Laura, to jolt her to her senses with a specimen jar. I remembered how she wanted to return our little body to the cold shelf where it had drooped for decades, and I stayed put.

By the time I quick-marched back to the coach station, over the footbridge and past the council houses, past the girl and boy and their syringe, I was stiff all over and my head felt bruised from staying awake this long. Even so I tried to walk with courage, with arms swinging, the same style as I heard Mum recommend to her women clients for going out at night. Mum herself didn't go out at night so I never really knew how she could say this with such cheery firmness.

The dark sky turned to rain. It felt like yesterday evening's rain on the rebound, misty and drifting, thickening steadily. As I completed the last lap of the High Street and turned the corner into the coach station forecourt the rain was full in my face with a needling vengeance. I climbed into the waiting Leeds-and-York coach wet to the skin, my socks squelching in my trainers.

The coach, thank God, was under half-full, and warm and dry. Air vents spurted hot blasts on to my soaked head. Overall the rain was to my advantage. It was to *our* advantage. The driver, ginger-haired and balding, took no notice of the kid in the rain-drenched hoodie, though, sidling in, I hovered in the shadow of a woman about Evie's age just to make sure. But, no, this twelve-year old travelling on his own in the middle of a school day didn't trouble the driver, not even the weird watery sounds coming from his luggage troubled him, as if a slurpy jar of tadpoles were knocking about in the bottom of his bag.

I chose a window seat, squeezing right up to the window, putting my bag on the spare bit of the seat by my right elbow where I could lock my arm securely around it.

The coach backed out of its bay, swung out of the station, pulled out on to Coventry Road leading north out of town. The driver cleared his throat to request us kindly to Belt Up, Enjoy our Trip.

I sat and watched as the familiar, old surroundings of Woodpark gradually grew less familiar, as the land rose up from our floodplain and grew bumpy. I remembered how Alice had laughed in scorn when our treeless Plain was renamed Woodpark to mark the expensive housing development along the railway line. The new name, we had then decided, must be to wipe from the memory of all purchasers of the future the thought that floodwaters move swiftly across waterlogged flat lands close to rivers. The thought that the drains around Woodpark had burped damp, brown odours for years.

We drove through the northern end of the city and into rolling fields. Here, on the right, was the zebra-painted speed camera that had been Dad's sworn enemy. There, on the far edge of town, where the motorway began, was the water tower shaped like an upside-down cone, its top lopped off.

With my finger I traced the fat rain droplets dashing the one after the other along the windowpane, top right to bottom left. I saw how my leaning head left a scratchy pattern on the steamed-over glass, like a ghost-kid's scribble.

I wanted to sleep but my thoughts wouldn't stop racing. When I arrived up north, would they be there? I asked myself. Would they be in? It was a Friday night; they might be anywhere. This African Lady, this Refugee, sounded totally the opposite to Evie. Probably she liked to go out, as Dad did. She liked to enjoy the City Lights. So would it be him to open the front door for me? Or would she, in her best Going-out Outfit? Would they be annoyed, maybe shocked? Would he call me weird-and-strange, as he sometimes had before?

'It's your doing,' Dad had shouted at Evie one evening after work when I'd four or five times "ignored" him when he'd called me down to say hello.

I think I'd genuinely not heard him, he was so often away.

'You let him daydream all day long,' he'd roared. 'If you don't look out he'll become a real weirdo, a really weird-and-strange weirdo. Even now I look at him and don't see my own son.'

I'd come down by then and seen Evie turn away from him. She had connected eyes with him in the mirror over the mantelshelf, and smoothed her hair with the flat of her hands as she always did in a quarrel.

'What can I do, Danny,' she'd said quietly, 'when you're never here?'

I leant in and spoke softly to my fish-mannikin, my gentle rubbery pod. 'We're making our getaway,' I told him. 'So far so good.'

It made me feel better talking to him. It kept me in definite mind of our rescue, our day's big goal.

Around me the six or so passengers I could see had their eyes closed, their heads propped against the misted windows. A lady in a woollen hat three rows behind us was breathing with a loud whistling noise, her left ear poking pinkly from under her hat's rolled rim.

I bent my mouth right close to his bag.

'Got to conserve our strength. We forgot to pack food, see. Food and water. Left in too much of a hurry. Got to buy something at the next stop. Try not to get wobbly, thirsty and wobbly.'

My fish slopped in sympathy.

I tapped gently at his jar. 'Sit tight,' I said. 'If we sit tight we'll be there before we know it.'

Now the sky turned black, like night-time at lunchtime, and a hard rain began driving down. The darkness increased the pressure growing in my forehead. I remembered the eclipse we'd had a few years ago, when I was about nine, when I'd had this same squeezed, headachy feeling.

11.11 a.m. and a shadow had fallen over everything. The birds had prepared for bed and the colour had faded even from the laundry on our washing line. Mum had called me in and locked the backdoor. She'd had a client and worried that I'd be tempted to look into the sun if she wasn't there to mind me.

Being pulled indoors in the middle of that shady, other-planet quiet gave the same tight feeling in my head as now.

With the cold rain pelting down, the condensation in the coach evaporated and I could see out. I could see how the roadside banks and hedges made a continuous low wall of green; a smooth, bright-green ribbon that ran beside the coach, unscrolling and unscrolling without a break. I could see the occasional church spire and the occasional electricity pylon sticking up out of the land. The big, trembling raindrops went on streaking the window.

I was a sealed capsule projected along this rushing motorway. That's how I felt. Safe in my seat, my seat belt safely on; projected headlong, no strings attached. This was how I'd reach my destination—bulleting northwards clasping my fish and talking to no one, a capsule speeding through the rainy, empty air.

*   *   *

The man touched down from nowhere. It was like the tail-end of a film I once caught on television. A silver man from outer space had popped up in this young boy's life without notice, mostly when the boy least needed him, when he was minding his own business, maybe riding home on the bus.

Suddenly this man, older than my dad with rosy cheeks and a black hair-dye shadow, was sitting right next to me. My shopping bag and the jar inside it were squeezed tightly between us.

To myself I said, '*Damn*.'

I had slept through the stop at Leicester. Earlier on the driver had announced the stop at Leicester. The man must've joined the coach there, which meant I had dropped my guard. Before falling asleep I should've stretched my legs over the empty seat beside me. I should've taken good care and cordoned off the space.

I saw it had stopped raining. Low orange light streamed out from under the dark clouds banked on the horizon. I guessed that the light must've woken me. The sun was full in my eyes and my new neighbour was gazing into my highlighted face for all he was worth, as if he might find in here the answer to a long-protected question.

'Well,' he said, 'so the world continues pretty much as it always did.'

He had that nasal way of talking that Evie called *cultivated*. She said Mrs Silver with her manicured raspberry nails, Evie's doing, was cultivated. 'Clients like Mrs Silver are gold,' she said.

To the man I said nothing.

'Yes, nothing new under the sun,' he continued regardless. 'Boys playing truant from school. Sagging, wagging, whatever it's now called. Going on big adventures. Heading off into the wide world all by themselves.'

At this a powerful new charge of fear knocked my chest. I made as if to study the brown road-sign up ahead: *Alton Towers*. 'Shit!' I swore at myself some more. 'Damn-damn-damn!' My capsule of safety had crumbled in an instant. Never trust an adult: Alice's words when I first told her about my dad leaving to set up house in the north. No adult ever, Arnie, and certainly not parents. She'd spat a plug of mucus at the word *parents*. 'The more they think they know,' she'd added, 'the stupider they are.'

I clenched the arm still resting around my fish closer to my body.

'Don't worry,' the man said. 'I'm not in the business of snitching or indeed snatching. I'm not about to spoil your big day. There aren't enough challenges for you children now-a-days; I see that, no big horizons, no void to touch. Excitement is on-screen and that's as far as it goes. So I'm in sympathy. Wouldn't dream of getting in your way.'

I looked around the coach. The lady in the woollen hat was still there, her one ear cocked, the seat beside her free. *Why oh why* had he come to sit beside me?

He was holding out a bottle of Volvic, unopened. 'Water?' he offered.

I looked at the bottle, at his knuckly, liver-speckled fingers. I looked at his face. I couldn't read his expression though his eyebrows were raised by his question. I looked at the bottle again and checked the seal. Unbroken. The sight of the water rippling inside the pale blue plastic worked at my thirst.

I took the bottle from him. Hadn't strangers offered each other water since before history began?

It was after I'd handed back the water that he sprang his trap.

'You're pretty thirsty for someone carrying around what sounds like a gallon of drink. Swish-swish the whole time we've been travelling. What's it you have in that bag, son? Thermos of milky tea like a proper boy scout? Bottle of extra-outsize vodka for your girlfriend?'

'Not vodka,' I said. 'Not old enough.'

And could've kicked myself. Why give anything away?

I glanced down at my creature. Till now I hadn't managed to check on him. Though my willow-pattern bag was held tight and secure against myself, I saw that the movement of the coach while I was asleep had worked its mouth open. Either that or the man's fidgeting and shifting about, which he did the whole time, as if he couldn't get comfortable. The bulk of the specimen jar still nested inside my browny-white fleece but its top had jostled itself free. The raised *rr* of the *Kerr* name was just about visible. The rim of the copper-and-glass lid was clearly visible. If the man had wanted to see more, a single tug would've laid everything bare.

I leaned my elbow down hard on the jar top.

The man drank from his Volvic bottle. Then he put the bottle between his feet and jigged his knees impatiently. His hands were between his thighs, rubbing together.

After a while he said, 'You're a funny kind of boy. An interesting boy. It takes one to spot one.'

'One what?' I said, again biting back too late.

'One curious customer. God knows what you've got inside that swag of yours but whatever it is, my advice is, Be careful. I know what I'm talking about. All our adventures are monitored. All the time we're watched. Go on this excursion you've got planned, do your thing, then go home. Put every little thing back where it belonged.'

He pressed his leg purposefully against mine and the specimen jar pushed forwards, dislodging its swaddling fleece by another few inches, unveiling a curve of bumpy whiteness behind the glass: a shoulder. I identified the bit of our fish it was, straightaway, but my companion, too, saw something more than just a jar. Maybe he didn't quite spot a *body*, but he saw enough to be getting on with. He looked, then looked away. Then looked again. He passed the back of his hand over his forehead. He breathed hard. He drank more water and smacked his lips. But he said not a word. I was waiting for a hue and cry, an outburst, a lunge, but nothing happened.

Finally he gave a deep sigh, almost a rattle in his chest, and at once, without knowing how I could be sure, I knew he'd keep quiet. I knew that he'd received a hunch, some *feeling* for my difficulty, but that this was as far as it would go. He wasn't keen to act on his information. He was in fact *put off*.

At that moment the importance of my fish-mannikin shifted. I saw it was to him that I owed this rescue. It was to him, my genie-in-a-bottle, my protector. Our positions suddenly had changed. I saw that he'd helped me, his helper, his rescuer, out.

I let my pressure on his jar lid slowly relax.

I said, 'I don't know where this thing belongs.'

'Sorry?' the man said.

'You said I should put every little thing back where it belonged.'

'It's a job worth doing,' he said.

A curve in the motorway angled the rays of the setting sun from my face onto his. I quit squinting and could see the man in full colour. His skin was lurid, his eyes feverish, his nose netted with broken, purple veins. He had folded his thin arms so tightly across his chest that his muscles stood out like plaited rope.

By the next stop night had fallen. The man said 'Nice—' before he stood to leave. He aimed the word at the coat-rack overhead.

We had arrived at a dark city standing cheek by jowl with the motorway. Its coach station was noisy and underground, drowned in exhaust fumes. During the fifteen-minute stop I bought three Kit-Kats from a dispenser. I put my fish between my feet as I worked the coins and the keypad and I thought of my dad and his cold hands. I thought of Alice and the funny movement her forehead made when she ate chocolate, kind of wrinkling. The thought sent a wave of something confusing moving through me. *Alice*. At the end of the day, Alice often said, peeling back her chocolate wrapper like a banana skin, a bit of chocolate is all you need to feel OK. A bit of chocolate feels like home.

And she'd pop the chocolate into her mouth, her forehead wrinkling, and then sneeze like a horse.

At the end of the day, Alice often added, is brilliant Leonardo diCaprio's favourite expression. She collected these useless facts along with her odds-and-bobs medical know-how. She had a brain like a turning kaleidoscope, Alice my friend. Whatever had happened between us, I now saw, I could begin to miss her. The afternoon she had cut up our dog's eye, when for the first time I'd despised her, even then I'd missed her. I had begun missing her at the very same moment as I'd thrown myself out of her garden gate.

Leo diCaprio, Alice would solemnly say, thinks his favourite expression captures *the very essence of finality*.

Back on the coach at the end of that strange day, our fish-mannikin in my lap, I broke my Kit-Kats into fingers, and ate each finger in two-three bites, thinking of Alice. I looked out across the sulphur streak of the motorway lights and tried to spot the stars coming out. They seemed very few, those stars, or else the darkness tonight looked very great.

Alice had a line about darkness like she did about everything else, I remembered. Dark matter, she said, fills the universe. Dark matter fills the universe *fully everywhere*, like the white does an egg.

It was in the papers, she said only last week, one day when she invited me up to her bedroom to look at her new *Astronomy in Colour*. The universe was full of dark matter and, as if that wasn't enough, full of dark energy on top of it, which meant there was very little in the universe anything like ourselves. To call us a lonely planet was putting it mildly.

Trying to fight off sleep I fell into a kind of dream. I was aware of the orange-and-black sky and the coach engine noise, but still I was dreaming. In my dream the coach was racing alongside white articulated trucks driving in convoy, looking like the trucks that the coach was in reality overtaking, except that in my dream the sides of the trucks were blank, without a scrap of logo or writing, and I could see through them. I could see no *Van Esselen, TLS Vehicle Hire, Brakes, Eddie Stobart*, and I could see into the inside of the trucks. I could see in cross-section rows and rows of tiny plastic incubators, all filled with greyish-bluish pods of flesh. I saw that the trucks were transporting northwards hundreds of these little babies, little baby foetuses housed like battery chickens in cages.

I couldn't tell from where I was sitting if the bodies were alive or dead but I could see for definite that none of them was moving.

I woke from this waking nightmare sweating, determined not to fall sleep again. All the way to Leeds I stayed awake by slapping my face with sharp smacks till my cheeks stung.

91

Chapter 6
Alice

About two miles out of town, off the road leading south through Woodpark to Dorchester, lie two ancient mounds close together, surrounded here and there by Iron Age barrows. The countryside here is flat, mainly flood-plain and water meadow, so that the mounds and the thickets of beech topping them can be seen for miles. The mounds, the Winborne Clumps, have been a lookout and stronghold for centuries, from before the time of Romans. Here, all locals know, the Celts brandished arms against the Latin invaders from the south, and centuries later, the Romans' descendants gave way before the shaggy-haired Saxons. In the fields around about, the lucky seekers who visit on weekends can pick up Iron Age flints and arrow heads and bits of Roman pottery.

The Winborne Clumps lookout this Friday afternoon is Alice's destination. Her bones tell her, intuition tells her, that this is a place where Arnie could likely have gone to ground. There's not a kid in the Woodpark area who doesn't know what mysteries and treasures stud these ancient fields.

She sets out on foot directly after school, pacing hard. She knows the way well. She visited the mounds for the first time as an eight-year-old Primary School kid. And then again several times last summer, when the City Archaeological Society ran a dig here and Laura put in work-experience helping the archaeologists on one of the barrows. Her job had been to sift out potsherds and wash them clean. Broken bits of cow bone and oyster shell, leavings off Roman Britons' tables, she was allowed to take home. A pointy, serrated length of bone she gave to Alice for her knife collection. 'Like an Ashanti blade,' she said dreamily as she handed it over, 'the cutting edge of some proud and warlike African empire. A true warrior's weapon.'

But Alice didn't like to mix the bone with her knives in their black velvet pouch. She didn't want it knocking up against her blades and blunting them. She keeps the bone on her bedside table instead, so she can handle it in the dark before settling to sleep. So she can run her thumb along its sharp edge, and wonder what kind of soldier might in fact have used it, in what distant age, and whether in deserts or on plains, or in some dense forest, and if for conquest or for revenge.

At the Londis on Selvon Street she buys a bottle of water and a Twix bar. She eats the chocolate as she walks the main road south. After finishing the chocolate she is carrying only her house key around her neck and the water bottle. Her arms swing free. She feels unburdened and sharp-eyed. She does not detour via Albion Street. Today her pouch of knives will stay at home beside her bed.

She passes the Cote Dazur chip shop, closed for the afternoon, then the Angling Emporium where she notices for the first time that the display of fishing rods in the window is sprouting cobwebs. The Fox and Flagstaff pub is open but quiet. The City Council Waste and Recycling Centre is open but quiet. All down its length the main road is intersected by streets crammed full of cars, streets lined with low, hunkered-down houses. 'Could be anywhere,' thinks Alice. 'Housing Development X, Anywheresborough, southern UK. Any one of the old browny-samey places you see on the South-East news.'

Beyond the Recycling Centre Woodpark peters away into a football field, a few more houses, then dense blackberry thicket and hay fields, the southern limit of town. The road continues on to the giant out-of-town Tesco. Alice takes the sandy public footpath that veers off at an angle from the road. She follows it across a stretch of fields and several stiles, the route Laura took last summer along with the other teammates who travelled on foot. It's not long before the two Clumps crop up on the horizon, the trees on the mound tops waving from afar like banners.

The fields around about are silvered with splashes of puddle. It rained earlier, around lunchtime, Alice checks back, when she was indoors sweeping out the lab. The sandy path is dry but the long wayside grass droops under a weight of sparkling droplets. And look at that! Between two outlying barrows just beyond the next stile hangs a small fog patch like a bit of earth-bound cloud.

It excites her, all this, being on her own in these very old lands, breathing this air that's so fresh and clean and new. She's never really been by herself in the open like this before, she realizes. Not entirely by herself, with the surrounding space full of hidden things and mighty secrets. It feels as if something incredible might happen all of a sudden. As if the deep history of the mounds and barrows might suddenly rise to the surface of the land, stretch open and sing out.

She'll forget that difficult business last night, she decides, the quarrel with Arnie, the fruitless waiting, Laura thrashing about. Today's a new day and it could bear good fruit.

She presses on. The path meets a narrow road that runs between hayfields. In the middle distance the Clumps swell up.

On her Primary School trip, Alice remembers, they travelled in a hired coach that crawled along this back road at something like walking pace. The class objective that day was to examine and sketch the resident Winborne Clumps wildlife. The sketches had to be labelled in one of two ways, the teacher explained. First label the *natives*: she shouted the instruction as they clambered out of the coach. Draw and clearly label the *natives*; then mark out the *foreigners*.

Natives were grey squirrels, small deer, owls and wood-peckers. *Foreigners* were mainly moles and rabbits, mainly pests.

Alice finds herself sucking her teeth at the memory. She thinks of Farouq Khan, her foreign father, and the unruly corkscrew hair she has inherited from him. She wriggles her toes in her trainers, the broad, splayed-end toes that she's sure he has passed onto her, too. Foreigner or native—how would she be classed? A stranger, a local or a pest?

By contrast with herself and Laura, Jilly has long, bony toes: 'tree-climber toes,' she says. She says that with these long toes her ancestors dangled from crooked tree branches and kept clear of the swamps of Britannia. Jilly claims her ancestors have lived in these parts forever, right here on this floodplain, close to where the Chartwell River meets the Thames. She says it's amazing how creatures will bed down in a landscape no matter how watery and sloppy, no matter how runny the mede.

Her own broad toes, Alice thinks, wriggling them some more, are dry-land toes, desert waders. They belong to her father's wide, dry spaces around Khartoum. On splayed feet like these in ancient times, she imagines, the riches of Africa came to Europe. Across the unforgiving sand dunes of the Sahara journeyed the patient traders and their undulating camels, their huge, swaying packs of gold, cowries, ivory, dyed and patterned cloth, serrated bone blades and maybe boy and girl slaves.

She checks her bearings. Over there by the stone wall and the three poplars is the grassy verge where they parked on the school trip, where last summer she brought a picnic in a backpack to share with Laura. Which means that around here, a field or so further on, will be the barrow area the City Archaeological Society opened up and where Laura helped.

The ginger-colour, adult-size skeleton with one cheekbone in the mud, one eye-socket raking the sky; Alice can *see* it again in the closest of detail though she never saw it in fact. Laura, excited to the point of shrillness, told her and Jilly all about it. It was a wonderful, extraordinary thing.

On the second-last day of Laura's dig the team found a full human skeleton lying on its side in a three-foot grave, its legs drawn up: an ultimate reward. Laura came home that evening exclaiming the news as she pushed open the front door, her eyes white and blazing in her dusty face. Although the skeleton was buried relatively close to the surface it was at least Roman, she said, second- or third-century Roman. It had been burnished to its mellow ginger-colour, almost nicotine, by the brown, surrounding clay. Burnt barley remains were mysteriously stored at its feet. And a silvery mark, probably a scraping from a plough, shone like a jewel on its bony forehead.

The dig had to be extended by an expensive two days to allow the team to get the bones out intact. The volunteers and work-experience people like Laura had to pitch in and lend a hand, a super-gentle hand. To pull out a buried skull, the dig-leader warned them, never use the eye sockets as these easily crack.

On the second-last day of the extended dig, Laura reported that the skeleton had been confirmed as male:

about twenty, extremely tall and strong, and male. He was so tall in fact, his thigh-bones so very long, his skull so high and domed, that the dig-leader had speculated he might have come all the way from the far southern and eastern reaches of the Empire, from Egypt, Nubia, even Libya perhaps. There were numbers of African soldiers fighting in the Roman army in Britain in those early years, he'd said. They'd send him for carbon dating to make sure.

He could have been a Moorish legionary. Laura spoke her thoughts aloud to Alice, her voice wobbling with some powerful emotion. Or even a Nubian officer from a prosperous town far down along the Nile; a Sudanese man, one among the tallest to walk on British soil, brought over to patrol the Empire's coldest frontier.

There was no mark on him, nothing to suggest how he might have died in these marshlands far from home, wounded perhaps in a skirmish, or laid low despite his great height and health by a fever or a cold. And then, burying him, Laura suggested, some kind friend, a fellow officer thinking of happier times in sandy lands far away, had placed the burnt barley offering at his feet.

Watching Laura maniacally dust and brush, dust and brush, for hours on end, the dig-leader told her not to worry quite so much; the crouched Nubian gent might seem special but he was by no means one of a kind. The fields all over here were studded with skulls and skeletons like gold-bearing rock with nuggets. Treat him carefully by all means, he said, but remember he's not cutglass, not a chap like that with femurs like poles.

'How can I help it?' Laura had come back at him. Her brush traced an arc in the air, up from the skeleton and towards her chest. 'When I'm staring Africa in the eyes in the middle of this Thames floodplain, in my own backyard? When I'm face to face with myself?'

Standing in the shadow of the poplars, within the wide shadow of the Clumps, Alice feels a tendril of chill wind itself around her spine. She doesn't want to think too hard today about the buried skulls, British or African, ogling at her from underground. She doesn't want to think too hard right at this minute about dead things. She takes a deep breath. Thing is, Laura's skeleton is not the only dead person she associates with these ancient fields. As she knows well and Quiet Arnie, too, knows well, there is another, fresher skeleton lying somewhere close by here, not far from the Clumps.

For several months the rumour marinaded richly through their school.

How late last year Darlene Miller, the Year 7 supply teacher and a local Green Party activist, chose to be buried somewhere in the Winborne fields.

How on her deathbed, due to sudden calamitous septicaemia, Darlene had asked for a tree burial close to a copper beech on the slope of the left-hand clump.

It was Jilly who first passed the information to Laura, and Laura of course passed it to Alice (who then passed it to Arnie). The left-hand clump, the taller one, was Darlene's favourite destination for a walk. She believed that age-old routes and paths crossed here. It was an important crux in an ancient-of-days network of ley lines. She believed in the powers of plants and magnets and wore a beautiful fiery crystal around her neck. She said her bones would be in touch with a place of special force. And her nail beds would sprout green moss.

People have said Darlene wouldn't have had a coffin, that is, not a coffin to speak of, not one of your common-or-garden ones, just one of those eco-friendly cardboard boxes. To think of it, Laura said Jilly said this over a low-fat, ready-cook lasagne lunch while Alice was at school. Even as we speak there are roots stretching around her skull and through her ribs like through a loom.

A series of very cold chills now darts down Alice's back. Though the late afternoon sun is shining with force, she's all at once disheartened. Coming here is not as good an idea as it at first seemed. In fact it's a deeply dismal idea. Now that the fog patch and puddles have melted away, the emptiness of the lands is more obvious. The absence of other living human beings is very obvious. Even Laura's dig has left no mark. Grass grew over the trenches months ago. Grass grew over Darlene months or at least weeks ago. Standing in these empty fields she feels at one and the same time alone and yet exposed, laid bare—a single, isolated figure in the landscape.

Since yesterday, since their genie flopped out of its jar, she's been a sucker for her own bad plans.

She looks back at the town, a brown deposit on the far edge of the hayfields. She scans the Clumps. There's really not a soul to be seen in any direction, not a living soul, not even a sheep. Truly, in spite of her hopes, there is nowhere in these green fields a single trace of Arnie.

She turns again and looks about her. But there's nothing, no one, no stooped figure gingerly carrying a foetal foundling, no one bending to place it in a safe corner in amongst the sheltering trees.

Goosebumps creep across Alice's scalp and down her legs. She's brought this funk on herself, that's for sure, thinking these grisly and gruesome thoughts. Why not remember Darlene Miller as she was, a comfortable woman with pulpy upper arms whose crystal whacked your ears when she checked your spelling? Remember instead the sociable buzz of Laura's dig whenever she, Alice, visited. Think of the row of caravans set up just here by the stone wall, the scuffed wheelbarrows, the smelly portaloos, the coloured marker pins in the ground as if in preparation for a fair.

She begins to walk on but her legs have lost their purpose. The flat unchanging profile of the path resists her feet almost as if it were going uphill. It stretches her Achilles tendons and depresses her spirit. Sweat collects on her temples. Until the land suddenly rises up to the Clumps, the fields stretch on levelly, on and on. They'll be stretching on for a good while yet. She realises that she won't be making it as far as the higher ground today.

She selects a spot of wayside grass, a tussocky, soft spot, and sits, then lies down. Her body is heavy with tiredness. She is stretched out on the ground staring up at the late afternoon sky. There are birds far above like snips of darkness against the thin blue light, and wisps of cloud that suddenly appear and melt away. A micro-light clatters into view and for a time hangs suspended in the space between the two Clumps. In the tall grass netted around her ears she hears the tiny rustle of creatures, whirrs, clicks, trills, the natives and foreigners both making small noises together. She feels her bones, hipbones and scapulas, even femurs, crammed up against the hard ground.

It's a pity it was drenching down so heavily yesterday, she thinks. Had it been drier she and Arnie and their lost-and-found might have made it past the Angling Emporium and the Fox and Flagstaff out here to these open fields. Had it been drier, had they not fallen out about that thoughtless cut, the road out of town mightn't have felt so long and strange. They'd have extended their walk. They'd have been together when these thoughts of bones and burials began to stir. They'd have talked. They might've said, 'After the mess we've made we owe it to our small basket of bones to find him a resting-place.'

Not extinction but absorption, Laura's dig-leader told the team the day they found the tall Roman skeleton. This is a place not of extinction but absorption. When Laura relayed the message home, she rounded her lips and boomed her voice, making it sound like a sermon.

It's the right sort of place for afterlives, Darlene Miller would have agreed. Green, lush and full of special energy.

It's so much the right sort of place for afterlives, Alice thinks, she was until now *almost* convinced that Arnie would've thought the same. That he would have remembered about Darlene and the old Roman and made the connection. That he'd have brought along their lost-and-found to add to their number.

She sees the two of them digging with bare hands, maybe using the copper lid of the Kerr jar with its red rubber seal to break the earth. It would be better than yesterday's ice-tray at least, and better than her metal file. They'd choose a safe spot between tree roots, she imagines, like where Yaz always buries her sandwich crusts. A place they could find again if ever they wanted to go and lay flowers. And they'd not talk. They'd be busy with their task and aware of their responsibility. Their cheeks would be long and stiff with the unusual formality.

They'd sink the jar straight down into its shallow grave. Or maybe, thinking of Darlene Miller and her cardboard box, they'd empty the thing out of its glass walls in order to guarantee absorption. *Absorption not extinction.* Or maybe Arnie would take off his hoodie, wrap the body round and lever it, steady on now, into the earthen hole.

Either way, lying or sitting up, it would be buried crouched. This is what it says in the black-and-white photograph under C for Celtic in Jilly's *Short Longman's Encyclopedia* at home. "Crouched" is the native way.

The grass begins to scratch at Alice's legs and neck. Sand has somehow found its way into her ear. Time to call it a day. Or at least call off the job. She'll have, at the end of this long day, to take serious stock.

At the end of the day is stunning Leonardo diCaprio's favourite, dangerously optimistic expression.

She starts back in the direction of town and begins to

hum, a *ta-tum* hum in time with the movement of her feet, the swish of her legs. This is how she likes to walk when she's feeling a little crestfallen like now, a little disappointed—walk to the beat of a tune. She likes to make her cheekbones resonate with sound. She's rolled up inside this ball of her own humming; she's a planet floating alone in its orbit, over the last stile, up the road, past the blackberry thicket, past cars queued at the traffic lights and piled high with Tesco goods. In the direction of the Recycling Centre two seagulls wheel and swoop, dive-bombing one another with beautiful accuracy, swerving at just the last minute. On any ordinary day she'd pause to watch them but today she's not bothered. Her humming encases her round.

As she nears the Fox and Flagstaff, the tune resolves into a low chanting song. She blends it in with the music emerging from the pub: Moby. The pub jukebox or sound system is playing Moby: *Why does my heart feel so bad?* The song pours out through windows that shine a friendly yellow. '*My heart feels so bad*,' she murmurs up against the roof of her mouth, replacing the word *heart* at each repetition with some other body space; *head, back, chest* and *gut*.

At the bus stop between the Angling Emporium and the Cote Dazur chippie sits a one-legged man scratching the stump of his thigh. He is carrying over his shoulder in a clear plastic bag a collection of empty water bottles: Evian, Sourcis, Volvic and Caledonian Spring. Alice turns her face away. He could be a bad omen. Arnie would definitely say he was. His face is red-raw and wasted, blasted by weather. But she'll refuse to credit the omen. The world is full of grown-ups who've fallen off the tracks of life.

At the Recreation Ground she takes the new concrete walk-bridge across the stream. She trails her finger along the thread of fresh silver graffiti that decorates the railing. *Amused* is what it could be saying? *Amazed?* Her legs feel leaden. Rip-tear-scrape sounds come from the skateboard rink on the edge of the Ground. Her tune is loud in her head. *Why does my body feel so bad?*

She has one final task to carry out before she turns down her street, a final detour past Arnie's house. But there it's as she imagined. His bedroom curtains are drawn and his window is in darkness. She moves on quickly.

She spots the white note pinned to the front door of 7 Albion Street from across the road. It's a bit of paper, doubly folded, marked with her name. She dashes over; tears it down. Her vision is suddenly blurry with fright. Arnie, what's...? *Damn!* If he comes to grief, what'll she do? Fingers will be pointing straight at her.

Dear Alice—says the note—*Things got worse. Couldn't stand it any longer. Took myself off to the hospital. A and E. Please don't tell Jilly. And don't worry. Luv, L.*

Why, Alice's head hums, does my heart feel so bad?

Chapter 7

Arnie

Hare Hills. Harehills. The name suddenly jumped back into my brain. In my mind's eye I saw Mum in her white salon overcoat reading the address off the back of Dad's padded envelope, the one he used to send the chocolate egg at Easter time. I saw how she clamped her lips, turned her eyes to the ceiling and then said, *Hare—one word—hills*, gingerly tasting the foreignness of this new name. I remembered how the words transmitted a picture of Easter bunnies bouncing across bright green hills, like something from the *Teletubbies*.

That picture of hills and big cutout daisies came back to me now. Harehills, Leeds.

The Leeds coach station was even gloomier than the gloomy one further south, and it was a lot colder. It was nothing but rows of bus shelters lining oil-stained concrete bays, open to the four winds, without chocolate machines. Except for the low-level neon lights, damp darkness drooped everywhere, darkness darker than the inside of my eyelids.

For a while I had kept my eyes firmly shut, my squeezed-shut eyes making the skin all over my face feel tight and shrunken. I had sat under the shelter where the coach had dropped me off, keeping myself to myself, thinking things through. Where did I go now? That was a big question. And how? Exactly *how?* That was an even bigger question.

Two Major Problems faced us here on arrival, I thought. Number One: the city was large, a lot larger than expected, busier and more built up than I'd expected. I'd planned to walk to Dad's house. By now I could see that this was no plan at all. Walking might take me hours. And without a map I'd definitely get lost.

Problem Number Two was the question of Dad's address: Grange Terrace, but which number? The figures that at home I'd stored so safely in my brain had dislodged en route.

Keeping my eyes tightly shut I had sat for a time facing my Problems till the taxi's ear-shattering revs just about jolted me off my seat.

Reversing at speed from the nearby taxi rank the white Toyota drew up alongside with a rip-roaring screech of its tyres.

The taxi-driver was leaning so far out of his car it looked like he was escaping through the window in a hurry.

'Grange Terrace, Terrace Grange, which way about? Can be both, nah, can be anywhere.' He was barking at me, but not evilly.

'Harehills,' I suddenly blurted. There! The name had popped up at last, in *Teletubbies'* colours. 'Harehills. 29 Grange Terrace, Harehills. But I can't go with you. I can't pay.'

It was best not to waste money yet. We could be spending tonight outdoors. We could be buying breakfast in the morning. Dad might be away for the weekend. He never was reliable.

The taxi-driver firmly shook his head.

'I watch you sitting there nearly a half-hour, son. In this cold. With no coat. I let my last job go to keep watching you. Is somebody picking you up then, I wonder? Nice kid like that must have someone to pick him up. Can't be walking to Harehills this time of night, with a big bit of motorway in between, and a couple of "no-go" pubs.'

'If I set out and walk I'll get there in the end.'

I didn't mean to sound cheeky but he rolled up his window in disgust and gunned the car back to the taxi rank.

I sat tight some more, legs drawn up into my hoodie, the willow-pattern bag pressed cold against my stomach. This time I left my eyelids open just a fraction. Was there a coach station shop somewhere hereabouts that had maps on sale? Or even a map taped up in the window? With Dad's address now in my head, all I needed to press on with was a map.

But alongside the station precinct the low row of shop-fronts stood in darkness. The newsagent, the coffee shop, the off-license, all shuttered up so securely it was as if the proprietors weren't planning to return for days. A pub across the way was open but I didn't want to go in, not with my shopping bag. I didn't want it knocked. I could see a group of men standing in the pub's front window. They were packed close together, watching a game on an invisible television, their heads tilted back. Occasionally they punched the air and pummeled one another's arms. It looked like they wouldn't take kindly to being disturbed, to a kid half their size, lady's shopping tote in his hand, bumping into their legs.

But disturbance arrived on the scene anyway. Disturbance all too soon made an entrance and found me out.

From a distance I saw the two teenagers, about sixteen or seventeen, come cutting across the coach station precinct from the direction of the pub. It was as if they had unpeeled themselves from the darkness of its door. They closed in on me with speed, propelled by some pressing purpose.

Even nearby I couldn't see their faces clearly. Looming closer they blocked the available light. I guessed they'd be about as old as Alice's sister's Phoenix. The neck and head on the taller bloke made one solid rectangle. The shorter, thinner one kept twitching and fidgeting; touching now his ear, now his chin; endlessly pulling his shirt and hitching his trousers.

The scary thing was they didn't talk at first. They came to stand dead in front of me, towering, their clothes almost grazing my legs. It felt like every joint in my body suddenly got looser. I knew I couldn't trust myself to run. Instead I bent over my bag. I wanted to be sure that my Fish in his shopping bag wasn't feeling threatened.

'Here's a sick 'un,' the taller one said. 'The kind that makes you sick just looking at 'em.'

'Very sick,' agreed the shorter one and shuffled closer still. 'A right idiot. A waste of breath.'

I could feel the pressure of his legs on mine.

Fish murmured liquidly in his jar, though not so loud as to alert them.

'What's in the bag?'

I meant to say, 'None of your business', but the words didn't make it out of my mouth.

I felt the shoulder of my top yanked upwards. I meant to duck to the side but the movement didn't happen. The yank was so hard the cloth of my hoodie cut into my neck. My Fish gurgled once again, louder this time though still inaudible to the two of them, set on whatever prize they'd clocked in me. His gurgle sounded about as unsettled as my heart but even so it was steadying. I remembered that there was someone else here, something to worry about that wasn't just me.

This feeling of Fish nearby cleared a cool, quiet space in the centre of my head. Inside this space a part of me stood by observing and saw what to do. I saw we should lay everything open. We should flatten their intentions with our total openness.

The thin bloke maintained his grip on my top. Craning round with difficulty, stretching the mouth of the willow-pattern bag as wide as I could, I began to take my things out one by one and lay them on the seat behind me: my toothbrush, the clean pair of socks wrapped in a tight ball like Evie had taught me, the red platypus beanie baby, which I put up against my leg.

My money envelope was folded into a roll inside my tracksuit pants pocket. I tried to ignore its edges pressing into my skin.

Last of all Fish came looping. After my encounter with the dyed-hair man I had wrapped his jar more tightly, folding the ends of the fleece into triangles like for a birthday present and tucking these against the bottom and sides of the bag. I lifted out the bundle in a smooth curve and put it on the seat beside the stuffed platypus. I had to go very carefully now. My palms were slick with fear.

At that moment the teenagers broke into laughter. Ragged guffawing burst from their faces. The thin one released my top and, helpless with laughter, just about fell on top of his friend. I felt the knot of tension under my ribs tighten. Was it the platypus that had set them off? Had they spotted it here by my leg? Such a babyish toy for a secondary school boy! Or was it the big jar in its fleece? What kind of a kid, after all, goes on a journey with a huge pickle jar in tow?

In the end I never did find out.

'So what's that?' the taller one pointed at random he was laughing so hard.

He must mean the jar.

'Something my Mum made for my aunt,' I said. 'I'm spending the weekend with my aunt. It's a present. Pickled onions. It's a jar of pickled onions from my mum.'

For a minute they laughed even louder, fit to burst, cackling *weekend present!* and *pickled onions!* Then suddenly, like a stereo switching off, they stopped. In place of their laughter came loud revving noises that reverberated against the corrugated metal of the shelter roof. The taxi driver had drawn up alongside a second time. He leaned back and threw his rear car door open bang in front of my face. It was two steps to climb in.

'Eh you,' he said. 'Beat it. Kid's smaller'n you. You got to watch your step. I seen you loitering round here before.'

He turned to me. 'And you, move it, too. Get in. Gather up your things and get in here.'

The lads were gone even before I had finished scooping my belongings into the willow-pattern bag. Fish's jar I wedged safely in the crook of my elbow. As I got into the car I lightly stroked his glass where his back and shoulders were. In some mad-brained way I wanted to thank him. He had in his own way stuck to me, I thought. He had given me courage.

* * *

For a while we drove without speaking, the taxi-driver, Fish and I. My bag sat on the seat beside me but the specimen jar I kept snug, my small lap-monster stowed between my knees. My body all the way from my feet to my neck felt like some piece of laundry that's been through the washing machine once too often, worn thin and creased by the day's events.

I leant back against the padded seat. The neck rest I noticed was covered with a crocheted comforter in red, yellow and green.

We sped along an elevated motorway, and then another, the fiftieth or hundredth motorway today, then plunged down a ramp into a valley. On either side the land sloped up steeply, ribbed everywhere with rows and rows of houses, the hills beyond humpbacked exactly like, well, sleeping hares. There were so many of these streets crowded with brick houses and no gardens that I could see, that the place emitted a kind of dull brown light. Even the traffic islands sprouted brown pebbles and enormous grey hoardings instead of grass.

At a red light the massive calf of a white woman reared up over us, smooth, hairless and shiny as a seal. The lights changed almost as soon as we drew up or I'd have memorised for Evie the name of the beauty product that the picture was advertising.

'Well, at least it not rain tonight,' my newfound saviour said as if continuing a conversation that had been progressing for some time. 'They say a 50 per cent chance but it turn out we're lucky.'

He spoke via the rearview mirror. What I could see of him from the backseat were his eyes in the mirror, dark-brown eyes behind small glasses, and here, nearby, the grizzled back of his head, his hair close-shaved above an ironed shirt.

I couldn't think of anything to reply. There was money on my mind. I didn't have loose change to pay my fare. And definitely couldn't dream of approaching Dad.

Not much hope of him stepping out of his front door with a smile of welcome for this bolt from the blue if the first thing I did was demand some cash.

We travelled in silence for the length of several more traffic lights.

'Not long now,' the taxi-driver made a second run at being sociable.

There was the immediate result of a loud whine from my stomach but if he noticed he didn't let on.

'Did you know, son,' he continued, 'that's how womenfolk do it back in my country? Send big bottles of preserves exactly like what you got in that jar. Woman to woman they do it. Pay off debts and the like. And eh, what a fuss they can make.' He put dramatic expression into his voice, the kind of expression teachers say we must use when we Read Out Loud. '"Don' open dat window dere, Marla, my marmalade still boiling, it go chill and spoil." Or, "Dulcie, Dulcie, how hot you want this sauce? What's in all those chillies try and hide?" Yes sir, pickle's an important household item where I come from.'

What hadn't my new friend spotted? Seemed like nothing had escaped him. He'd seen the bulk of the big jar perched on my lap, that was for sure. He'd heard what I told the teenage boys. He watched me now in the rearview mirror as I hunched forwards and clutched my travel companion closer.

'That's right,' he nodded briskly. 'Must've been that ol' jar you got hid there got them all work up.'

The Toyota was beginning to climb yet another hill. There were shushing noises of the wheels on a cobbled road. I crunched my nails into my palms, resisting these heavy arms and legs, these dragged-down eyelids. *Don't*, whatever you do, fall asleep. The taxi-driver pressed a button on his car radio. Applause burst into the warm gulf of the back seat, followed by the explosion of an orchestra, a yelling and chirruping of violins, and I jumped.

'You surprise?' he chuckled. 'You not expect a black man to listen to this kind of stuff? You expect some *Afrikan Riddum*? Or why you startle?'

'Just the noise. Surprised me.'

He turned the sound down so low I could barely hear it. It felt like an invitation to explain myself.

'I know a bit about Africa, you see,' I said. 'My best friend's father's from Africa. But he lives there so she doesn't see him much. Actually, hardly at all. "He lives on the banks of the Nile," her mum says. Sometimes he drives a taxi, like you, and sometimes he runs a passenger boat, a falucca. "He fishes for a hobby," my friend says.'

The last bit of this was mainly invented, using the help of our classroom poster on Egypt, but I didn't care. I was getting comfortable and making conversation.

'Son, here's news for you.' He changed his voice to sound what I'd call funky, Rastafarian. 'I not from Africa, not directly, though black. I Jim Noelson from a lickle island in the ol Caribbean, a lickle bit of cricket ground in the blue sea. It flat-flat far as the eye can see.'

I saw his eyes in the mirror creasing up as I sat blushing.

When did you last put ears inside your skull, Barmy Arnie? I could hear Alice scold. The conclusions you jump to! Aren't I African, half, and not really *from* Africa at all?

'So is your ma send the pickle to your auntie or the other way about?' the man asked, still squeezing with his eyes. 'I hear something like that from you at the coach station.'

'My mum,' I managed to say. 'The jar comes from where I live, down south.'

'And your ma not sew your destination into your pocket, or put a paper with an address in your bag?'

'I memorised it,' I said truthfully. 'I thought it was clear in my head.'

'Well, don't you worry bout a thing, we'll get you there before you know it. This street here is already Grange Hill, and then next is Grange Road, and after that Grange Terrace. Is a right hiding-go-seek of street-names round here, even for us taxi folk.'

We rumbled up a steep street paved with round black stones. A web of telephone cables and electric wires covered the sky overhead. The end-point of my journey was moments away but I couldn't move, couldn't lift a bone of my body, not even to make sure of Fish on my lap. The seat against my back was so soft, the neck rest as if built for the shape of my head, and meanwhile, out there in the dark, the closely-packed back-to-backs were a foreign country.

It was several seconds before I realised he was asking a new kind of question.

'You not truly-truly taking a jar of pickle onion to your auntie, are you now, boy? Truly-truly? You not truly off to see your auntie?'

'*P'dn*?' I almost swallowed the word whole, then tried again, 'Pardon?'

'What I saying is, is my feeling you not tell those boys at the station the truth. Why tell those boys the truth? In your position I give them a lie, just the same as you.'

Nothing to deny. I nodded at the rearview mirror, couldn't help it, then nodded again, not sure he'd spotted the first time. The car bounced around a corner. Grange Terrace was spelt in white letters on a black strip painted on a house wall. My friend drew up at the top end of the street, where the numbers were in the teens. He switched off the engine and swivelled himself right around and now I couldn't see his eyes, just the gleam of his glasses under the street lights.

'I want to tell you something,' he said. 'But first, give me your name, your true name.'

'Arnie. Arnie Binns.'

'And James Noelson, Jim, like I said. Think of the Christmas carol. We used to sing it when I was a kid, back in the ol' jungly bush.' He reached his hand over the back of his seat. 'The-First-No-el-the-ang-el-did-say. So, *No-el-son*.'

I brushed my fingers over his fingers.

'Well now, Arnie,' he said, still swivelled round, 'You listen to me and mind what I say. In my line of work I see a great many people in many different mood but I never see a boy look so knocked about as you. Or carrying so big a jar, kept so tightly under wraps, never. Now I don't want to know what you got hid there. If severed hand or sliced-off ear. Eye of newt, toe of frog, God help us. Strange things move on this earth nowadays, those bits of things, arms and torso and that, floating in our ol' Thames. I do know there's a funny smell in this car right now and I guess it come straight off your burden. Pickle indeed! But I watch you close and I think you not up to badness. I don't want to imagine where you deliver tonight or under what orders'—he peered down the street and then up at the streetlights—'but you yourself, you OK. In fact, I think the time come sooner rather than late where you need help with that load, so you listen up close. Just call me, you hear? Tomorrow I got the weekend off. Me driving to see my sister down in London. If you need a lift back south, if you got no money or you running scared, you call me. Understood? If you decide you gotta leave, you call. Jim Noelson's the name.'

Scissored between two fingers he handed me his taxi company card, the phone number bright yellow on red.

'Understood?' he came again.

'Thanks very much.'

'No thanks,' he shrugged with impatience. 'Is thanks enough if I know a kid's safe. I got no kids of my own but plenty nieces and nephews. Here and back home. I like to think someone do the same when they meet trouble.'

Trouble? I turned the shifty word around in my head. When Dad lived with us and Evie was cross she used to say he was trouble. A man with a face so red and hands so cold was trouble. An absent dad, on the other hand, was no trouble at all. A weekend dad to visit when the fancy took you, that was another question again.

Mr Noelson eased the handbrake and the car rolled down the street to come to rest opposite my father's house. There was the number in brass beside the door: *No. 29*. The house was a redbrick back-to-back like the others in the street, with two windows, one beside the front door and one up on the first floor, and painted drainpipes wrapped in barbed wire marking the house from its neighbours. The wide-open front door spilled light over the stone doorstep and there, in the middle of the pavement beside the doorstep, a domed barbecue set stood smoking.

I could tell there was something interesting about the house's painted drainpipes and painted window frames, but right this minute I couldn't think what it was. There was also something about the two cardboard cartons that stood on either side of the barbecue set, but again I couldn't properly take it in. This was 29 Grange Terrace and someone was home. I must get out to greet them.

Jim Noelson switched on the inside lights of the car, then straightaway switched them off again. A figure had reared into the yellow rectangle of no. 29's doorway, a woman, tall, very dark, with a massive headscarf stiff like a meringue dwarfing her head and shoulders. She cased the street, then peered at our car.

Breath sliced sharply through Jim's front teeth.

'So—is not just one African friend you got.'

My hand was fumbling with the door handle. He pushed my fingers aside and let me out.

'You not want to leave your burden with me? For safe-keeping?'

His questions were puzzles. I searched his face for signs of a joke, then shook my head. I slid Fish-in-his-fleece into the willow-pattern bag. Gently, levelly, I lifted the bag out of the car, the woman still watching.

'You don't worry about payment, OK Arnie? Just remember what I said. Keep hold of that card.'

He freewheeled the Toyota to the bottom of the street, switched on the engine at the corner and was gone. I had the clear impression he did all this in a hurry.

Between two parked cars close to where I was standing a small group of girls sat hunched, sharing a cigarette. To my relief they left me alone. As I walked towards the bright, open doorway I was aware of my feet dragging and my tired eyes threatening to roll in my head.

But this woman was my Dad's girlfriend, I reassured myself. She was with Dad—

Dad who once lived with us. Behind her I saw an armchair I recognised, its faded blue upholstery, one of the pieces of furniture Dad had taken with him. The armchair was unoccupied. She'd been sitting in it, I imagined. And Dad might be sitting opposite, in its faded blue partner. This was, wasn't it, my home-from-home?

I walked over and put my hand in her hand.

'It's Arnie. *Arnie.* Arnie B-Binns,' I stuttered, immediately running out of anything else to say. If once I'd had a clear aim, it had long ago zapped itself. Why was I here? Search me. What did I want? Maybe I once knew; now I'd forgotten. To Dad himself I couldn't have explained. The journey had been too long. It had evaporated my plans. I didn't even know this new lady's name. But in this case I hadn't so much forgotten the fact that Dad hadn't bothered to tell us.

The lady frowned deeply but she held my hand a long time. She almost pulled me up the stairs towards her with the force of her grip. Keep the jar steady now, *steady*. I lurched after her indoors.

'Your father's not in.' She pointed vaguely at the familiar, worn armchairs, their blue, threadbare armrests, empty of Dad's shape. 'You sit down. If you got good fortune, *if* you got fortune, he come here before too long.'

She swung round as if to take my things but I was already seated, my bag with my Fish in it perched on my feet.

Smoothly she translated the movement that had been towards me in the direction of a small sideboard. Under beaded netting stood a plate of charred sausages and a glass bowl of coleslaw.

'We have barbecue today, your father and me. The night not too chilly, especially for April. You want some?'

I sat opposite Dad's empty armchair with a paper plate on my lap and wolfed down every scrap of the four sausages she gave me. I felt a burp rise and swallowed it. As I ate she paced the tiny front room in silence, now and then touching an ornament, a table edge, the several things in here that were so familiar to me. These blue armchairs but also the nest of side tables that Mum still missed and talked about. The shiny Phillips stereo, the red-all-over car-boot-sale painting of an army on the march.

I could almost have believed I was at home if it weren't for the photos everywhere. The photos were different. Each and every surface in that room including the floor was loaded with photographs in plain wooden frames: portrait shots mainly with formal, painted backdrops and everyone in makeup. These especially she touched. She kind of held a finger to them for long seconds at a time. A wooden rack of keys nailed to the wall behind the front door she touched, too. She drew her finger along the hanging keys as if playing a kid's xylophone, making the same jingling-jangling noise.

The front door stayed open and it grew cold. On one of her circlings around the room she switched on the electric fire but left the door. Whenever anyone walked past in the street I started thinking it might be Dad, but she never flinched. Open door or no open door, it looked like she wasn't expecting him back tonight.

From time to time she snatched a sharp glance at me and I dropped my stare, but as soon as she paced on I swept my eyes back. Truth was, I *had* to stare, I *needed* to stare. I'd not seen anyone like her in my life before. It might have been rude but at that point I was as likely to burp out loud as to quit staring.

She was amazing. Her green-and-red swirly turban and massive wrap-around dress made her grand as a swan with spread wings. The shape of the turban stayed rigid no matter how low she stooped. Her big, long body and big, wide back made the exact opposite to Evie's thinness, I noticed. And her silky, dark skin reflected the light of the electric fire. It kind of beamed with the light.

What extraordinary thing had Dad done, I asked myself, to be able to ensnare this glowing person and bring her to this little house?

'You Daniel's boy then? Elder child?' she said at some point, beetling over to me.

"*Only* boy", I wanted to correct but she'd paced on.

And at another point, 'You stop here tonight?'

I nodded, but it was her foregone conclusion. She was back playing that row of keys.

I wondered what Dad had told her about us, about me. Had he said anything at all? Anything like, 'I have a Son Down South, and he looks like this and this, with dark hair, and he's a dreamer, and likes to have the whole world ship-shape?' From where I was sitting it looked as if none of the hundred photographs in the room showed my face. Or Mum's for that matter. Or any of our family, not even Dad himself.

It was then I realised that there were no photos of white people at all in that room, unless hidden behind others. With this thought a shadow touched me, and I wondered if I shouldn't feel unwelcome. But then I reminded myself the lady hadn't made me feel unwelcome. She had shaken my hand a long time. She had pulled me towards her. She had given me food. So a new thought came. Maybe this house was *hers*, I thought, and these were her people and

118

Dad was in fact the guest. Maybe Dad was a recent and not-very-settled houseguest.

By now I was tireder than ever in my life before, at least as far as I could remember. The lady's endless circlings could have hypnotised a wakeful baby, even if I hadn't already felt about dead. My head was knocking about like my neck was made of elastic. I wanted to stay awake long enough to greet Dad but there my head was, clunking against the back of the armchair, and my breath catching in my throat in a snore. I thought of Fish down on the floor with his legs tucked up. I was ready to envy any human thing such total and never-ending rest.

At some point I was aware of the lady tucking a rug around my shoulders that smelled of grass and her hands, just here under my chin, of peppermint. At another point a palm was held to my forehead and I was looking up into worried, incredibly sorrowful eyes. Later again the lights were out and I was sure she was sitting on the front doorstep and sobbing softly though trying to fight it, hiccuping and sobbing. The door was still open and the clean, grey air of the early morning was rushing into the house.

'Ma pickin, na wetin,' she murmured between sobs, or words to that effect. 'Ma pickin, ma child, ma pickin.' And she was rocking herself, rocking, rocking, and—I saw it as true as I sat curled there—she was cradling Fish on her lap. Fish was in his jar but his browny-white fleece had dropped down beside her on the stone doorstep and she was holding him.

Chapter 8
Alice

Laura sits upright in her white hospital bed by the window looking sheepish. The swing doors to the ward clap against Alice's shoulders. She charges at her sister's bed, ready to launch herself into her arms, but Laura's shifty expression holds her back. Laura's awake and conscious, it's clear, she's uncontorted by pain and in fact looks completely unscathed. The sight of her in bed with the sheets pulled up to her chin is about as everyday as a toothbrush.

Alice brakes at the foot of the bed.

'Hiya.' As offhand as it's possible to be.

'You OK, Laura?'

'Uh-huh, I'm OK. After all. At the end of the day.'

Alice shuffles her body into the crook of her sister's waist, a familiar spot. She slides her a sideways glance. It's true, Laura seems genuinely OK, her shape under the covers as skinny as ever, her eyes brighter than they have looked for weeks.

She takes in the rest of the four-bed ward. There are two other patients, young women about Laura's age, maybe a bit older, both flat on their backs, fast asleep, hair spread on their pillows. It's a scene from the illustrated *The Night Before Christmas*, her favourite childhood book, a present from B-J on her fifth birthday. *The children were nestled all snug in their beds, While dah-dah-dah sugarplums danced in their heads.*

She's aware of a vague disappointment at this general

tidiness and quiet. She checks for drips and heart monitors, bags of red-purple blood and yellow seepage dangling under the beds. There's nothing of this nature to be seen. She'd have liked there to be something moistly medical and organic to examine, some pendulous, *extracted* object, a discreet but tumescent bag of blood. Even a tray of stainless steel equipment would've been interesting to lay a careful finger on.

She can feel her own stainless steel collection, now returned to her trouser pocket, press gently against her thigh.

Laura has found her hand and is holding it tight. She launches into an explanation without prompting.

'I slept in this morning, Alice, thinking that if I rested a long time the stomach-ache and everything would go away.' She shoves up against her sister to make sure she's listening. 'Phoe swears by sleep, doesn't he? Sleep cures all ills.' She smiles at Alice's turned-down mouth. 'But the thing didn't go away, not at all. Actually it grew more intense, like suddenly. The discomfort was kind of slowly building up, like I said, and then early this afternoon when I got out of bed, my stomach—well, suddenly all this blood came out. My cycle usually isn't too predictable but this was different, just thick and pouring. It felt like the inside of me wanted to turn itself out. I cleaned up the floor but didn't want to lie back down on my bed in case I couldn't get up again, that's how it felt. I wanted to wait for you to get home from school and then I couldn't, I panicked. Jilly was having herself done at Arnie's Mum's like on most Fridays, thank God. So I borrowed money from our moneybox and called a taxi and came straight here. No parental involvement required.'

The mention of Arnie, Arnie's Mum, stirs and dislodges something in Alice. It feels like bits of her are sliding about in her chest.

Laura's apparently fine but Arnie's still missing. There are not one but two rescue projects to keep in play.

Keep watchful, she talks to herself sternly. Laura's self-help efforts give no reason to relax.

'And then?'

'Well, it was a really bad haemorrhage basically. It can happen, even to girls my age; that's what they told me; it's to do with our bodies still growing up and sorting themselves out. The sickness and swelling were part of it, too. I refused the scraping procedure they offered, though. Said it wasn't necessary, there's no way it was necessary.' She looks hard at Laura and narrows her eyes, as if to give emphasis to something. 'There's *no* way. So they put me under observation. That's what's happening now, I'm under observation, but, ahm'—she gives a weird little cough—'it's OK, it's all over now.'

In Alice disappointment rubs up against a rising feeling of relief. She has the clear sensation that the toys and the birthday candles have been put away before she had a chance to join in the party. Laura's OK, that's great, that's really great, but she wanted it to be her, Alice, to make it OK. She wanted to be Laura's No. 1 helper. She wanted so much to draw benefit from their funny, squashy specimen.

She can't help saying, '*Heck* Laura, after all that worry and bother! Even I could've told you it was some women's problem like that. At least it'll teach you not to spend your time dieting on so many fridge-loads of steak. It gave you that stomach-ache, I'd bet, and that load of extra blood. I could've told you that no one lives on just steak.'

To herself she wonders about the pills in Laura's knickers drawer, the medicine for bringing off babies in a hurry. When she peeks next time, will the seal on the box finally be broken?

'I know it's kind of awful.' Laura rolls her eyes but looks blissed out enough not especially to care. 'All I say is promise not even to *breathe* a word to Phoe. *Please.* He'll be waking up around now, having one of his afternoon breakfasts, I'd guess. He won't have missed me. Not yet. He won't have thought anything's the matter. I'll tell him in my own time.'

They gaze at the early evening sky framed in the window, the round clouds orange with the reflected glow of the city. Laura grips Alice's hand more tightly.

'The freakiest thing actually wasn't the bleeding. It was what I saw when they finished checking me over, after last night's ward round. Someone was very ill in a ward down the corridor, I heard the nurses talking. They'd left the door here open by mistake. The person was wheeled past when I happened to be looking out. I must've been feeling wobbly from losing that blood because the sight of it really did me in. The person, the body maybe, had a sheet pulled over its face and it was so still, just like an object, and I could see this beak-like nose sticking up rigid. This is what I couldn't get over, the whole thing, the object, was so rigid. I kept crying and crying. And now I can't stop asking myself, *what* are the dead, *where* are they? I keep thinking of how they lurk about the whole time, lonely, without us even noticing them ... '

Alice finds herself fidgeting. She doesn't want to hear about the dead. You could say she's had enough of dead things for today, for this whole weekend actually. She fights to swallow down the dry sob of some emotion, after-shock, collecting in her throat. She tries to think of something to entertain them both, a bit of chat. Steak-only diets ... the famous Bruce Lee ... she read a short piece the other day, it was in Jilly's *Hello!* ...

'Here's a thing,' she tells Laura. 'Did you know that weeks before a contest Bruce Lee the kung-fu star lived on nothing but pints of liquidised, raw horse steak? And then died of a heart attack. I found it in *Hello!* Says it all, doesn't it? The meat built up in him and then it killed him.'

Laura shoots her a puzzled glance, then looks away, lets whatever it was pass. She releases her sister's hand and turns on the light beside the bed. They both blink. On a television in a neighbouring room they hear a football match make a steady sonogram, alternate blocs of crowd chanting and crowd roaring. Alice is sure she's been awake forever.

'It's fantastic you came, Alice.' Laura pulls herself higher on her pillows, grimaces a little, bites her lip. 'I'll make it up to you, I mean it. Right now, though, we need to think about Jilly. There'll be enough questions from her to handle without you arriving home after dark.'

'I'll tell her the usual,' Alice shrugs, trying but failing not to sound deflated. Her big, red surprise balloon has burst and she still can't get over it. 'I'll say—well, that you're at Phoenix's, till late.'

She sits on for a while longer in the warm silence. The breathing of the young woman in the bed alongside Laura's is audible and uneven, full of soft sighs, gasps, tiny moans. Laura brings her lips close to Alice's ear.

'That one, she was crying earlier and tossing. Saying names in her sleep. Boys' names, James, Sean, a whole string. I was thinking to myself,' her voices descends to a bare whisper, 'you never know, poor thing, maybe she had that procedure today, that *scraping* procedure. It was so sad. Like she was rehearsing a new baby's names.'

'A new baby's names?' Alice mutters through the sieve of Laura's hasty hand, her cheeks warming at what she imagines she might be saying.

But her sister's face stays relaxed, connected. Her curiosity is genuine. She says *new baby* and doesn't bat an eyelid.

A bell rattles in the corridor beyond the swing doors. End of the evening visiting hour. The lift doors on the landing ping and swish. Alice stands up slowly. She feels the ache of the long afternoon walk in her thighs. She takes a few steps in the direction of the sighing young woman. Her hair is brown and freshly combed. Her face is shut up in sleep.

'Not what you think,' she turns back and bends to kiss her sister. 'Don't think she's had the kind of operation you mean. Not her either. She could've been saying her boyfriend's name, couldn't she? Or someone else she was seeing in her dreams? This anyway doesn't look like a hardcore ward. There's not enough equipment, drips and things like that.'

'You would say that.' Laura stretches out and closes her eyes. 'And I'm too full of Nurofen to challenge you.'

Alice observes her closely, cautiously, one last time. In case there is after all a secret message buried in that talk of boys' names. But Laura looks to be at peace. Partly stoned, definitely at peace.

'I'll come again then?'

Laura nods. 'They discharge me tomorrow morning, Saturday. So why not come when I get out? I'd like that. We could meet up outside, in the hospital garden. You'll have seen it on your way in.'

'I'll meet you in the garden, behind the carpark,' says Alice. 'Under the trees.'

* * *

That night the foetus works its way into Alice's dreams. She dreams that she's lying in her own bed, the selfsame bed she's dreaming in, and the foetus is in the room. Arnie has returned it and it's in here with her. It has somehow escaped its jar and is crouched on the rug close to the radiator. In the light of the half-moon shining through the window it takes the shape of a hunchbacked goblin. She can sense that it has something on her; something she doesn't want to think about; something about hurt, blades, cut-open guts. She can sense that it wants to frighten her.

She turns to the wall but the creature wants her attention. It gurns at her with its cunning face. She can tell that it's dragging itself closer, on its belly. She twists round, she can't help herself, and peers over the side of her pillow. And there, looking up at her from the floor below, is its domed skull, its sharply pointed nostrils, its high African forehead shedding a moony, unearthly radiance. It's calling her to a judgement, she's sure. The head is pointing to left and right, casing the area. Its tiny hands are folded over its gaping chest.

Her legs now struggle desperately but are dead weights. Their heaviness soaks into the rest of her body. 'Are those empty, ogling spaces really eyes?' She asks herself. 'How can a thing with lidless eyes seem to peer and gape? To look hell-bent?'

Hell-bent on her shimmering blades and knives, laid out in order of sharpness on her bedside table.

Though she doesn't wake from her dream, the next morning when she opens her eyes its after-image comes to her in exact, pixellated detail.

* * *

By 9 a.m. the next morning Alice is pressing her way up the hill to the hospital. Yesterday she took the bus to the hospital; today she needs to walk. The ache in her thighs has disappeared. She'd be feeling completely fine if it weren't for this strange discomfort in her chest, a snarl of muscle that aches like a stitch, as if last night's monster-baby dream had left some scar.

Is Arnie her partner in crime? She wonders. Is it to do with being worried about him or to do with missing him?

She doesn't know where he is, and, even more, she wants him back here. She wants his company. She wants him here with or without the specimen jar, the feeling's that strong. She wants him here regardless of the invisible link that connects them. In point of fact, this stitch pain is so strong because right at this minute she can't feel the link between them. Since last night the line's gone dead. The discomfort in her chest is the scar of a connecting cord gone dead. Laura's useless, stupid false alarm has produced this totally real predicament.

She'd never have thought it, she who always tells him what to do, how hard she'd take his not being here. His not being here *and* not knowing where he is. Forget the foetus. Whatever he's gone and done with it, it's him she misses. The surprised look of greeting that travels up through his eyebrows and signaling what's up?—she misses that. And how his face, his trembling chin, betrays exactly what he's feeling, much as this annoys her *to death* when they're together. And she misses picking him up on the way to school. Even this morning she resisted the temptation to detour past his house, just in case. She didn't want to risk bumping into Evie on her doorstep. Evie awaiting her first Saturday morning client and hoping to talk about Arnie, to discuss the birthday sleepover or school outing or sponsored walk, he'll have used as his excuse for being away.

On the hospital side of the city the houses display newer, cleaner double-glazing than in plain, flat Woodpark. The front gardens have space for silver-grey four-by-fours, lined up everywhere like expensive garden pagodas. The ground now begins to rise steeply. Alice passes a picture framers, a wine bar, a shop with a single dress hanging in the window, untidy as a dropped poppy; a nail bar called Dilys's. She remembers Laura talking dreamily about this nail bar's fame and excellence. It was last summer, after the dig. Laura's nails were *ruined*, she said; they were *totally talons*.

She'll have to tell Laura she's seen the place. It well-and-truly exists.

The hospital rises up ahead, at the top of a long straight road. It's a grey block built of weather-resistant concrete that squares off the summit of the hill. One end of the block points into thin air. The building looks like America, thinks Alice. Or, anyway, doesn't look very much like England. A flagship hospital, people say proudly, even though it resembles a chunk of art more than a hospital.

The hospital must somewhere, she decides, other than in Laura's vicinity, contain rooms piled with pieces of the most satisfying, cutting-edge, state-of-the-art stainless-steel apparatus.

At the barrier gate she turns and looks out over the pale green trees of the city to where the hills around town are just visible through the late-spring morning glare. The view up here is good. Far off to the left in the shiny grey she can just about make out the shapes of the paired Winborne Clumps. At their base is the strip of yellow-green water meadow. Beyond, the two copses of trees, are the highest points on the horizon.

Laura is waiting as arranged on a wooden bench under the row of chestnut trees that lines the hospital garden. She's waving and mouthing before Alice comes within earshot.

'I'm fine,' she says loudly, 'I'm fine,' though Alice hasn't asked. *To the memory of Polly St John who loved this place*, reads the brass plaque over her left shoulder. She shifts over to make room. 'I wanted you to see this,' she goes on. 'Look!'

This is a sunken garden-within-a-garden. They are at a distance from the hospital's glittering car park and the wooden bench looks out over the sunken garden. From here the cars make small sounds only, their wheels on the gravel like remote radio static.

There is something curious about this garden. Alice has to sit a while and sharpen her ears before she picks it up. The garden is full of tinkling sounds and twinkling lights, that's it. It's full of wind chimes. There are clusters of glass rods, bamboo and metal tubing hung on the trees and inside the rosebush hedges planted in rings in the middle of the garden.

'That sunken bit must be an old swimming pool,' says Alice. 'It's the shape of one.'

'It's a memorial garden now,' says Laura.

'Not *another* memorial garden.' Alice sighs, momentarily dropping her guard.

'What do you mean? *Another*?'

'I mean, I don't know what I mean. Must be something about a hospital. Makes you think of the sick, the unwell, like you said yesterday, the dead. We're not that used to hospitals, Laura. I mean, maybe it makes me think of the assistant at school who died, Darlene Miller, who had the nature burial at the Winborne Clumps. I was out there the other day, yesterday, thinking how the land around about has kind of become *her* memorial garden.'

Keep to the bare minimum, Alice tells herself. No point in offering the whole sticky story.

Laura makes a noise as if to speak; stops; begins again.

'I remember Darlene Miller really well. When I was in Year 7 she was always happy to help me with my reading. She was so patient. She'd have wanted to blend in peacefully. The parents of the little kids lying here eventually want them to blend in, I'd guess.'

Alice checks her sister's face for signs of a Nurofen overdose. Sounds like the ghost of Enid Blyton warbling through helium is coming through Laura's mouth.

'What do you mean, little kids?'

'That's what they are about here, little kids. See, this garden belongs to the maternity section of the hospital.

The women's wards are just behind us. This is the place for the parents whose babies don't make it. So they can hang their wind chimes. They can place ashes or flowers. The girl in the ward told me all about it this morning. I'm sure she did have some problem. She kept talking about little babies cut off in their prime. Even at three months their corpses look human,' she said.

'Stop it.' Alice shifts about impatiently. 'At three, four months it's not babies, it's *embryos*. It's not even *corpses*. The biology textbooks all agree. I'll show you the diagrams. We don't need a graveyard to learn any different.'

Laura refuses to be nonplussed.

'I think it's quite beautiful here actually. And it's not a graveyard. There are no burials. It's *not* a place of extinction. Absorption, not extinction; remember what that archaeologist said last summer?'

Alice jackknifes upright as if to dump the shadows of the garden unceremoniously from her lap to the ground.

'God Laura, won't you shut it? Has something here in the hospital got to you? Last time you said that you made a joke of it.'

Laura grabs the belt of her trousers and as abruptly and unceremoniously pulls her down again.

'*You* shut it! Stupid. Look what's behind you.'

Alice looks. Winding between the trees comes a solemn procession of four women of various ages dressed in shades of black and grey. The woman who leads is the youngest of the group. She carries a small wooden box pressed into her stomach. A Winnie-the-Pooh balloon on a ribbon tied to the box bobs in the air. The woman at the back of the procession is singing a Rolling Stones' song feelingly though self-consciously: *When Tears Go By*.

As soon as the procession is out of earshot in amongst the rose hedges it is Alice's turn to drag at her sister.

'I think we don't belong here.'

130

They see the women kneel down in a circle holding hands. The box has been placed on the grass between them.

'I disagree. I feel good here. I feel *well*. We're not disturbing those people. Personally I think that by sitting here I'm respecting what they're up to, facing the past, thinking about the dead. That's my whole beef with Jilly; how she hides from most of what has happened in her life. Those people there are looking their past in the face even as they're doing their thing with that box and tying their baby's balloon to a bush.'

'And so what? I mean, it's just a story they're weaving. Did their baby actually have a life? Did it have a past? Probably not. Meanwhile all over the world there are wars and people dying. There are enough dead and dying people to be getting on with everywhere not to worry about the dead half-people, the little embryos.'

'I'm happy to remember these small dead people, Alice, no matter how tiny they were.'

Laura seeks out her sister's eyes but Alice fixedly looks away. There's an uneasy pause, then Laura makes a sudden, impatient movement.

'God, Alice, don't you see, I'm partly talking about *us*? Myself. Maybe I see these things the other way about. Maybe it's to do with being dyslexic. The past and the future, death and birth, for me they're upside down and tumbled together. It's to do with remembering. Think of Jilly with her long-winded stories about her lovely time with Farouq Khan. Isn't it funny how she talks about the past without ever really *dealing* with it? Look at us; take a good, long look. What's our past really? It's not exactly like we spring from this soil, not wholly. I won't accept that we find ourselves here by some hippy-hippy-shake chance, just some passing romance of Jilly's.'

She gets up and begins to kick at one of the bench legs. Alice wants to grab her foot. She wants to put her arms around her and persuade her to be still. You've been poorly, Laura, please take it easy. Life is *all* chance, she wants to say. Most deaths are a combination of chances. Not one of her books has ever given a different point of view.

She waits till she's sure she won't blurt.

'I don't have a problem with our past, Laura. I just don't think about it much. I don't have a problem with life being random cells, or with the stories of old Farouq K. I understand your thing about him not belonging to you like he does to me. But what difference does it make, really? Do we ever see him? For all we know he's been dead and gone years. Some sandstorm crushed his house. A Nile flood swept him right out of his bed and he's never been seen again. So what? There are pictures in the *National Geographic Yearbook* you showed me of women launching miniature rafts into the Nile, to ask the river gods to be kind and not take away their crops. Floods and things happen all the time.'

Laura leans down to Alice and makes a Silent Scream face.

'But I have a problem! I happen to want to *feel* belonging. I want to know where our random cells connect us. Maybe my Dad was Sudanese? OK, but he might equally have been Guyanese. Or maybe Haitian, maybe Moroccan? And that's fine. I don't care *where* my Dad, our Dad, was from but I do want to *know* where. I don't have a problem with our skin colour but I would like to pin it down somehow. Since that dig at the Clumps last year I've been looking stuff up, making notes even. I've been finding out about the old African kingdoms, their incredible ancient cities. I don't get how you can't relate to that, when you're always cutting things up, poking about, dragging your knives around.'

132

Alice grows more thoughtful. Laura's time in hospital has obviously not siphoned off her anger.

'Thing is, Laura, you can go on and on searching but at the end of the day there'll never be enough answers. I see how our colour makes us African, but you could just as well say that it makes us local. It depends how you look at things. Didn't Jilly once show us a map of where Farouq lives? Didn't she herself say that Europe has always been on Africa's border? Think of the guy you dug up, that tall, old Nubian skellie. Haven't these places talked to each other for thousands of years?'

She breaks off as the mourning women file past on their way back to the car park. The youngest woman is now at the rear of the group. She is empty-handed and dawdling, her face woebegone. Her hands are still clutched together at her waist. One of the older women gives a nod of greeting. The group is measuring its steps to make sure that the sometime-mother-to-be keeps up.

The young woman drops a white tissue not far from their bench. The sisters see it, make to reach for it, then keep sitting. The sight of that single, dropped tissue on the grass worriedly recalls the painful stitch in Alice's chest. *Where the hell's Arnie?* In this garden of dead memories she almost can't think about the question. He should be here with her; so where the heck is he? Is he lost? Is he hurt? What terrible thing has happened to force him into hiding for all this time? If he were back, wouldn't he have sought her out by now?

Her head feels suddenly feel hot and uncomfortable. A horrible, dry, choking sound escapes from her throat.

Laura's arms come around her shoulders. 'Oh Alice,' she says, 'It was so sad, that sad lady, that tiny box.'

'It wasn't that.' Alice presses her fingers into her eyes.

'What is it then? Is it the Dad thing? You're upset about me being upset? You want us to have the same Dads. Well, we do, really, we do. Let's just say that, we do.'

Alice rubs her cheek on Laura's shoulder.

'No, no, it's not that.' Now she's diving into a shadowy lake, depth unknown. 'It's not that, Laura. It's Arnie.'

'*Arnie Binns?*' Laura pushes her to arms' length, gives an unpractised arch look, hugs her again. She whispers into her hair, 'Didn't know you were that crazy about him.'

'I'm not *crazy* about him. It's just that we're friends. We're, well, whatever—we see eye-to-eye, we're the same age basically.'

Saying this she sees the truth in it. They *are* close. They're closely matched even though they're all at odd angles. They're misfits together. Despite his dreams and her love of facts she sees how they map onto one another. Arnie and Alice; both oddballs, both otherwise.

Then, sniffing, wiping her nose, she gives a rough account of the past forty-eight hours, but without the complicated bits concerning the demonstrate-the-baby plan and the specimen. She says there was a disagreement, a misunderstanding, something about schoolwork, a school project, and now Arnie has careered off on his own, leaving no trace, and the forces of guilt and blame are gathering at her back.

'And, Laura, I'm so frightened. Not for myself but... There're only so many places...'

Laura's listening smile grows provocative, as if she's about to offer a long-promised kiss.

'I've got it,' she says. 'It's simple really. What we do is we hunt for him ourselves. Haven't we got all weekend? You know where he'd bolt to; you're right there are only so many places. We'll take Phoe's car. I drive him home from parties all the time. We'll try to follow Arnie's tracks. The only thing is to focus. Try to imagine it for yourself, where would a kid your age head to?'

'He'd not go far.'

'He'd go to family?'

'Might do. But there's not much family. His Dad has left Evie and gone off north. There's a nana somewhere not too far away at Aylesbury. She lives alone. She paid an afternoon visit once. I remember her saying she hadn't spoken to another human being in a month, apart from cashiers in shops. Her teeth had kind of left dry indent marks on her lower lip.'

'We find the dry-lipped granny. Is she a Binns? We need to find out where exactly she lives.'

'We could ask Evie.'

'You want to involve her?'

'If you're there to back me up. Say we drop by and ask, making conversation..., Ahm, how's old Mrs Binns, Arnie's nana? The add-on advantage is that we discover if she suspects anything about Arnie.'

'We'll need a pretext though. Why are we visiting on a weekend when he himself isn't around?'

'History project?' Alice is as impressed as always at her powers of invention. As if all were worked out beforehand, the railtracks of her scheme click smoothly into place. 'How many times a year does the school ask us to do community work for free? Litter blitzes, old clothes collections? Let's say we're doing a local history project. Say we've been told to speak to older people in our area about their memories of childhood, the fifties... sixties... about rockers and baby boomers. Or no, let it be *your* project, a pretend Sixth-Form College project, preparation for when you go back next year. That way she doesn't ask why Arnie's not participating.'

'It might work, Alice. But first I'll call Phoe, see if the car's free. Or no, first we call a taxi and head home for lunch, a lunch of no steak at all, no meat. And then we see.'

Chapter 9

Arnie

There was no choice in the matter. I stumbled upright, walked over to the open door and stood beside Dad's girlfriend on the front doorstep. Could have left her to it of course. Her sobbing was heartbroken and private. She was clutching Fish's jar to her chest as if he was a real baby. I could've pretended to wriggle in my sleep and to turn my back to the door; could've pretended nothing was wrong. Except for us being there. Except for me and my friend Fish, us unexpected interlopers. So I walked over to the door and stood beside her for good reason.

Three very good reasons: A, B. and C.

My worry about Fish. What she might do to him in the heat of the moment. That was A. To remind her I was still there. Present, if unwelcome. Which was reason B. And then C. Finally there was something, to do with wanting to put an arm around her back. I wanted to stand close to her. I'd barged in and taken a roof for the night, hadn't I? The cheek, I heard Alice say. I wanted to make things all right and touch my hand on her back and put my arm around her shoulders.

I came to stand slap-bang beside her but she took no notice. Maybe her sobbing quietend down a bit but, really, she wasn't bothered who was there and she didn't look up. I definitely could tell she wasn't bothered from what happened next.

Next she put the jar down on the step and wiped her nose with the back of a hand. I noticed she'd taken off her head tie and put it on the sideboard. Her head was bare, closely shaven, almost as closely as my own head. She reached down for my fleece, Fish's fleece.

At this moment her body blocked the movements of her hands or I'd have called out. I'd have spoken or made a noise. When next she rocked back against the opened door, Fish was held to her chest, in a snug, tightly wrapped bundle. I mean Fish's body. Fish now was out of his jar. Only the top of his wrinkled head showed above the folds of my browny-white fleece.

'Too cold in there.' She spoke solemnly, looking straight at me. She was a nurse, I remembered. 'Too cold and too dry. Even for a dead one.'

The last shreds of my secret ripped clean away.

Faced by that straight look of hers, the heavy weight of what I'd done hit into me hard. Worry cut my guts like a knife. This was my father's house, or as Evie always said, your *absent* father. I'd brought a thieved, dead foetus specimen to my *absent* father's house, under wraps, by night, while wagging off from school, and his girlfriend, a nurse, had caught me in the act.

She had caught me in every facet of the act, Fish's bad travelling conditions included.

I'd been looking for safe shelter. I'd been looking for chill-out time from Alice, maybe. I couldn't remember what I'd been looking for.

'When's my dad coming home?' I'd meant to ask. I'd forgotten to say a word about him, right up till now. What would she be thinking? The boy hadn't been bothered to see about his dad.

Even now I didn't speak, couldn't. Couldn't do a thing. Didn't snatch Fish back. Didn't move. I just stood and stared at the top of his eggshell-white head. In the pale, early morning sunlight I thought he looked worse than deathly, like a visitor from another world, a kind of embryo-spirit.

Our genie-baby was well out of the bottle. Launched into the air; not home, but dry. Drying out.

She patted the stone step beside her. 'Sit down now. You wait small and see.'

She said this quietly but it wasn't an order to refuse. I sat down at the other end of the step. I left enough space for a person to pass between us.

For a while she crooned in the back of her throat. That's to say there was a humming sound that came from somewhere around her and filled the air. The humming seemed to weave in with the dark birds wheeling through the white arch of the morning sky over the houses opposite and with the invisible birds making a racket in nearby invisible trees. I thought of the people getting up at this time, of the milk deliverers, nurses and rubbish collectors, and of Alice and the people still asleep, like Evie.

From my doorstep perch I saw why the house's window frames and front door had looked unusual in the dark. They were painted in diagonals, sky-blue and bottle-green, the green stripes decorated with rows of white dots. It was this lady's doing for sure.

The barbecue arrangements would be her idea too, the shiny, new-bought black barbecue set boldly in the middle of the pavement, and the Pampers nappy boxes used as seats. For Dad special dinners, even Christmas dinners, were a waste of money, so he used to say. Why go to all that trouble when what you wanted was to fill your stomach? All special dinners were a waste, he said, except Christmas dinner. The *twaddle* of a barbeque especially was a very big mess and a very big waste.

'Katrina,' she nodded over to me eventually, ducking her chin so as to point to herself. 'I not say last night.'

'Katrina,' I said. It was a relief to be told.

She ducked her chin a second time. 'And he?'

'He? Fish is a he?'

'Maybe so.' She clutched him tighter. 'Is Fish, you say? You call him Fish?'

I nodded, half-wanting to put my hand on him, too.

I noticed she was crying softly, almost without making a sound, and gently rocking herself, the wooden bracelet on her right wrist clicking against the doorframe each time she swung. She had a rhythm going...to and fro, click, and her heels slightly rising, falling and rising. It was a kind of drumming, very quiet. I wondered whether she'd been crying all the time I'd slept.

And then she began to talk. A long stream of talk came flowing from her mouth with only now and then a pause for breath. It was the strangest thing. Where last night I'd struggled to catch her meaning, now every word was plain. The only problem was that sometimes she called herself "I" and sometimes "Katrina", as if she was standing outside of herself, so it wasn't till later that I understood clearly parts of what she'd said.

'Now then, Danny's boy Arnie,' she said. 'You think why I help lift your heavy burden? I tell you why. Katrina born five, six, pickin in this life. She bring her five or six children into this life, but not bring one for her house. No pickin. No single one live. They come from Katrina perfect like this one here, five or six. Some early, some late, only one they take a knife to open my belly so the breeze rush inside. That one have a nice, round head; his body fine, too, but all-the-same he die. The other ones have long, smart heads like this Fish.' She cupped his head, she rocked, the bracelet clicked. 'Fact is,' she went on, 'Katrina know very well how new baby look. She has midwife certificate, she seen plenty. She seen poor, sick pickin born with brain hanging down their back like raffia. And heart outside body, and too-small arms like little wings. I think Fish born small like this and head frontwards, very ordinary, but then like my pickin he choose not to live. No, not at all. Maybe he got hole inside him somewhere, so his ghost leak out. Or maybe he take one look round and think no way, not this world, it too raw, not for me, just like each and every one of the pickin Katrina born.'

She cradled Fish up higher between her chin and her shoulder, as if he was a violin.

'Off my babies go, and then come back, and again and again and again. *Ogbanje child* we Igbo call them in the muddy river delta from where I come. *Ogbanje child* always knock at the door of the same belly, the same mother, and yank her hair, want to try the thing one more time. "Please, let me try another little bit of this life," they say. "I want to put these arms around you, make you feel warm, give it a go one last time." And the mother say "yes, 'course, come"—how can she not?—and the child rush in, and lose the hope and hunger to live even while they rushing.'

I tried to shift my eyes towards Fish nestled there on her shoulder but was afraid. I'd heard about long dead things laid far from the eye of the sun. How, when the air and the light touch them, they shrivel away to nothing. What was left is a wisp of dust at the bottom of the sarcophagus, an oily streak. I was afraid that Fish out of his jar a second time might suddenly begin to shrink and change colour. Go purple, weep like a wound. But when I forced my eyes to the spot where he lay, there was only that pasty, whitey-grey top of his head against her smooth, shiny neck.

'In my work,' Katrina said, 'I find many women with big-big woman problem. Their belly go wander, their belly flesh go move round their whole body. They grow baby from the lining of their spleen. Womb-cramp attack their chest and knees.' She semi-closed her eyes and shushed her lips, as if trying to coax Fish to sleep. 'Katrina is blessed for having no wandering belly. Just the one wandering pickin who come back and back to tease me. Tease me and hurt me, five, six times.'

I noticed she was patting Fish's back, winding him.

"Course in my country the elders got their remedy for them, the wandering pickin. It a good one. Katrina a modern nurse; true, she not listen at first. But then, by-and-by, when she find herself a stranger in this place here, year-on-year a stranger, their talk fit sit in my ears. I, a good nurse, certificate aplenty, but still I get trouble to stay on here and live. People meet me the first time and ask, '"Well now, when you go home?" The Home Office folk drag their feet on my Leave-to-Remain. And so when trouble comes, when I feel bad and grieving, the elders' talk come back.'

She put her lips close to Fish's head. "Do something powerful to that returning baby," the elders say. "Bury *ogbanje* baby like that deep in some swamp, under a tree, on some Yorkshire moor, so his soul can't get free and come back." At home we sometimes break their arm and leave them in the forest where no one go. We stick them in a clay pot and stop up the mouth and put them far away, many miles walk, so they no fit find their house back. We dig up their spirit tokens, magic stones and shells, and we crush them to nothing, give baby a chance for everlasting sleep. As for the mother, the mother put mud in her ears so she no hear them call. The mother must travel a far, far way to lose *ogbanje*'s spirit, like Katrina travel far, very far, to reach this place. Katrina make a fuss in her country with the government so they not even want her back. She collect money for her leaders who sit in gaol. She curse the bad leaders who sit in Government House. But nothing help. Katrina still sit and dream about all the lost children. She sit and dream, nurse the pain inside.'

She loosened the fleece as if to give Fish room to breathe and for the second time I was faced with his face, just a moment, till I had to look away; his wrinkled, old man's face with the tiny, bluish, blanked-out eyes crumpled all over; the picture of a once-upon-a-time. She followed my eyes and gazed down at him for a long while. She didn't seem to mind the look of him because next she began to speak to him in a cutesy, sweetie-pie voice.

'Aren't you a handsome one? Good shape all over, head and everywhere. Strong, firm skin, after all the years you spend. Some smart, thinking person even give you a special cut, take a razor to your chest so your wickedness can dart out. So we can mark you. So you think twice before you return to make your mother gnash her teeth. Unless you stubborn. One I had come back with a dark line on the breastbone where the razor touch. Small baby, if you mine I make three special cuts on your two shoulders, so I can recognise you always. And then I fit wrap you and rub you warm, lay poultice on your cut. And maybe your spirit decide to live, in spite of all. If I weigh your heaviness here in my hands is like a livin' pickin almost. If I rub and care for you, maybe you think, "Ha, this is good!" And try harder and take the noose of life round your neck. And your body grow full of lice, colds, mucus, like any other pickin, full of everything in the world.'

As she spoke she stroked Fish's back and unwound the fleece and then swaddled it around him again, adding a red scarf of her own pulled down from a peg by the door. My head leaned itself against the doorjamb so as not to topple off my neck with how sleepy I still was. Fuzzily I wondered if there was a bed somewhere to stretch out on, just a strip of carpet maybe to lie down on...when she made me jump.

Suddenly she straightened her back, quit staring at the baby, gave a deep cough, and said, 'So, Danny's boy Arnie—'

The change in her voice especially made me jump. She had switched for no reason I could see to a new accent, an everyday nurse's voice, something foreign and ordinary at once, African and Northern bundled together.

She said, 'So, Arnie, here's a plan I think you like.' This was her practical self, I guessed, the one she used on the wards, talking to people on the street, up and down Grange Terrace. 'I think we take a walk, an early morning walk. I know a good place where to go, a nice, green, open space, the kind that are nowadays few-and-far-between. We go there, have a look round, breathe some air, and on the way back maybe catch a hot drink and a breakfast. There's a caff close to here, next door to a panel beater your father knows. Maybe we even find him there, our Danny. I find him there on other mornings having breakfast after a night's drinking.' She sniffed, 'Drinking and whatever.'

I must have looked puzzled because she leant over and patted my neck. Her hand was moist from touching Fish's body, I could tell, because she left my hoodie sticking to my skin.

'Now don't you worry yourself,' she said, her nurse voice almost sliding into her sing-song. 'I'll change my party clothes, can't walk in them. Your father and I have a small celebration party last night, you see, with barbecue meat and beer. It my weekend off.'

So smoothly she said this that I almost felt I could ask, 'Where's my dad now then?' But she didn't give me a moment. Her talk soldiered on.

'And we take your pickin on our walk, of course. We take baby and show him the place, or what you think?'

I couldn't think...whether to smile, frown, say yes, no—no idea. But I must've given some sign in spite of myself because she stood up with a sharp click of her knees and laid Fish ever so carefully on the blue armchair I'd spent the night in. She disappeared upstairs, each stair squeaking as she went, and within minutes came down without her wrap-around. She was wearing jeans and a white shirt, ironed just as crisp and smooth as my own best ironing.

She placed Fish in his fleece and a new red scarf in his willow-pattern bag. It was strange seeing her bending over Evie's familiar tote. Then she thought better of it and lifted him out again. She created a pouch around him using the scarf folded double, and bound the scarf round her chest, so that he made a small bundle on her back. A small, very flat bundle. She took the willow-pattern bag containing his fleece and all my things and stood waiting with her hand on the door handle.

It was obvious she was totally not bothered that I was standing like some spare part in the middle of the room and all this time hadn't said a word.

'My Dad?' I hiccuped uncertainly at last.

My hands were itching to claim my things. Lay hold of my Fish. Get my grip back on that tried-and-true willow-pattern handle.

'Oh,' she tossed her head towards the lower end of Grange Terrace, 'he come one of these days, one of these fine hours or so. I told him last week I hate his face when he's—'. She searched for the right word; it was Dad's word, *Blattered*. 'He's not very much my friend when he's blattered. Especially when we have a nice party together. For what does he want to get blattered? For what does he go down the pub with friends after a party at his very own house? With his girlfriend? A nice party with meat and beer? What thing eats him? What kind of friends is that?'

It didn't seem like there were straight answers to these questions but still I said, 'He liked the pub when he lived with us. The mornings after he got in my mum used to beat his smoky pub clothes with her carpet brush.'

'So then, some lives never change. Me, I throw his smoky clothes in the bin. But wait, my child, I think a thing.'

She stepped round me and began rummaging in amongst her photograph frames, eventually choosing three or four. She covered the faces with her hand as she picked them up, but I was sure it was framed photos of her family she was sliding into the bag. I was glad then that poor Fish wasn't there with them, walled in by photographs like some stunts magician in a closed glass box.

All the same I worried about him. Stepping down into the street after her I worried about the chafing of the woollen scarf on his skin. I worried how he'd stay balanced on her back. I worried about the cold. I could myself almost feel the cold penetrating through his covers, the air drying his skin, flaking it, the skin slipping off. Didn't Alice and I agree way back yesterday that we should try as hard as possible not to let him dry out?

In the street I turned to check on Fish's jar. It was standing by the door where Katrina had left it. Shouldn't we take it along like a portable bath and dip him in it if necessary? But it was too late. She was locking the door and hefting the bag over her arm. She gave Fish a shrug, shunting him into a more comfortable position on her spine, suspended between her shoulder blades.

We climbed the cobbled street in the direction I had come last night. We turned the same corner and then walked in a zigzag pattern through the streets of back-to-back houses; left, right, left, right, each street at right angles to the last. There wasn't much talk. She strode like a woman with a mission, pulling ahead and waiting with hunched shoulders if ever I paused to catch my breath.

Our destination was a green space on a hill. She pointed it out on several of our turns, stretching over the brow of the slope we were climbing. For a time the place looked like a park with dark-green, spreading trees and a friendly wooden gate with a trellis. As we drew closer, I saw the gravestones standing higgledy-piggledy round about, stained with early morning dew.

At the gate Katrina took my hand to lead me in. Her hand had the same firmness of the night before. She tugged hard. I could tell there was no choice in this matter of the graveyard. I glanced up at the bump on her back that was Fish and saw how easy it was to imagine him alive and real. The up-and-down movement of her body as she walked gave the clear impression that there was something in her bundle that was breathing, that could stretch out, make sounds, squirm, roll over.

We made our way across several aisles of gravestones, heading over to the left-hand side of the yard where the ground was higher. Tall, dew-drenched nettles brushed against our legs. Katrina knew exactly where to go, it looked like, and I struggled like a desperado to keep up. Before we had gone very far my tracksuit bottoms were wet to the knee and plastered to my skin.

At the brow of the hill she took my shoulders and spun me round. We were standing in amongst a wavy row of stone slabs and fat marble crosses. There were dark firs at our back and dandelions flowering everywhere in the long wet grass. Between the stone crosses lay a view of the city blanketed in blue morning mist, stretching for miles.

'Oh,' I said. I heard how deflated and unimpressed I sounded.

I sat down on the stone slab directly in front of us, panting. Acid-yellow lichen had grown thickly across the top of the stone and masked the engraving. I poked a finger into the grooves remaining but found no letters I could recognise.

As for Katrina, she was un-puffed, breathing hard but

steadily, sounding almost as if she was deep asleep. She busied herself laying things out on the stone slab. First she drew the photos from the bag and placed them face down. Then with a nifty, unplaiting motion, done blind, she loosened the red scarf tied across her back and levered Fish down and round, the top of his head just peeking over the fleecy wrap. She laid him in the middle of the slab on his side. I wanted her to check how he was holding up but she was busy knotting and reknotting around her waist a triangular shawl I hadn't noticed before, that she must've carried in the bag. She reknotted it about ten times till she was happy with how it sat, all the while talking softly to herself.

'I stranger for this country, so they say over and over, but I say one thing. Best way to plant the feet is make a pickin.' She knotted; she unknotted. 'Make a pickin, born a baby. Always I get trouble keeping pickin alive but this a new place, a new start in a new place. And Danny's boy bring me a sign. Sign from God knows where, hospital clear-out or whatever, but sign all the same.'

She bent over Fish folding something, I couldn't make out what.

'This one special, with a special cut.' She whispered so low it was difficult for me hear. 'Someone mark you for the forest, eh pickin? Well, you come to the right place. Yes sir, this place with all the stones and all the deads is close enough, peaceful enough.'

I looked out across the crosses bristling aslant and askew all down that hillside. I couldn't work out what she meant, so I squinted, looked again, and then, like a blow to the head, it hit me.

A blinding white light suddenly played around everything she was saying.

She meant to leave Fish out there among the ancient and crumbling dead like a sacrifice. Remember that stuff

147

she said about the elders, about abandoned baby corpses damned by their parents for refusing to stay alive? She meant to offer Fish up to the gods or ancestors or spirits, I was sure of it. The pictures of her family were like a warranty. She was laying them down so as to plead that she who had lost so many babies, wouldn't lose any more. Daniel's *elder* child, she'd said to me. She was saying she wanted a baby of her own here in England with Danny Binns and she wanted it *live*.

Some fierce force fuelled my legs and arms. I threw myself at her. My head drove into her middle. I buried my nose in the loose-weave black crochet of the shawl. I grabbed her arms, feet drumming the ground. Somewhere a voice was yelling. 'Can't, can't, *can't*. *Mine*, he's mine, mine.'

Untangling from the shawl I swung round and reached out for him lying on the stone, balanced awkwardly on his side. I made an effort to slow my movements so as not to damage him. He felt like nothing, a capsule of cold air. At the same moment she gripped my shoulders and for a second time this morning spun me round. I faced her, holding Fish in my hands. My emotion powered me to meet her eyes. But her expression was kindly, serious but kindly.

'Child, child, let's get this right,' she used her nurse's voice. 'That small baby's yours, no problem. I not mess with him. I say nothing different than you. But I give you advice, yes. I think you must give him a chance for sleep, a long, long sleep. I think you must open his lips and let him breathe himself out. But at the end of the day what you do with him is for you to say.'

She took my hands. Gradually, by inching and tweaking, she worked Fish out of my fingers and into hers. I let her do it. My skin had turned rough with goosebumps, my teeth were chattering. She never stopped talking.

'For me, Arnie, it enough to see the baby and hold him, a lost one in this place just like me. A one with no papers just like me. It enough to lie him here with my pictures, my own children's pictures, and pray and hope for the best for him. For him and for them and for me. His special cut make him special to me. He bring me luck.'

I looked hard into her face. Her eyes were pools of longing. I wanted her to understand that I was trying to understand. It flashed through me then that Alice and I had somehow committed magic. Though we never could've thought, never imagined, our actions yesterday had become kind of electric. Alice yesterday had made Fish's cut in curiosity, because she was a pre-teen surgeon-in-waiting and because she hated me standing up to her. And then it turned out special. She had given him a special cut and it would mark him always.

Let him breathe himself out, Katrina'd said.

'I ask you one thing now, Arnie. You listen up. I ask you one big thing and also one little thing. Depends what you think's big and what's little.'

I dropped my eyes, looked at the ground, the dewy grass, the dandelions like miniature suns.

'I ask you go away. Leave my house, leave this town, not right now, but soon. That a big thing, OK? It a tough thing, as we only just met and you come all the way to see your father. But you a sharp child so I think you understand. After a time you come back for a proper holiday, a proper celebration. You come on the train, I get you at the station. And we pour water on the ground like we do in my country for a blessing. Pour a libation to thank all our ancestors for everything they have given us. But for now you go away, go back to your home. Katrina needs to be alone. Katrina doesn't want children round her, dead or alive. Some women's lives are too full of ghosts, ghost babies and baby spirits crowding in, hounding them and punching with tiny fists.'

She sighed heavily.

'And then there's the small thing I must ask you... small thing or big thing, depending. Leave me quiet with your tiny one just one half-hour. I entreat you this. I promise I handle him gently just like you seen. I sing over him. That wound in his chest is raw. I close it with my fingers and hold it closed a while and wrap him tight. You go on a short walk. Buy a cup of tea, milk, Fanta, whatever you like. The caff I mention is down there in the last street we come through. Then we go back to my house and you head home with your Fish in his jar, safe and sound. You leave me to my quiet and eventually you find a quiet place down in the South so he can take his proper rest.'

She placed her feather-light bundle on the slab and briefly laid her hands on my forearms. Her touch was full of certainty. Then she crammed money into my palm, a whole £2, and turned back to the gravestone the second I began to walk away. Over the sound of the long grass swishing against my legs I could hear her crooning, humming and crooning. I didn't look back.

It was the thing about the special cut that convinced me it was OK to leave. I had the feeling that without even knowing it Alice and I had worked along with her hopes.

Chapter 10
Alice

Laura turns the car key; Alice settles back in her seat. They pull sharply out of the tight parking spot beside the twins Isla and Amina's house, at 8 Albion Street. The twins are standing at their front window waving, two identical curly heads, two identical sun-coloured pinafores. Laura straightens out the car and shakes back her hair in relief. Alice waves at the twins. She is surprised at how expectant she feels, how hopeful. Cars are a novelty to their licence-less family, so much so that even Phoenix's fifteen-year-old Fiat with its cracked windscreen and dodgy handbrake feels like a treat, a big day out.

She winches back the passenger seat so she's lying as if in a hammock. She imagines she's a stone in a sling, a ball in a giant hand. She wants to be thrown forwards. She wants to be projected bodily into this pale, dry Saturday afternoon, into some open space in the nearby future where the tough decisions are all already made.

Their meeting with a brisk Evie Binns was easy. She dashed out to see them in the middle of an appointment. She'd applied her client's facemask; she could take a minute. She stood in the hallway in her white salon coat studying her cuticles and barely mentioned Arnie. 'Yes, he's off on some school trip,' she said lightly. 'How many of these do you get in a year?'

Was the *local history* project Laura's or Alice's? Was it full-on or small-scale? The sisters didn't get round to saying. As Evie scribbled her mother-in-law's name and address on a pink sticky note she was already walking backwards up the stairs.

'They're making you work hard at Woodpark I'm pleased to see,' she said, glancing at her watch.

Their success in getting hold of the sticky note has set a merry cork bobbing on the surface of Alice's thoughts: *Mrs Daphne Binns, 17 Beecroft Road, Aylesbury*...17, exactly Laura's age. They've come a stage closer to wherever Arnie's hiding, she's sure. He has done exactly as expected; told his mum he was on a school trip. She's reading him, his white-lie excuse, his quiet scheming. The two of them somehow have re-established their connection. She's transmitting to him and he's transmitting to her. She suspects that even her guess at his whereabouts won't be too far off the mark. She and livened-up Laura have in any case settled on a destination. They have a way to go, a road to drive.

London Road leading out of town opens dry and shimmering under the sharp, grey light. The brown terrace houses on either side are backdrops in a film-set: the United Kingdom, 2002. Green wheelie bins stand to attention behind low garden walls. White bay windows frame slatted Ikea blinds. A dream-catcher swings in a kid's bedroom. Almost every third house is a B-and-B festooned with hanging baskets and Vacancies signs. And everywhere is parked cars, winking burglar alarms and parked cars.

Laura changes into fourth gear and begins to unwind a long string of talk. She wants Alice to know how *well* she feels. She's kind of *aerated*, light, full to the brim of frothy bubbles. She has this definite feeling things will work out for Alice and Arnie, too. How can she not have this feeling considering yesterday's small-but-beautiful hospital cure? She's convinced that by the end of the day Arnie will be located and all will be well.

She stumbles over her words and says Arn-ice, to rhyme with spice.

Alice, not minding, slumps lower in her seat, shuffling her shoulders into the soft fissures in the cracked plastic upholstery. Traffic light after light shows green as if a magic switch inside the car engine were working them in their favour. A way to go.

Alice doesn't believe in anything she can't see or touch and yet, she lets herself think, today she could almost make-believe that their foetus had transmuted itself into an invisible force propelling them on their journey. That it had changed from a lump of dead matter into this energy jetting them through these green and yellow fields, flashing past one-pub towns, small retail parks, mobile phone masks and Countryside Alliance hoardings like a bullet.

'I do *so* love Phoe's silences,' Laura says, 'I love how he watches a situation and draws his own conclusions.' Her breathing grows light and quick, as if she's gazing into a chest full of desirable treasures and deciding which one to take out next. 'He's been so fantastic during the tough times with Jilly. He listens to me and holds me and says I'm beautiful. What more could I want?'

Alice through half-closed lids watches a red kite hovering overhead. She remembers how Laura swore her to secrecy about her illness. Promise not even to *breathe* a word to Phoenix, she begged.

'I *do* see Jilly has a point,' Laura says, 'I do see why she worries. Maybe I am pretty angry all the time. And I suppose there is, *was*, the diet, *all* the diets, the Lo-Carb, the Weight Watchers Club, the McKenzie, the Slimsize one that was all about eating salads. I'm sure Jilly worries I self-harm. Masses of girls do it. She thinks that I hate this bloated, brown body, that I'd want to cut it. Then again, they always say how it happens in families where you least expect, and our dad-free family is where you'd *most* expect—'

At the mention of cutting Alice moves infinitesimally to feel for her thigh pocket, her collection of knives. There's the squidgy give of the velvet pouch beneath the combats' cotton, the cold hardness of the metal against her skin. Beside the pouch lies a longer shape wrapped in cloth, the blade she usually leaves behind. Grandad's tapered 1930s cut-throat razor, extracted from its new, post-dissection hiding-place between the wardrobe and the wall.

'You really do find it in the strangest places, though,' says Laura. 'People giving pain, taking pain ...like James Dean. Who can imagine anyone more gorgeous? But after his death, you know, in the car accident, they found James Dean's skin was covered in cigarette burns. I've read about this. All the skin normally hidden by clothes, it was like chickenpox. I mean, *James Dean* getting into that, imagine. The burns were everywhere.'

Alice circles the cut-throat razor with finger and thumb, making sure of it. She slumps back as she was. As they were leaving the house she ran back for the blade in its cloth wrapping, in case it came in handy. She knows she'd like for it to come in handy; she'd like to do something special with it. She's been thinking she'd like to give it to Arnie as a peace offering, to bury the hatchet. Set a knife to bury a knife.

Laura has been talking a very long time so Alice chips in, 'Wonder if Leonardo DiCaprio is into harming? You know, *at the end of the day*? What with him having it all and being so brilliant and beautiful.'

Her own barely veiled sharpness takes her by surprise.

But Laura doesn't notice or else doesn't let on. She's playing the piano on the steering wheel and smiling at some sunny thought.

'He looked like I felt that night,' she says. 'Phoenix I mean. He looked on edge. It was only the second time we'd met. It was in the same club. I looked at him and knew we could be soul mates. Romeo and Juliet would have nothing on us at our best.'

Alice lays her head to one side on the passenger headrest, refusing to meet her sister's sociable sideways glances. This is one day she definitely doesn't want to hear about Phoenix, or silent signals in the dark, or anything to do with teenagers in love. And Laura seems to get the message. Her remarks grow erratic. Her voice mixes in with the sound of the tyres on the asphalt, the shush of overtaking vehicles. Eventually she's not saying anything anymore. Time shrinks to the dimensions of the narrow band of roadway opening seamlessly in front of the car.

Alice notes to herself that her sister this afternoon has avoided all reference to Farouq Khan of far-off Khartoum.

There is the sudden screech of a hubcap on concrete. Laura mouthing *ffff*—front teeth clamped on to lower lip—turns the wheel and banks the car on to the pavement beside a petrol station. 'I think we might be there,' she says, reaching across Alice's face for the map lying on the back seat. 'Aylesbury...or anyway close to...spitting distance or closer.'

* * *

It seems they are expected. The white door to Daphne Binns's bungalow on suburban Beecroft Road is waiting wide open, as if the welcome party has briefly abandoned its watch to go and switch on the kettle for tea. Glazed pots of wilting petunias stand on the doorstep in the warm afternoon light.

The sisters knock, first with soft knuckles, then hard raps. Silence. Gently thudding fists, then a sharp blow to the middle of the door. Not a sound. They chirrup 'Mrs Binns', and then, more loudly, trilling, 'Mrs Binns?' Same result. A gleamy black cat slips like oil between their legs and slants into the shadowy interior.

Down the passage Alice sees a white Toy Town phone with an outsize keypad perched on a pinewood table, its receiver dangling to the floor. A collection of china owls is arranged on a wooden wall unit. Here, close to the door, a pair of lace-up outdoor shoes stands heels-together on a newspaper dated September 2000. A medium-sized beige raincoat hangs by its hood directly above the shoes.

Someone must be home.

Laura and Alice look uncertainly at one another. Still calling 'Mrs Binns, hello?' they tiptoe indoors, abreast.

Scenes of desertion and neglect. The small sitting-room to the right is a mouse's nest. The floor is thickly littered with paper, bits of tissue, newspaper, used envelopes, all torn into strips and crumpled. The settee, single armchair, and tiny side tables wade in the paper flurry. On the tiled mantelpiece a bunch of skeletal chrysanthemums slants askew from a stained cut-glass vase.

The door to the main bedroom opposite is ajar. This room has witnessed a windstorm. Some force has swept through pulling the bedclothes in a tangle from the bed and the clothes in massive, woolly granny knots from the cupboard.

The girls sidle past. Alice, ahead, looks back over her shoulder.

'*Weird?*' Laura mouths at her, eyes fixed and panicky.

Weird, Alice nods. Or did Laura maybe say *dead*?

The kitchen is the worst. Here the damage is of water. The pink gingham curtains are drawn, the floor surface gleams in the half-light. Then they step into it. The lino is under an inch of sudsy water. Shirts and coils of underwear are adrift like boiled pasta. Draggled pantyhose in flesh-colours make seaweed bunches.

Alice removes her socks and trainers and picks her way over to the washing machine, the obvious culprit; its door burst open, the plastic catch loose, broken. Her sister pokes distastefully at the load of unwashed dishes in the sink.

Mrs Binns herself they find in the back garden. Alice, stepping out of the kitchen door, is the first to see her. She grabs Laura's wrist in warning.

The old lady is standing tall and pole-like against a bank of rose-trees at the end of her short back garden. One shoulder is oddly stooped as if by cramp. Her white hair is matted into stubby tufts. She is wearing a viscose cardigan over a pale orange pyjama suit and her chalk-white stick arms protrude like caricatures from the sleeves.

As Laura follows Alice onto the kitchen step, Mrs Binns whinnies through her nose. It's not annoyance, Alice senses, flicking the wet from her feet; it is animal fear. They have both started too suddenly from the backdoor. Maybe they do the elderly lady an injury by approaching head-on like this, but they have no choice. The concrete path leads straight down from the kitchen step to the rosebush hedge.

Mrs Binns's face is unrecognisable. Not even the mouth corresponds to the shape in Alice's memory. These are not the imprinted dry lips of that one-time visit to Arnie's house. This face is a drought. It is as if it has suffered a blasting, a scouring of windburn. Skin is peeling from the face, the ears, the neck, in ragged, filmy strips.

Alice doesn't offer her hand till the last minute. She brings her arm up slowly but Mrs Binns's expression stays alarmed. Her round eyes are fastened to Alice's face and the raised hand escapes her notice.

'It's Alice. *Alice*, a friend of Arnie's, your grandson. We met once, a while back. This is my sister Laura. I hope you don't mind. We've come on a bit of a surprise visit...'

'Albie, *of course*. Dear Albie,' Mrs Binns cuts in, producing a vast, wan smile. Her sprightly way of talking contrasts with the stiffness in her body. 'I always stood by

Albie even when the others said— I knew he was right, you see. The road runs to the river and goes over the bridge, that's what we all thought, just follow the road and find your target. But Albie knew better; he'd bunkered there for months. He knew you can't go that way. He knew how people whisper their secrets and there'd be hell to pay, the place crawling with their men. And all the parachutes! Albie never stopped believing, you see. "There's always the other way, the roundabout way," he said. "There's always this and that, the one thing and then the other." We know now he was right. Albie knew the business and what's in the bottom drawer.'

Alice steps off the path into the grass to give Laura a chance to say hello, but Mrs Binns seems to be cringing back, pulling away from them both. If it weren't for the fact that something is preventing her from moving anywhere at all she might overbalance with this effort of pulling.

'You seem to have a bit of trouble in your kitchen, Mrs Binns.' Laura has come too far forwards not to say something. 'Your washing machine seems to have—'

'It rained so hard this summer, you see. You're right, but still you wouldn't believe how it started raining, even indoors. The buckets and basins we put down! The racket of the rain in the basins! And so cold! That rain made it so cold indoors. We had to get out our jumpers. Came into the garden to get away from the horrible, slimy rain.'

'We'd like to help you. Help clear up.' Alice inserts herself in front of Laura. 'It's lucky we came over looking for Arnie. If you have some towels we'll spread them round and soak up the worst. Any old towels, dishcloths, newspaper, torn-up bits of newspaper.' She steals an uneasy glance at Laura. 'You never know, Arnie may arrive back before we're done. Arnie, you know, your grandson.'

'Wouldn't dream of that in a thousand years.' Mrs Binns's eyes become round like headlamps. Her hair starts away from her skull the more violently at the nameless indignity she has suffered. 'Not in a thousand years! I mean, how could you, my dear? I'd have expected more. You *know* I wouldn't let a soul in, with the linen cupboard so neat, all my spick-and-span piles. *Any old towels*! I could've won prizes, couldn't I? Folded corner to corner, well-stretched, and every one of them starched, in their piles.'

She makes a tiny movement and winces dramatically. It dawns on Alice there's a special reason why the old lady looks trapped. The fact is she *is* trapped. The rose bushes somehow have trussed her up.

So as not to draw attention she circles around Mrs Binns's left. Sure enough, there's some tangle here involving the taller of the rose trees. Alice gestures to Laura to keep talking, keep her distracted. Her sister's face looks contorted, as if her tongue had met some bitter taste.

'Different generation, obviously.' The old lady's tone is suddenly confidential. 'Gob-stoppers were our thing. After the ration years you couldn't fill your mouth too full. But we were taught how to present our linen, us girls, even so. Even our bobby socks, just so, the frilly tops turned down. All straight and proper, neat and nice. In the drawer the same as on your legs, the socks tucked into the turned-down cuffs. The cupboard is your character, see, couldn't be a more private place. Wouldn't let a soul in there to poke about, not for the world. Brown and dirty hands touching all over.'

Alice hears her sister suck her teeth. Laura senses offence like the princess senses the pea.

She herself can't afford to get stuck on details. Peering over Mrs Binns's raised shoulder she sees how, skewered and pinned at several points, she has become a prisoner of the woody rose-tree. Her Berkertex cardie is a spiderweb strung across its thorns.

Earlier, Alice thinks, maybe when the washing machine began spewing water, or when she and Laura came marching through her open front door unannounced, Mrs Binns hared headlong down her garden and became entwined in the roses. She caught her cardie on these scary thorns and, when she tried to free herself, probably became more tightly snagged in.

She places a hand on Daphne Binns's shoulder. The old lady's skin is like soft wax, wax sliding across surprisingly sturdy bone.

'Stay still for a moment, Mrs Binns,' she says, pleased to feel her arm relax under her hand. 'Hold it there just a moment.'

She takes a step closer. It's a checking motion, bringing one leg up against the other. Along her thigh is the heft and glide of her knives in their pouch and beside them the cut-throat razor wrapped in its cloth.

With her eyes on Mrs Binns's face she slides her hand down to her pocket. Her fingers first encounter the Santos penknife. Its blade is sharp and strong but its point too thick, no good for snipping a thread. It has to be Grandad's razor. Today it will have found its niche. She'll put its sharpness to a different test, a quick precision job, totally bloodless.

Provided the patient stays calm.

Gently she slides the blade free.

When the knife appears Laura nods. She gets it. *'Talk to her,'* Alice mouths. *'Work with her?'* Laura queries. *'Talk,'* Alice whispers, *'talk,'* and adds, in a normal speaking voice, 'Just as well it's not raining, Mrs Binns. We'd all be soaked by now.'

'You never can tell, though,' says Daphne Binns. 'The same with rain as with roses. Roses and rain, they creep up.

Evie said only the other night. 'Mum,' she said, "the roses down our way are playing up too. Yellowing, petals dropping." She's tried everything. Dishwater, special spray, all her tricks, flick of the hair. Still they catch you when you least expect. The road goes over Arnhem Bridge.'

'So Evie's been in touch?' Alice lines her blade up to the thick snarl of fabric just behind Mrs Binns's captured shoulder.

'Of course, yes. Evie's always in touch. In touch the livelong day.'

She flings out her free arm to give the effect of all day long. At the same moment Alice slices through a puckered loop of cardigan thread. Too deep. The cut will leave a hole in the cardie, a small nick but visible. She firms her grip on Mrs Binns's upper arm.

'And Arnie? Arnie's in touch, too?'

'Arnie? My dear I said Evie. *Evie*. I told you before. She's about, but not so as you'd expect company. I'd have liked her to come out with it. The why and the wherefore of who'll be visiting at this hour, Saturday afternoon, when everything's so busy, everybody rushing about. Nice girls and all, I admit. But climbing into my linen cupboard, you know, where it's all kept nice and neat. Snooping. And not expected for a moment.'

Mrs Binns jostles her shoulders as if pestered by a wasp.

The jostling movement dislodges a single, pearly cardie button hooked on a wily thorn. Alice helps it off with the tip of her blade. The left side of the cardigan swings free. Laura stands poised in case the old lady, disengaged, will tumble forwards like a collapsing puppet. But she stands firm; she remains tethered. Alice ducks around Laura to begin work on Mrs Binns's right.

Here the job is less of a knotty tangle than first appeared. She gently lifts and severs a few snagged threads but mostly she is slicing and pricking at the air. The old lady stares into the space of lawn between the rosebush hedge and her house. She appears not to notice what Alice is up to.

The final snag in the fabric is the lowest down. Alice skims her blade along the line of Daphne Binns's spine like a violin bow sliding across an octave. The catch severs, the cardigan drops back into shape, the old lady's shoulder at last comes down and she steps away from the rose tree as if nothing had happened. Laura, waiting with arms outstretched, is pressed out of her path.

'So what about a cup of tea?' She smooths both hands over her cheeks, then looks at them levelly. 'I heard you two girls say something about helping in the kitchen.'

Alice wraps her cut-throat razor in its cloth and slides it back into her pocket.

* * *

They plant themselves in the sitting-room with their wet feet buried in paper and newsprint. Alice has closed and bolted the front door. She serves tan-coloured tea in newly scrubbed mugs. Daphne Binns sits round-shouldered in her armchair. A ragdoll has replaced the odd-angled puppet of the garden. Laura and Alice are side-by-side on the two-seater settee.

Laura kicks her heels, making the torn paper scurry through the room.

'Like stirring up bubblebath,' she volunteers helpfully.

Alice bends over her tea-mug and presses her lips together. Drawing attention to the mess won't help win Mrs Binns's co-operation.

But the old lady's face shapes itself around a tidy, contented smile. In the afternoon with light slanting through the net curtains her flaking face radiates a shimmery aura and her hair makes sun-rays. The bolted front door and steaming tea are working a special chemistry at last.

She waves vaguely at the papery chaos. 'What I say when spring-cleaning. Best is to make plenty of space. Break it down small and get rid of build-up. How you cut your butter into your flour. The smaller it is, the less easy to see.'

She moistly slurps her tea.

'The smaller the more mixed up,' Laura slowly suggests. 'Like letters. Me, I see letters and numbers very mixed up. When the print is small I can hardly read them.'

Daphne Binns dismisses the remark by dusting down her front, as if she had eaten a large amount of crumbly cake.

'You break it down, you cut it up small,' she pronounces tersely. 'The most important things nowadays are invisible.'

'Like what things?' Laura asks. 'Things like love, having fun—?'

Alice can tell from the tightness in Laura's back how hard she's trying to keep the conversation going.

'Not what I mean.' The old lady presses her fingers to her cheeks. Skin flakes dance in the light. 'Staying at home and never leaving; that's invisible. "Don't leave the house if you don't want to," said my father. "Never mind what people say; make yourself an invisible nest. Stay at home and stay out of trouble." And so I did. Didn't darken the doors. At the kindergarten they all wore smocks, even the helpers. Couldn't stand how the starched ruff rubbed your neck so I headed straight home. Made to feel welcome there even though not expected back, not so soon. Like others I know. Darkening the doors though not expected in the least.'

Alice looks at the framed school photographs of Arnie on the tiled mantleshelf: Arnie at six, his summer freckles and no front teeth. His sulky nine-year-old gaze shifting about in the space behind the camera. Quiet Arnie aged twelve with a tightly closed mouth and hooded eyes.

All three pictures in fact have hooded eyes.

Laura prods her elbow into her sister's side. 'Your turn now.'

Alice tests the device of naming him one last time. 'That must be Arnie, then,' she points. 'Arnie, your grandson.'

'Evie's work,' says Daphne Binns firmly. 'You can tell from the teeth. Runs in the family. Gravestones, pillars of the community. Come to think of it, even Evie has them though she's not family proper, not *blood*. But she helped out our Danny after the first wife, you know, God bless her.'

'You've seen Evie lately?' Alice persists. 'You said she's often in touch?'

Laura creeps her hand over the settee and pokes Alice in the thigh (the thigh free of knives). Mrs Binns is beginning noticeably to fuss. Over and over she rubs her face as if to scrub the skin clean away. She pushes at the paper around her feet. She taps a fingernail against her empty mug.

'I'd wish they'd say who they are,' she grumbles resentfully, 'when they've gone into the cupboard and all to get the dishcloths. Earlier it was the wonderland one, very sharp. I can tell the sharpest. Such blades she had, like a griffin's beak flashing. The ice-skating on the telly flashes no brighter. Not to be let loose in the community, I daresay. Not to go about invisible.'

'Mrs Binns, you mean me, Alice?' Alice asks. 'The girl who helped you free of the roses? We, me and my sister, we didn't mean to frighten you, promise. Thing is, Arnie's my friend, Arnie your grandson, and he's gone off on a trip; we don't know where, and, well, I was hoping you might help, you know, to find Arnie. I was hoping he might be here.'

It isn't working; Laura shakes her head; give it a break.

They sit in silence. Alice feels a gummy despair block her throat. So that's it. So much effort and—nothing.

They'll have to start again from scratch. Only this time they won't know where to begin. Where-oh-*where* in her stupidity has she driven Arnie Binns?

'If you must know,' says Daphne suddenly, extremely regal and confident, 'he died.' She takes an audible breath and once again busily scrubs her face. 'If you must know, though I have no idea why you ask, my dear brother Albie died nearly sixty years ago this autumn. Missing in action in the last year of the war. Battle for a bridge too far. Filthy night. Missing presumed dead. And we miss him still. Even on telly they miss him. Talking war, always talking war, stirring the pot.'

Laura nods sympathetically. Alice feels her face is set in stone. Earlier she caught sight of the black-and-white photograph of the serviceman on the kitchen wall, alone in a desert of faded rose-sprig wallpaper. A shy smile yellowed by half-a-century's summer sunshine. Arnie's long-dead Great Uncle Albie, it seems, buried in Europe in an unmarked grave. Now that Mrs Binns says it Alice remembers Arnie mentioning something in passing, but today for the first time the idea gives her goose-flesh. This talk of missing, of dead. Teeth adrift in mud. She can see it clear as day. The clods of earth in his eye sockets; his blackened bones and broken, scattered teeth.

The bleep of a mobile phone jumps all three from their seats.

Laura reaches down for her bag. Mrs Binns pats her pale-orange pyjama pocket. Both produce silver Vodafones. Mrs Binns's phone is incredible, a state-of-the-art fold-out scallop of a mobile. Alice has a sudden urge to begin to shout and block her ears. It's too much to take. What if it's the police? Someone in Authority? What if an anonymous stranger walking a dog has found an as-yet-unidentified body in a shallow grave? Its eye-sockets smashed to pieces.

But the text is for Laura: a ☺ from Phoenix. Alice leans over and sees the round, un-reassuring logo gurning at the top of the little screen. Funny how close together its eyes; she'd not noticed before. So she gives herself room for one last, tiny hope. Arnie has sent a message via Phoenix. He knows Laura takes her phone everywhere; it's just that today he forgot her number.

As if... the idea's ridiculous and she erases it cleanly. As if Arnie on the run would send a message to anyone, let alone Phoenix, let alone even Alice and Laura.

'He's woken up,' Laura says comfortably as though referring to an elderly relative. 'He always sends a smiley when he gets up, no matter what time of day. You know, Alice,' she whispers, 'I've just realised I've not seen Phoe for nearly two whole days. Two-whole-days. And, boy, do I miss him.'

'Funny that,' Mrs Binns chips in. Her phone is clipped closed and back in her pocket. She gets up stiffly and bends down to the newspaper rack where a single piece of untorn paper still lies. She picks the paper up and drops it on the floor. 'It's been on the tip of my tongue to say. He called earlier. Albie, I mean Arnie. *Arnie.* He should be along any minute. Evie phoned to say to expect him. Not the others of course. The sharp one and the gawker, they weren't expected at all. I'd been thinking to mention it. Come, why not make another cup of tea and by the time we've drunk it he'll be here? Evie wanted me to look out for him. Arnie, I mean Albie. He could be along at any minute.'

Alice and Laura look at one another in disbelief. Disbelief softening into newborn, uncertain hope.

Laura takes Alice's hand and squeezes hard.

166

Chapter 11

Arnie

'Well Mrs Binns,' Jim Noelson said familiarly through the open window of his Toyota, 'Must be about the first time in history this taxi company arrive at the door of this house in daytime.'

Katrina chirped her tongue and glared up at the clouds. She let go of my hand. We had been waiting on her front doorstep for Jim's car. I took the chance to slip round to the Toyota's passenger side and climb in.

Jim let his sunglasses slide down to the end of his nose, making it look like he'd enjoyed himself in relaxed conversation with Katrina before. 'Must also be the first time in history I arrive at this house and not collect Mr Binns drunk and incapable.'

'Ah-hah. Capable, incapable. Capable enough to step into your taxi sharp-sharp whatever the hour. Capable enough to walk into pubs and carry on the fun of the night into the morning. Down by the varsity where the drink is cheap.'

'And not even come home to see his nice and polite guest here. This good young gentleman.'

I saw Katrina purse her lips and shake her head as he said this, wanting him to shut up.

'The child was not expected,' she defended herself, themselves. 'I happy whatever. *Whatever*. At least this way Boyfriend not make trouble. So this lady here can carry on her life and keep house without fuss. At least he takes his stupidity off to wherever you drive him and not bother me witless.'

For the second time I caught her mouthing a round, silent word at him, signalling something, maybe *No*. But I didn't mind. I didn't mind Katrina and I didn't mind Jim Noelson so I didn't mind what secret language they shared. Katrina was powerful and steady. You could move like a small fish in her slipstream. And she'd given me a fry-up this morning as good as anything Evie and I ever served at home—diced chipolata sausages stirred in fried onion and tomato.

As for Jim, his style was off-duty and laidback but he had pitched up even so to give me his promised free ride to London. His yellow-and-red taxi card in her hand, Katrina had phoned earlier to confirm it, her eyes gaping as she dialled, surprised at how well she knew the company's number.

Just as promised, Jim had arrived on time, at 11 o'clock sharp, grinning a welcome; a far cry from my Dad who hadn't pitched up at all and was even now, Katrina had muttered sourly while cutting sandwiches for the journey, sleeping off the night on some friend's floor. It was then that she'd first remarked, 'Mind you, pickin, we not expect you. You pop up in my doorway unexpected like a ghost.'

Now she leaned down to speak to Jim, her wide hand spread across his wound-down window. A tiny smile creased the corners of her mouth, in the fold where her lips met her cheeks.

'Funny that so many Good Samaritan is busybody one way or other,' she said. 'Look at you, Mr Taxi. You spend so much time finding out who got pain and why as regards the walking wounded, one of these fine days you pass the dying man bleeding in the street.'

Pleased with this last statement she drew herself upright, marched over to her doorstep for the goods that were stashed there, then round to my side of the car. There were all kinds of bits and chunks and things balancing on her arms but I had eyes for the Kerr jar only. She held it unwrapped, the glass misty with fridge condensation. I took the jar from her first thing, lowered it to the car floor and stowed it between my feet.

Fish neither gurgled nor sloshed. An hour ago, about as soon as we'd arrived back from our green hill graveyard walk, we had returned him to his jar. I'd asked. I'd been so worried about his condition I'd almost snatched him. Feeling him between my hands all stripped and naked I'd glooped his body straight back in, let him bump down to the bottom. I'd seen the tiny threads of fleece still sticking to the skin around his neck.

It had been Katrina's idea to pour away the last of the years-old, used-up formalin and bathe him to above the skull in white vinegar. Up to his lid, there was hardly an air-bubble remaining. 'That'll keep him cool and peaceful,' she'd said, emptying a catering-size bottle of vinegar into the jar mouth, then chafing the side of my face with her knuckles.

When Fish was stored safely on the floor of the car I could look up again. Katrina was waiting patiently. Next she handed over an enormous plastic lunch-box with clip-down fasteners like on a suitcase. Inside, I knew from watching her, were double portions of cheese, roast turkey and pickle sandwiches: 'Extra if Jim want'. In the corners she had tucked little bananas and small loaves of the dumpling breads she called *bun*, an explosive sound.

After the lunch box came my willow-pattern bag newly stuffed with a bottle of water, a clean T-shirt of my Dad's and a pair of warm socks 'in case it get cold'. To this she added, leaning into the car window, a folded hank of new cloth, indigo and white, that had a fresh smell and evenly frayed edges. 'For your Ma. Will cheer up a table.'

Last she offered her business card. It was tucked into a used envelope addressed to Grange Terrace and thickened with green Nigerian stamps. I peeked in at the card, nodding to acknowledge it. It was one of those DIY cards you fix for yourself at the machines in Woolworths. I saw that she called herself *Lecturer in Nursing Practice*.

Jim was beginning to whistle through his front teeth. 'Cha, Mama Africa, you think I not got it in me to look after this child same as you?'

Wait! She held up a warning hand. Her arms were now empty. Her face looked a whole lot more easeful than it had yesterday. '*One last thing*!' She raised a single finger of her warning hand and disappeared into the house.

Jim sat scraping at dirt on the steering wheel and grinding the gearstick. He studied the profile of his nose from below in his rear-view mirror. He poked out his eyeballs like a schoolboy.

Minding Fish I didn't move.

But she wasn't long. When she emerged for this last time there was something hidden in her tightly clutched right hand. Eyes locked on mine she pressed whatever it was into my palm, a wooden thing with curves, edges, whirly imprints. For a moment she gripped her two hands around my one.

'Look after that and it look after you,' she said in a hurry and glanced at Jim.

But he had picked up something. He had quit grimacing and fidgeting and kept silent.

'In my country amulet like that watch where you go,' she said, singing again despite her rushing, almost but not quite stumbling over her words. 'In my country amulet mind everything you make with your life, every load you carry. It the map of where you are. If you lost, you look on it, find its scratches and markings, study them. It the road back for your house.'

I opened my palm. She had given me a carved wooden face, a narrow mask nearly as long as my hand, its straight, thin eyes half-closed. On the reverse side there were complicated swirling patterns that looked nothing like a map. A metal ring was fastened to the mask's topknot.

I remembered seeing an object a lot like it hanging from one of the keys on Katrina's rattling keyrack. I remembered seeing knick-knacks almost exactly like it on sale in reed baskets in the Oxfam shop on the High Street, at £1 a piece.

I closed my hand over the carving. So what if it was an all-seasons stocking filler? It was also Katrina's parting gift.

'That my advice,' she said. 'Hold on to it.'

She pushed herself back from the car door and seemed for an instant to lose her balance. As she tipped, teetered and splayed her feet I thought I saw her betray something. I thought I saw her betray a secret. As she teetered and came close to overbalancing she gripped her stomach very suddenly and winced in pain.

A second passed, the single beat of a second, when everything was very still, and then she grabbed the door again and her face was suddenly back in the car. She spoke so softly I had to lean forwards to catch her words.

'Listen what Katrina tell you, Arnie Binns. I want to ask you one other last thing. You take your gift home and, if you can, give me one back. This morning I ask you to find your special Fish a quiet place to rest, breathe himself out. Now I also ask, make sure that place is a place where he truly belong, if you can. Where you imagine he can belong. You a smart and bright son. Make sure he find his own true home, somewhere like Africa, like Africa is my own true home. He a lost one so you find him a way. Tether him back to where he belong. A gift for a gift.'

The whole time she talked I watched how her hands grasped the wound-down window and her knuckles stood out pale.

Then Jim let out the handbrake and the car began its roll down the street, riffling briskly over the black cobbles. I turned to wave through the back window. She stood up straight and towering with both arms raised, her eyes glittering. The window with its blue-green pattern of dots and diagonals framed her like a picture.

I twigged then; how I twigged. You're *so slow*, Arnie Binns, you're so very, very slow! I wanted to hit my head on the dashboard and kick myself, except that Fish was sitting between my legs. I twigged the word *already*. I twigged that Katrina was maybe *already* carrying a new baby. She'd used Fish in the graveyard to bless a baby *already* on its way into the world. Saying goodbye I could've been within a hand's breadth, within millimetres, of my very own flesh and blood.

For a while then I forgot what she'd said about a resting-place for Fish. All I wished was that someone could've told me her news straight out, no fuss.

As the car gathered speed at the bottom of Grange Terrace Jim turned the key in the ignition and we pulled smoothly around the corner and off down the slopes of Harehills.

I folded my arms tightly. I gripped Fish between my ankles till his jar lid dug into my skin. The mask key-ring thing sat on my thigh looking at me with an expression that was both crafty and sleepy. *Hang in there*, it might be saying. Or, *Watch yourself*.

I turned back once to look up the hill, at the staggered rows of houses, the graffiti rambling like succulent black ivy, the damp brown roofs. '*Hang in there*,' I whispered to myself.

I imagined Katrina pulling her painted door closed behind her, letting out a lung-deep sigh of relief. She had her place back, her home-from-home. I saw her leaning against the door, resting a quiet hand over her stomach, letting a finger rattle along the dangling row of her keys where, towards one end, an open space gaped, where the mask key-ring had hung. The space was making a break in the continuity of her rattling.

Not a word passed between Jim Noelson and I till we reached the motorway. Once or twice he snatched a look at me as if something worried him. I could guess why. Probably I wasn't looking so great. In actual fact I wasn't doing so great. A muddy tide of miserableness was washing right through me.

I was an abandoned house. So I felt. I felt how that house feels when the furniture is removed, the pictures taken down, the place left empty. A moment ago there were children running through the echoey passages, pressing grubby hands on the walls, but now they're gone. The doorways are vacant. The house has no power to call them back. And the river in spate at the bottom of the garden is threatening to burst its banks.

'So, so, so,' Jim finally said, squinting across. He was speeding us along the bottom of a green Yorkshire valley. 'So your auntie send another kind of pickle to give your ma in exchange? In the very same jar?'

I said nothing.

'Look like super-exotic chilled pickle to me, eh Arnie? Chilled chilli, like?' Smiling at his own humour. 'Is that pickled snails now, if you not mind my asking, or cold frog legs? Look damn close to something animal. I just curious, you understand. And I like food.'

'It's been in the fridge.'

All I could think of to say, and then I looked down and found with alarm Fish's misty curtains of fridge condensation breaking up into droplets, beginning to clear the glass walls of his home. Jim had the car heating on.

And I had no covering for Fish. This was a new problem brewing. The plump look of my willow-pattern bag when Katrina had handed it over had put me off my guard. I had forgotten that my fleece was not in there. My fleece was left back at her house. She had laid it on the blue armchair by the front door as we came in after our walk. There it lay, even at this minute, waiting for hungover Dan to come and plant himself on top of it and ask whose kid had been visiting.

To block Jim's view I shifted my bag so that it stood side-by-side with Fish's jar, a barrier. I saw him lick his lips as if savouring a dish, caught up in his talk of food.

'Down on some of our islands in the Caribbean,' he said, 'we have this thing called *kwis grainoo*. Lovely stuff. Made from the big tropical bullfrogs. Seasoned with plenty of sea-salt and cardamom. Look to me like your auntie prepare something like that. You feel tempted when you get home, you think? Try a little *kwis grainoo*?'

'Don't know.' Feeling overheated and sweaty. 'Guess I'll find out when I get there.'

And meanwhile Fish down on the floor was quietly roasting. Second by second the heat stripped back his thin-as-steam disguise.

There was silence. Jim was cleaned out of things to say concerning squishy things in jars. He began to hum a tune, a nonsense rhyme about bee sucks and cowslips I didn't bother to follow. The miles passed. Hare-backed hills followed hare-backed hills. Thick rainclouds rolled over us but it never seemed actually to rain. The motorway skimmed south across a greeny-brown landscape wrapped in a shiny cling-film of wetness.

Beside the cooling towers at Sheffield the traffic ground to a halt. A large, slow truck decided to overtake a little truck and we weren't far behind. I noticed from the shape of the surrounding hills and those cooling towers that the coach station where we stopped last night had been here in Sheffield. I recognised that kids' toy shopping centre to the right, this raised motorway here. I remembered the Mars bar dispenser lit up like a lantern in the grainy dark of the coach station and the night sky full of stars.

'That Mrs Binns, I have wonders about that auntie of yours,' Jim charged up his chief topic again. His thumb on the steering wheel repeatedly beat his nonsense tune, *In a Cowslip's Bell I Lie*. 'Is she as magic as she look, Arnie Binns? You'd know. Does she keep a big old shrine in her top room, full of totems and taboos? Trinkets like what she gave you? Masks and flywhisks and such?'

He nudged his elbow in the direction of the carving lying on my knee.

'Don't know. I never went to her top room. Her house has only two rooms: the sitting room and the one above it. I'd say the second room was private.'

He studied the side of my face. 'It private because she weave her magic circle there, you think? She weave her magic circle and keep her drunk-'n'-crazy boyfriend well out? Powerful stuff her magic. Like I say, it make me curious. Thing about your auntie is, she don't care. She don't care what people say. Or anyway it don't look like it. She don't care about giving a kid like you funny pickle to take home. She don't care about sticking right out, wearing her big turban like it a sore head. I different in that respect. I an older generation and I mind badly about fitting in. From the day I come to this place here, I mind.'

I looked up at the curve of the cooling towers, wondering how they managed to make concrete that smooth and evenly curved. I closed one eye; closed the other. I pressed my hand against the window in line with the curve.

'She cares,' I found I said at last. 'She made me feel at home. She talked to me a long time. Maybe there's something about her boyfriend she likes.'

Her boyfriend my dad, I added to myself.

'I don't mean she don't care for people, Arnie. I mean she got no worries about fitting in. What did we use to call it, me and my friends? Fashion nation. She got no fascination for fashion and none either for this nation here. *Fashion nation* you see. Me, when I was a small schoolboy in Jamaica, I sing songs from Shakespeare at my school. This song I'm singing now, we chant it then. When I arrive in this *fashion nation* here, this *You-Kay*, this Grand Britannia, I *expect* to fit in, nah. Why not? I work hard, all hours. I sing the songs of Mr Shakespeare. *Where the bee sucks*, I sing. I sing: *And the rain it raineth ev-very-day.* So why I not fit in?'

I could tell the last question wasn't for me. I could tell the frown on Jim's face was directed somewhere beyond those crawling trucks ahead, somewhere down south, at the end of this long motorway. But what he said about Katrina bothered me.

'My auntie has got worries,' I told him. 'She worries about people, people getting on, getting on together. She worries a lot.'

I surprised myself. These words burst out of me. And really, I didn't know what I was saying. I didn't know Katrina. She hadn't in any case told me her secret. That is, if there *was* a secret to be told. She hadn't really included me in her doings at all; me, Arnie Binns, her boyfriend's son, who at a critical moment in her life and maybe in his life she'd packed off to the caff for a Fanta.

Jim looked startled. My outburst had surprised him as much as it surprised me. He quit beating his tune on the steering wheel.

So I persisted. 'I think she worries about, you know, the world.'

'Don't we all, son? We all worry about the world. And most especially when we stuck in this kind of traffic.

Maybe it only in traffic that we see we all really belong together, enh? Each guy in his car, each one for themselves, but at the same time all stuck in it together?' He inched the taxi a few yards forward. 'I do know that when I locked in traffic, and that's often, I not too worried about fitting in.'

The large truck finally edged ahead of its competition for the slow lane. The queue of backed-up cars began shooting into the gap it had opened.

'Look now, to change the subject,' Jim shifted to fifth gear to make his point. 'Why don't you tell me where you're headed, young Mr Binns, so I know where to drop you off? Just *South*, what your auntie tell me, is a big old place.'

The cooling towers dropped away on our left. The car swept across a broad hill and another broad hill and then through patches of field broken by flashes of river, eruptions of trees. I didn't have a word to say in reply. My mouth opened but no sound came. I was a proper fish, gulping air. Meanwhile my own Fish hunkered at my feet and grew warmer and warmer.

'I don't know exactly.' I had to answer something. 'Can I say a bit later?'

And wouldn't I be perfectly happy if for the rest of the day this car seat right here could be my single destination?

He shrugged, 'Seem to me your path pretty clear. Is not home to your mother?'

'I'm thinking about that,' I said slowly, very softly. 'I need to decide something.'

'Well, Mr Arnie Binns, you say when you ready. If you need to use a phone, mine's there beside your right knee. Your auntie, by the way, she seem to have some idea where you headed. But it not for me to play Nosey Parker. My sister, the one I visit today, Gracie, she work in the Smith's in Terminal 4, Heathrow, Duty-Free Area. That pretty central. I can take you plenty places from there. She not expecting me till five or six or so. So we got time, nah? We got world enough and time.'

'Thank you.' I hesitated, then said, 'See, there's a reason I can't go home today.'

But Jim didn't want to hear. 'Son, like I say, it not for me to press. You just remember to take care. After I drop you today Mr Jim Noelson not there to help watch your back.'

I gripped my crossed arms tighter together.

The problem was, I thought to myself, I really didn't have a clue: what to do or where to go, no clue. How today would end, just a grey blur. If I'd be in my own bed tonight; if I'd see Alice. Couldn't even guess at the shape of the rest of today. I looked down the motorway and I saw a grey horizon, a grey sky. I imagined Alice camped in the hydrangea bushes beside my house, lying in wait for when I'd get in. I imagined her dark-in-the-face with worry; worry and blame knitted together, rearing up from those same bushes the minute I hoved into view. I tried to imagine myself standing up to her. I saw myself planting my feet and straightening my back, saying with all the force in my voice, 'Alice, Have a Heart.' Piloting Fish to Safe Harbour, who wouldn't? Scooping him out of Harm's Way, wasn't it the Best Thing to do?

About forty miles further down the motorway—in the Land of Robin Hood, the road signs said—Jim cleared his throat.

'Ahm, if you don't mind me saying, Arnie son, your auntie give you some all-time-powerful vinegar in your lunch-box there. You check if she not get you some good ol' Yorkshire fish and chips? If she wrap it in paper and stick it in your bag?' He rubbed his stomach as though a big meal had recently taken up residence. 'You not smell it, this vinegar smell sitting in my car like it's come to stay? Making me ravenous, fit to eat a mountain.'

178

'Katrina gave me sandwiches.' I stuck to the facts. 'Cheese and turkey sandwiches.'

'Then maybe that pickle jar there is leaking, because, Arnie man, this smell is savage. You not get it? Look, here's a plan. At the next Services we stop for a snack and you take the chance to check your pickle. Make sure that screw-top lid on tight.'

* * *

The Motorway Services sign cropped up suddenly. Jim had to veer sharply or we'd have overshot the exit. As I eased my stiff legs out of the car I stowed slippery Fish in the crook of my arm. I folded Katrina's hank of indigo cloth over the top of the jar and snug round the sides. Just as well she had given me it to cheer up a load of old pickle.

A new instinct now pushed me forwards. It was something to do with the heavy hints that Jim had dropped. The long journey had produced the careless feeling that he and I were somehow in league together, in partnership. That he knew everything, saw right through my disguises, into the heart of my plans. Jim's warm face took for granted you were his mate, so who was to say this feeling was wrong? His eyes magnified by his glasses stood out a little, which heightened the effect. It was as if he could see out of the corners of his eyes, and round the side of his head, and then some more again.

In the Motorway Services coffee shop most of the chairs seemed to stand at odd angles and the yellow lino was scuffed to blackness under the tables. Tina Turner singing through her nose played loudly over the sound system. A large, silver speaker poked out of the wall above the entrance door.

Jim bought himself a super-tall coffee and a cheeseburger and me a hot chocolate. I refused his offer of food. I had left my lunchbox and all Katrina's double-portion sandwiches in the car on purpose. Some sadness, grumpiness, I couldn't tell, had closed my throat. And Jim was right. The vinegary smell that was Fish's new smell was razor-sharp and off-putting. I thought I could smell it even on my skin.

The Services coffee shop was built on a bridge over the motorway and its walls were glass. I'd never been inside a building like this before. Looking down from our table we could see the traffic streaking towards us at speed and away from us at speed. It was like having a giant TV showing a Grand Prix stood next to your seat. The endless movement and busy-ness made you feel that the life of the country depended on it. That if the traffic stopped the country would collapse from lack of motion and sink into the sea.

Jim eased my brimming hot chocolate from his tray to the table in front of me. I was stowing Fish in his usual spot at my feet when he said something that since this morning I knew he had to say and yet at one and the same time hoped he'd not get round to voicing.

'Put your jar up on the table, Arnie Binns,' Jim said. 'Like I say, I not Mr Nosey Parker but I think we both know that what you got in there is no real-live pickle. It very different from pickle, isn't it, son?'

My hands were on the jar. Bent over I rested my eyes on the traffic. The longer I watched those cars the less thinking I could do.

'Enh now, Arnie son, come, let's admit it. Jim Noelson isn't blind. What's in there is *not* mango pickle though it preserved. I'm going to say in fact that what's in there was maybe once upon a time a Real Live Something Else. Kind of *kwis granoo* though not true *kwis granoo*, if you get my drift.'

I paused just a moment longer to give someone, Fish, me, Alice maybe, the benefit of Jim's doubt, a stay of execution. But he was right, there was no point to the cover-up. I lifted the Kerr jar and put it on the table beside the paper cup of hot chocolate; leaving a space between the two, still taking care not to overheat him. The folded white-and-indigo cloth had come loose at the sides. I made to tighten its edges, to wall him round. Even if Jim had guessed everything, that didn't mean the whole world should share the privilege. The fattish fiftyish man slurping soup just opposite, for example. The family of three girls in mauve dress-up fairy-dresses lined up along the stainless steel barrier at the buffet.

Jim patted the table like he was soothing the head of a small child. I tried to meet his gaze but his eyes were busy elsewhere, busy staring. Today destiny had decided to remove any make-believe that I might have wanted to stick on Fish. My careful wrapping of the Kerr jar had, as it turned out, created a slipknot effect. The more I tugged at the indigo cloth's corners and edges, the more the whole camouflage structure unravelled. Jim now stared with 100 per cent full attention. It was obvious at what. Between the fallen folds of cloth he had encountered the face of Fish, a full frontal view.

To improve his line of vision he lowered his head till his chin was sunk inside his coffee cup. He squeezed closed his eyes; opened them. He angled his head to one side, then the other. I saw a single pale tear slide down his cheek. My stomach turned over. Now what? In these last forty-eight hours Fish had triggered a long series of unpredictable reactions. Looked like a new instalment was about to arrive.

'Well now,' was all he said at first. '*Well now.* Well— now... In all my born days as a taxi driver I never think to have such a one as passenger. Such a little one, such a very old, very little one.'

He sounded matter-of-fact. I hoped he'd stay matter-of-fact. I turned down my mouth; made a serious face. I shifted my seat round so as to block the view of Fish from everyone and anyone but Jim. If I gave no comment he would create no fuss, maybe. He would stick to the matter in hand and take Fish as he was, a once-alive, almost human thing. The ones to watch were those like Katrina, like Alice, who saw him as other than human: a spirit, or a charmed foundling, or a chunk of rubbish.

I sat tight behind my jar, my Fish's home. I could see his scrunched left hand, here, very close to my arm. I could see the wrinkles of his waist and the doughy hunch of his miniature back. For nearly two days I'd managed to steer my creature from harm. But I'd failed to keep him out of sight. My failure was now laid bare. It felt as if some foot was repeatedly tripping me up and as if my bones were turning fragile as eggshell. As if the Kerr jar were spidery with cracks and about to shatter into a million pieces.

'Arnie, Arnie,' Jim resumed patting the table. 'What I say is this. You can choose to ignore my questions, I fine about that. But, well, this is very curious, I do have to tell you that. In this day and age it unusual to find so big a baby in a specimen jar. Obviously you know this or you not hide him so. I love to know where you get him. Is it Katrina magic or not? I see this one been dead a long time. And I see that for whatever reason you mad about him. But, man, how he stink, enh?! He carry a very bad smell. Vinegar *and* whatever lie under it. Dead mouse.' He tapped the jar with his thumb. 'Baby, how you do stink.'

Then he caught sight of his forgotten burger.

'Look here, Arnie, maybe we put him away a minute? We three all well met now and it time for food. Put him on the seat beside you, cover him with that cloth.'

He sunk his teeth into his burger. The melted cheese squeezed out of the sides in shiny globules that he licked away. I raised my hot chocolate to my mouth but my stomach stayed determinedly closed. I lowered the mug to the table.

After a while Jim sighed. He looked at me mournfully, hesitantly, above all mournfully. I couldn't think why. Fish was small and shrivelled but was that enough reason to make a grown man look so sad? With two hands he reached across his plate, right across the grey table, and lifted Fish's jar. He tucked his camouflage half round him, on the public side, which I appreciated, and put him down under his nose. He pressed a handkerchief to his face. For the second time he lowered his eyeball down to Fish's level. I saw the round of his eye behind its spectacle lens enlarged through the wall of the glass jar. Then he shook himself as if something beggared belief. He rubbed his glasses clean on his shirt and peered again.

I wanted to wrap my hands around the jar to block his staring. No one on earth should be stared at that closely, least of all, like Jim himself said, such a very old little one.

Finally he said, 'Well now. Well I never. These are strange times, strange, *strange* times, with strange things walking the land. Too much funny magic. You gotta be careful, Mr Arnie, son. See, I get a very strong feeling here. And I should know.' His nose was almost stuck onto the jar, his glasses tapped against it. 'Blow me down if this isn't . . . Arnie, look, you mind if we lift your pet out of his glass cage?'

Wouldn't be Fish's first weekend outing. Wordlessly I shook my head. *Don't mind.* Didn't want to agree but couldn't help myself.

How Jim managed it so fast I don't know. The lid came off with a single twist. For an instant he had his hand over Fish's skull, then he pulled. The same swooshing, glooping noise sounded as before, of slithering into the open in a hurry. We both looked around, on guard. Fish's stink knocked a steel pin straight up my nostrils. Puddles of vinegar covered the table. But things were OK. The fattish man was still eating soup. The mauve girls were filing out of the exit doors with their mum and dad.

And now Jim did the weirdest thing of all. Tucking the indigo cloth around Fish's body, wetting the cloth through so badly it would be impossible ever to give to Evie, he laid him in his two cupped hands and began to rub his plasticene forehead. He took the balls of his thumbs and stroked his temples and cheeks hard, like he wanted to iron out each and every one of Fish's wrinkles.

I had to clutch my hands into fists, to stop them from grabbing Jim's arms.

He looked at me over his glasses. 'Arnie, can you tell me please, is this thing here, this baby, to do with your alleged auntie up north, your Katrina? I know I say refuse my questions but I think I need to know. It important.'

I shook my head with energy. *No, no.*

'You sure? Really sure?'

I shook my head some more and found something to reply. 'Katrina did see it, him, like you're doing now, but he, it, doesn't belong to her.' I rubbed my forehead in sympathy with my Fish, exactly where Jim was rubbing him. 'The jar's from the lab at my school.' And now a gift came to me, a word. 'My friend and I, we *liberated* it. You know, set it free. Like a dove.'

He looked disbelieving.

'This the African friend you mention? Half-African?'

'Yes, but that's got nothing to do with it.'

'Well Arnie, this where I not sure. We African people need to be careful. Folk like to tar us with voodoo and juju. Give us a bad name and say we up to no good.'

'*Voo-doo?*' I repeated to myself. '*Juju?*' But that couldn't be right. *Juju* sounded like calling up the devil. Voodoo was vampires and darkness, something about the newly dead, blood still warm in their veins.

There definitely was no fresh blood in Fish's veins.

Stiffly I said, 'It's been OK looking after him, this specimen. Though it's been a job keeping him safe.'

'No doubt, son, no doubt. I must put it to you however, job or no job you on the run, categorically on the run. At some point yesterday you peel off from your friend and now you running, with your dodgy pickle jar in tow.'

I took shelter behind my folded arms, my forearm skin red and sore from all the day's folding and clamping.

But Jim wouldn't let me retreat. He reached out a vinegary hand and raised up my chin and held it there till the acidic wetness made my skin crawl.

'Look, kid, there's something important here I must say. Got to say it out loud, recognise it. OK, maybe I not see straight myself. I got bias maybe. But this baby here, he move me. He *move* me. I want you to see why. Katrina, when she see him, touch him, she a nurse, did she say how old he is?'

'He's old,' I said, and again, stalling for time, 'He's *very* old. Me and my friend think he's nearly a hundred years old. The lab at school dates from the World War I.'

Jim chucked his head impatiently. 'No, I mean, his *age*. How long he live, you know, in the womb?'

Womb. Womb meant something else again and I didn't want to think about it, no way. *Womb* pointed to some other human being lying beyond Fish in the chain of life, like how my own mum, my other mum who carried me, lay in my chain of life. Womb meant a body full of blood and organs that had closed Fish round. A body that had itself been born, been closed around. One body inside the other, and the chain extending further and further back in time like Russian dolls.

I didn't want to think about that.

No, I wanted to have Fish single just as he was, sealed off in his jar. Not connected, not a son.

185

Hadn't I seen him cut with my own two eyes? He'd been solid but, no, there wasn't a drop of blood in him, not a single drop. Just tough grey skin offering resistance to Alice's knife.

Jim ignored my hesitation. 'Katrina'll have known, won't she Arnie, or guessed? How old was this body? Did she say? How long in the womb?'

I had to give way, stop him repeating that sticky but hollow word *Womb*. 'She said he must have died not long before birth,' I mumbled. 'Around birth. He was a, a returning baby.'

Jim thumped the table like he'd just received the answer to a £1,000,000 question.

'I knew it! I *knew* it. Arnie, come close, look here.' He was rubbing those tiny grey temples and tiny neck so vigorously it was making my own temples ache. He pressed his thumbs into Fish's catlike shoulders, smoothing out the creases. 'See, this baby here got markings on him, here on his forehead. Maybe on the shoulders too. Dots on the forehead and lengthways cuts on the collarbones. What we call *sick-a-tricks* or kickatrices. Can't even say it: C-I-C-A-T-R-I-C-E. Basically tribal marking. You see them on the ancient Benin heads, the household gods from Meroe. They have them in West Africa, where my people come from way back. I think this little half-kid has Africa marked on him. I think his parents mark him for a still-birth, just so, a returning baby. To me he maybe even has Africa *in* him; he look African. Earlier, when you unwrap him, I saw it then, his forehead, how his cheekbones rise up.'

'I don't think Katrina noticed anything unusual about him; I mean, any markings. She would've spotted something like that, wouldn't she?'

I could tell how sulky I sounded. Couldn't help it. It was tough to tell Jim a lie. Trouble was I didn't know half of what he was on about. It sounded like he was reciting from a book, a fairy story. And I couldn't see a thing under his big hands. Couldn't tell if the marks he said he was finding weren't just crinkly Fish's own indelible wrinkles.

I saw how Jim was frowning, turning Fish's face this way and that, his thumbs planted against his forehead. I saw that he believed his own story for sure.

I managed to say, 'Katrina did call him special.'

'Special and African. And dead. One of the trillion dead African babies laid on this earth, born to die. You never know, maybe whoever birthed it saw herself that it a special baby with a special destiny, some important after-life. See here, Arnie, how his markings embed, how deep they go.'

I didn't want to look. I turned my eyes to the racing traffic, going north, going south. I rubbed my temples in sympathy with my Fish.

To me there wasn't any noticeable marking on Fish's face or body, other than his wrinkles, other than his cut. And his wrinkles spread everywhere. I had my own worries about those wrinkles. Fish had been released to the open air three times now, three times in two days. This afternoon his forehead skin clung to Jim Noelson's thumbs.

I sat as quiet as I could but Jim picked up some signal. His coffee untouched he was suddenly standing upright, tucking away his handkerchief, wrapping the indigo cloth any old how, handing the bundle over to me as if it was some everyday thing, some old bloomer loaf. I had to grab it, no choice. He soaked up the vinegar spills with paper napkins, threw his burger wrappings in the bin. '*Come*,' he beckoned. He picked up the Kerr jar of white vinegar, empty of Fish. His free hand steered my shoulder.

'See, Arnie, your task here even larger than you think. It large exactly because he's dead. The dead aren't gone from us, finis, empty set. Your small one here's definitely not gone from us. It important to find ways of making terms with his kind.'

He was warming to some new story but this time I didn't feel as lost. Hadn't I tried to bring Fish into safekeeping? You could accuse me of many things but not of neglect, of underrating Fish's humanness, abandoning him in some skip.

Jim didn't expand his topic. As we wound our way through the trackless car park, all the cars either blue or black or white, he gave up talking and began to sing under his breath, something like, *Where are you keeping? Why you so long?* Or words to that effect, the same crooning sound as the *bee sucks* tune from the beginning of our journey.

We found the car eventually. Jim remembered parking close to a tree that looked dead, 'its branches stiff like the hooks on a coat stand'. There were five of these ornamental trees in the car park. We walked in widening circles around three of them and his car was standing a few rows behind the third.

Inside the car he gave the nod to ease Fish back into his glass home and in my hurry I let him plop out of my hands, making yet another wave of vinegar slosh over the sides of the jar. The level of the liquid now reached to Fish's odd, indented ears, that looked like nothing so much as squashed belly buttons. His invisible markings, if present, would now be half-covered, half-dry.

* * *

For the initial miles of the second leg of our journey neither Jim nor I had anything to say, or, if we did, didn't have the courage to speak it. The pit stop had done the exact opposite of what it was meant to do. Jim looked done in, I felt exhausted. In front the motorway stretched south without curve or camber, with no end in sight. In my case, it was particularly so. The distance between junctions felt longer than hours. The samey, browny lands on either side could have been an enormous skirting board pollyfilla'ed here and there with a retail park, a service station, a Travelodge. Jim's little tune wound through the air between us: *Where are you keeping? Why you so long? Where are you hiding, taking your time?*

From time to time I shunted Fish around the car floor to keep my circulation alive, but always so that my bag or feet blocked Jim's view of him. From time to time I sat up and even opened my lips, wanting to ask how he knew all that about tribal markings and still-births and making terms with the dead. Once I cleared my throat to speak my question but no sound came. I saw my speech collapsing on the air between us like a balloon run out of puff.

For all I knew, I thought, Jim's rubbing and pinching had created the *sick-a-tricks*, *kickatrices*, he said he'd found engraved on Fish's skin.

Signs for London, St Albans, Welwyn Garden City, Watford, began to crop up with frequency. Jim several times glanced in my direction. I could have been imagining it but he looked more lightened up than an hour ago while I only felt more weighed down. I'd soon to make my decision, very soon, though I still hadn't a clue. For two days I'd more or less had a clear route mapped but now I was lost, flopping around without purpose the same as old Fish in his vinegar.

Out of the blue Jim said, 'Now, Arnie son, look like you and me both shattered. Maybe it home time, enh? I hit you with too much back there. Better you just forget about everything I was telling you and return that jar quietly to your school lab, whenever you ready.'

I said *uh-huh*, though I didn't know what I was agreeing with. To feel better I tried pulling my legs up to my chest, where the seatbelt held me secure. I gripped my arms tightly around my knees. Shifting about trying to get comfortable I discovered, slipped under my thigh, Katrina's gift, the mask, poking me like a reminder. My fingers traced the carved whorl, that she'd said was a map for tough times. The sweeping swirls on the back ran against the rhythm of the deeply lined face on the front. '*The road back for your house,*' she said. For Fish, where was this house? Up one of Africa's big rivers? Jim seemed to think so. But, with my fingers tracing those swirls, a sticky heat creeping right through me, I finally saw that Katrina had thought so too.

A certain decision was beginning to punch me in the face.

If Fish was, like Katrina said, really-and-truly a baby-who-returns, I reckoned, then he deserved to go home, just like she had said. He deserved to return to where he belonged: to Africa. On top of the willow-pattern bag I saw perched the envelope Katrina had given me, plastered with green Nigerian stamps. If she had felt a special tie with him, I thought to myself, then I could imagine his home not far from her old home. I could imagine it in full colour, a swirling green-grey river, with dugout boats, trailing creepers, villages between the trees. No one could doubt her feeling and connection when she held Fish to her chest.

Always I was the slow coach but in the end, limping, covered in dust, I reached my destination.

How sulkily I'd received Jim's advice on this, when Katrina had pushed at the very same thing!

This morning when I'd walked up the graveyard slope to meet her, my Fanta can in my hand, what was it she'd said, even then? She'd spoken in her nurse's voice, her hand cupped over Fish's head still lying on the gravestone.

'To help put your baby to bed you must steer him where he come from, the resting place where he belong. Tell him a story to point him to that resting place, a story to match your feelings for him. That way you can be happy about his tiny life.'

And at the car, there was that other thing she'd said. 'Tether him back to his own true home,' she'd whispered. A gift for a gift.

I uncurled from my bunched-up position in the car seat. I balanced my mask, my mascot, on my knee. *Hang in there.*

'Mr— Jim, I know where you could drop me. I've got it.' My voice sounded suddenly loud and boastful in that small space.

'Well then, son, I pleased to hear it. You spit it out.'

'I want to go to Heathrow, same as you.'

'You want to come all the way to my sister's, to Gracie's? You welcome, Arnie, of course you welcome, but what about your family? They not expecting you?'

Jim wasn't completely happy. He navigated a roundabout with wobbling sweeps of his steering wheel.

'I don't think so. Another time I can explain. The main thing now is to get to Heathrow. I won't come along to your sister's, thank you. If you could drop me at a Departures hall, any Departures hall, that would be fine. My friends'll pick me up later, I know.'

'Well, if you sure . . . Heathrow a huge, confusing place, don't forget. Four terminals, and runways point in every direction. Every place looked like every other place. Once I spent an hour waiting for my sister by Terminal 1 that in my head is Terminal 2, where she used to work. You better hold on to Jim Noelson's phone number.'

I nodded at him with a face of immense confidence, straining just about every muscle and sinew in my cheeks and neck.

191

'In that case then I nearly done minding you. And what a pleasure it been, enh? What a time we had. Today I give a big young boy a long lift south and find I have a magic baby on board. When I get back to Harehills I let Katrina know and tell her all my speculations and fashion-nations. See if she invites me to one of her barbecues. And now I give you just one more piece of advice, Arnie, and that is, Take Care, Watch your belongings. You leave them sitting somewhere and after a minute they arrest you. Could be a funny bomb in that glass jar and they take no risk, not after the war we just had. You leave nothing sitting round and, more than anything, let no one see what burden you got. You never know what people think: *Missing youth meddles in black magic.* You can see how the papers'll love it. So I drop you at Terminal 4 where my sister works. It not as crowded as the others.'

I promised to take care. To prove my good intentions I began at last to unpack and eat my lunch, beginning with the Nigerian bun, which was salty and not flavoursome. The sandwiches had dried and curled but I forced one down. Eating some of the food would decrease my load.

Now that our destination was settled I couldn't help noticing that Jim's attention had moved on from me. There was a smile tweaking his mouth that wasn't meant for me or for Fish. I guessed he was thinking of his sister in Smith's; how good it would be to see her; where they'd go together tonight. A small part of my brain wondered if his smile also might have something to do with Katrina, if he was thinking of her magic and getting to know her better, of her singing voice, tallness and stunning wrap-around dress, and her meat-and-beer parties on the pavement.

A picture of the crowds milling at Heathrow now surged into my eyes. I had to use all my strength to force it back. I grasped my mascot key-ring tighter and called up a thought of Alice. Alice would like this idea of returning

Fish to Africa, I said to myself. It was a full-colour idea, a definite goal, a goal she'd like. Laura's wafty dreams about distant fathers annoyed her but she didn't mind her African roots. *'One day these splayed toes will walk the Sahara desert,'* she often said. Well, Fish could help bridge the distance. He could plot her route.

Alice, I thought, and saw her wide-awake brown eyes darting about as they always did. I thought about how sharp her guesses were, how much more quickly her ideas moved than mine. I hoped she'd stopped being cross. I hoped she'd locked her scary knives in her bedside drawer. Come to think of it, I hoped she wasn't worrying herself to pieces about what had happened to our Fish.

'Jim?' Trying to relocate the confident voice that had sat fatly in my mouth just moments ago. A polite but thorough cough did not revive it. 'Ah, do you mind, do you mind if I use your phone?'

He reached for it without looking down.

'In this car, Arnie Binns, you help yourself.'

Chapter 12

Alice

Alice and Laura sit stunned. Alice reaches over to hold Laura's hand. She wants to make sure her sister has heard what she just heard. Arnie called earlier. Daphne Binns just said it. He's expected at any minute? Can it be possible?

Mrs Binns nods smugly at them. Has she been withholding the news all this time, playing like a cat with two interfering but unsuspecting mice?

They can't look at each other in case they break the spell.

'What about that second cup of tea?' Mrs Binns asks. 'Nothing slides. Can hardly slip down for thirst.'

She flick-flacks her fingers back and forth between the door and her lips.

And then the spell does crack. Mrs Binns's phone really does ring. For a moment Alice can't work out how the weird, paper-strewn space of this sitting-room is connected to the everyday world in an ordinary sort of way, as in, through a phone line, especially when earlier the phone was off the hook. To her the bungalow is like a cottage tucked away in some distant wood, where a tall, once-lovely lady, a mortal princess imprisoned many long years awaiting the return of her pauper prince, has marked each day of her waiting with a tear in a sheet of paper...

Then she remembers Laura's stoop-and-straighten as they walked up the passage earlier with their steaming tea-mugs, past the dangling Toy Town phone.

There's a fifth ring, a sixth... Mrs Binns clutches her throat in fear. Alice jumps up and dashes.

The afternoon has been so off-the-planet she isn't surprised to hear her mother's voice.

'*Jilly*,' she voices silently to Laura just behind her.

Jilly, a deeply irate, high-pitched mother.

'Alice, is that you? Well, I can't say I'm surprised. I assume Laura's with you? You girls are in big trouble.'

'We're safe, Mum, don't worry. Laura's here with me.'

Laura is poring over the collection of china owls standing on the wooden wall unit. With a concentrated index finger she evens out the higgledy-piggledy spaces between them.

'I'm not worried about whether you're *safe*,' says Jilly. 'My worry is the mischief you've been up to. You've got some extremely quick explaining to do, Alice. You can't think what this means for us as a family and how people will see us. A rudderless, fatherless bunch of delinquents.' Her voice shakes. Alice hears her draw a rasping breath, as if she had suddenly overbalanced and in the nick of time grabbed tighter hold of the balancing rod of her anger. 'What can possibly have possessed you two, you little idiots?'

'Hang on a minute, Mum. Can we go through this more slowly? Laura's right here with me. We're safe in Arnie Binns's granny's house.'

As if her mother were able to see her Alice pokes her forehead in the direction of Mrs Binns. The old lady has wandered down the passage after her sister and is standing at her shoulder, teetering from foot to foot. To Laura, shunting china owls, Alice makes wide-open eyes, Get in here, but Laura coolly takes no notice.

'I *know* you're in old Mrs Binns's house. For god's sake, aren't I calling you there?' Jilly is yelping. 'What do you think I have been hearing from Evie Binns this past hour?

"What *are* they doing at *my* mother-in-law's?"' Jilly's outburst has successfully gelled her tears. Her sentences are hurled like bricks of ice. 'You, Alice Brass, will have to don your oh-so-clever thinking cap and set it all out for me. First about waylaying poor Arnie Binns. He's disappeared, you see, and his mum has no idea where he is. But she suspects, rightly I'm sure, that you'll know exactly. And then there's this question of unauthorized borrowing. The taking of school property. I've had Evie Binns *and* your science teacher on the line to me today, both upset, both up setting. "So-sorry-to-call-on-a-Saturday-*but*... " Where's Laura? Put me on to her. I'd have expected her to set a better example.'

Alice removes the phone receiver from her ear and holds it out to her sister. Points at it, at her, at it, sharply, jabbing her finger. Laura shrugs, adjusts the position of another owl, a tiny one made of seashells.

Alice leans over and pokes the earpiece into Laura's ribs. Their mother's voice squeaks on tinnily.

'*Laura, you going to take it?*' Alice's mouthed mime turns frantic.

Laura retreats two steps and creates an elaborate semaphore of saying no, her arms going like windscreen wipers. Mrs Binns vaguely echoes her motions, hands fluttering. Then she turns and shuffles away into the front room, Laura backing after her, her eyebrows making a fierce downwards arrow on her forehead.

'Mum, Laura can't talk, she's with Mrs Binns. We're helping her out.'

'Helping out? That'll be the day. God, *God*, how did you girls end up like this? Too fierce, too reckless by half, too, *too* much. Alice, did Mrs Binns by any chance request this treatment from you girls, hm? This *helping out*? I doubt it. Was this whole thing possibly your big idea? Somehow I suspect so. The stamp of your mischief's all over this. So maybe you *are* the one I should be talking to and Laura for a change is innocent. Haven't you thought how it looks, the fact that you're over there bothering your friend Arnie's granny? I mean, don't you think *someone* would've smelt a rat? This madness certainly speaks volumes to Arnie's poor mum, a single mother making do just the same as the rest of us. Arnie's inseparable school mate and her sister wander round with the grand plan of involving his granny in a school project. A very respectable-sounding school project indeed, oh yes, with Sixth Formers involved, collecting oral history. Wouldn't any parent think so? Evie certainly thinks so. Fine, she thinks, give the girls the information they want.'

Jilly comes to a sudden dead halt to catch her breath. Alice finds her heart pounding so hard the sound thuds in her skull. She presses the phone harder to her ear. Jilly panics with ease but today her anguish is steely, a force to be reckoned with.

'So the day wears on,' Jilly's saying. 'Evie takes her lunch break, puzzles to herself, shouldn't *Arnie* be involved in a project that includes his granny? And, oh, isn't Alice's sister taking a year out of school? Why, for heaven's sake, is Arnie on a school trip this weekend while his friend Alice Brass is chasing his granny for her childhood memories? A very old granny who, by the way, isn't very well and is frightened out of her wits by strangers? And so Evie calls me. Here I sit, minding my own business, and what can I tell her? My dear, I haven't the faintest where my girls are. Don't think Alice has a school trip, no. And Laura certainly doesn't. I suspect that at least one of my children slept away from home last night. More I really can't tell you. The situation's way out of control, I know, I know.'

The blood noise gallops in Alice's ears. She leans against the wall, propped on stretched-out legs. Her feet begin to slide out in front of her.

'Alice, answer me! Have you considered for a moment how very bad this looks? I mean, Evie thought of phoning the *police* before she called me. At some stage soon she *will* have to phone the police.'

'Mum, I can explain some things, I promise. Some of this *does* have to do with school. I mean, a school *project*. But I don't know where Arnie is. I *really* wish I did, but I don't.'

'Problem is, Alice, that I don't think Evie'll believe you. Right now isn't the time for the fibs you're so addicted to. Can you put Laura on to me? Where's Laura?'

Alice's back slides down the wall. Her legs splay out more widely in front of her. Her phone hand drops to her thigh. The plastic receiver clinks faintly against one of the knives in her combats' pocket.

The phone continues its tinny chirruping, Jilly's *too, too, too*. Alice puts the receiver down on the floor and shoves herself upright.

She finds Mrs Binns kneeling huddled inside the nest of paper covering the sitting-room carpet, Laura bending over her, patting her shoulder. It's not clear what's going on; if it's an awkward cuddle, a shying away.

'You'll have to speak to Mum,' Alice says dully, sitting cross-legged beside the other two, the scattered paper crackling under her. 'I said about the school project. Everything that's going on has to do with the history project, one way or another, I stuck to that. I said we didn't know where Arnie is. And that's the truth. I wouldn't mention the hospital if I were you.'

Laura's lips turn out in an expression of exasperation. She leaves the room raking her fingers through her hair in a way that makes her look exactly like Jilly.

'He always was a one, that Albie,' Mrs Binns whispers into the carpet. 'Disappeared for good the day we put him on the train. The bridge too far. So many, many boys tumbling down those sandy hills like sand dunes, between the green beech trees. Never could have guessed when he was stood on that wide, old concrete platform, waving goodbye.'

They hear Laura begin stiffly, haltingly, to speak. Mrs Binns presses her head into her bony thighs and pulls the ball of herself in tight. Alice puts a hand on the shoulder poking up like the pointy edge of a spade. The old lady strains her body away. She's right to cower, Alice admits to herself. You can sense the dark cloud of fear and foreboding that's leaking out of the phone and spreading through the house. Arnie, let's face it, is AWOL, missing, God knows where. Her mouth feels full of sand.

She pushes the sitting-room door closed and Laura's voice thins to a murmur. Mrs Binns resorts to a croon held in the back of her throat, something like '*Albie, Arnie*'. Or maybe, '*Albie, Albie*'. Arnie's obviously not the only one in old Mrs Binns's family to have left home without a promise of return.

Laura handles her side of the call with briskness. Considering how hard Jilly went at her earlier, Alice thinks, Laura flings open the door and marches back in long before she'd expected. She plants herself in the two-seater settee and twirls her hair. Her eyes are fixed on her pressed-together knees.

Finally she says, 'And all this time Phoe hasn't once called round for me.'

'Laura,' says Alice with exaggerated patience, 'You have a mobile. Why'd he call round at home? He texted you. You didn't in any case want him to know you were poorly. At the end of the day he's been in touch. Unlike some, by the way.'

'And what would you know, Miss Alice Brass Khan? Or should I say Miss Alice Frankenstein, wanna-be Junior Scientist of the Year, lost in her Neverland of smart ideas?' Laura finally raises her eyes and flashes accusation directly into Alice's face. Her top lip lifts in an ugly sneer. 'You're well in trouble. You could've told me, you know, before leading me on this wild-goose chase.'

She points a raised big toe in the direction of Mrs Binns.

Alice meets Laura's stare head-on. 'Don't know what you mean.'

'You don't? Then why not use your incredible scheming brain to decode me? Turns out your science teacher, what's his name, Brocklebank, has something on you. I remember Brocklebank, bad beard, minotaur head. Anyhow, in *his* call to Mum today he said he'd spent the morning working in the lab at the school, laying things out for next week like he does, like you know well he does. Looking around for equipment he found something important was missing from the back lab storeroom. Something really special and important. He wanted to ask if you might have anything to tell him about the specimen collection on the top storeroom shelf.'

Laura dips her head and stares levelly from under her straight, black eyebrows. Alice can't think what her own face is doing. It feels like her head is about to split in two and the two halves fall to the ground.

'Course he was being polite about it but you get his drift.' Laura begins to speak in runs and gasps, as if her indignation is threatening to close her throat. 'He said he knew you'd be concerned to hear that one of the most valuable of the specimens has disappeared. He knows how you love biology. "You're one of his keenest helpers," he told Mum, "one of his most curious helpers." But he wondered, he couldn't help wondering, if you'd maybe borrowed, you know, something for the weekend, for some extra-mural experimentation, while of course planning to return it on Monday. He was calling in good time, he said, so everything could be nipped in the bud. So you or whoever could slip the stuff back into the lab and no questions asked.'

Laura's fingers twirl through her hair like spinning tops. Since she returned to the room, Alice notices, Mrs Binns hasn't once shifted her bunched position on the floor.

'So,' Laura says, 'It's all news to me, I must say. Apparently Brocklebank also told Mum that he'd arranged quite recently for the lab's specimens to be moved to an anatomy museum somewhere in London. Where, not before time, they'd be stored in better conditions. And, God, Alice—what a mess! Couldn't you have *said*? Do you think I'd have driven you all over the countryside like I have if I'd known you were carrying dodgy scientific specimens in your pockets? If I'd thought you had some *preserved item* in tow?'

The pounding noise in Alice's ears has grown deafening. Her T-shirt is wet all down her back and in her armpits. Her skin has turned slimy all over. She's never in her life felt anything so moist and repulsive.

At the sight of her Laura weakens by a degree, she leans over and puts her palm against her sister's hot cheek. 'We had our plan together, Alice, you and me. You could've said it related to a bit of science as well as a lost friend. You could've involved me more than you've done till now.'

Alice waits till Laura leans back and takes her palm away. Then she picks up a piece of Mrs Binns's scattered paper, an old electricity bill, and tears it in half. She tears each piece in half again. She can't think what to say. She can't think where to begin the story that Laura's insisting on. The story that's been unfolding alongside the hospital saga across these past two days, if only she knew it. There aren't the words. What's been going on isn't just about a borrowed specimen. It's about many things, basically. It's about, well, the Whole of Life—at the end of the day.

And that's why she wanted to have her sister see the specimen in the first place. To say: 'See, Laura, I wanted to bring the two of you together, you and this *something-for-the-weekend*. Hard to believe but here, in this jar, is where everything begins.'

But even if Laura weren't an interested party, her thoughts run on, she, Alice, has no way of showing her now, right at this moment, what it all means, how much it all means. She's horribly empty-handed. She can't deliver Arnie and she can't deliver the specimen. Boy and foetus have vanished together, on her call, and she must face the charges.

She counts to herself by pressing her fingers one by one into Mrs Binns's carpet:

Specimen Snatching, *a.k.a.* Body Theft

Damage to stolen goods

Damage to a Body

Wilful and severe damage

Disappearance of a Friend

And no way of making use of Mr Brocklebank's *no questions asked* and claiming the benefit of his doubt.

God knows, Arnie could've fly-tipped the foetus hours ago.

Or been fly-tipped himself.

She shuts her eyes tight. She can see the shape of the cut in the foetus's belly like a weal of fire. The cut of her razor blade. It was mainly a straight cut, except at the one end, where it dipped slightly. A slightly concave cut. She opens her eyes and sees the shape of the cut curve in the empty air between her sister and herself.

It's like the Cheshire cat's smile in *Alice in Wonderland*, upside down.

She feels a strange grimace knot her cheeks. She plucks at the places where her T-shirt has stuck to her body.

The odd thing is how it's not Mr Brocklebank who has triggered this meltdown, she thinks, even though Jilly left the dreadful mention of him till last. She suspects that in spite of what she's done she's not at the top of his hit list of problems to tackle. That he might eventually, if anything, owe her a favour. That she gave him a pointer. Eventually, at the end of the day, her wake-up call was sent not to Laura but to him. Her weeks-long enthusiasm about the storeroom, her dawdling and dusting and staring, maybe alerted him to the embryo collection's value, or why else is he now handing it on? The disturbance of the shelves spoke to him of quids, of how to turn dust into brand-new lab equipment.

No, it's not the thought of Mr Brocklebank on the warpath that has got to her. It's fly-tipping; it's weals and blades; it's the thought of Arnie's uncertain, saucer eyes.

So? Laura shoots her a straight look.

Alice says, 'How did you leave things with Jilly?'

'Jilly was very clear, for Jilly. Come . . . Home . . . Right Now! That was about her message. So I said we would.'

Alice points at Mrs Binns and frowns, What about her? By now the old lady must be fast asleep. Her breath is whistling loudly in her nose.

Laura stands up and makes her semaphore of refusal. She tiptoes to the front door, eases it open and looks out. She beckons Alice into the front garden. Laura's been entrusted with way too much information already; Alice thinks, it turns her spiteful somehow, spiteful and unyielding. But she finds herself getting up and following her.

They face one another over the diamond-shaped stones that pave the front garden. A chilly burst of wind rattles the rose bushes along the wall. The spring so far has escaped these bushes. It seems to have escaped this whole street of bare-brick bungalows, tightly closed windows and scraggy hydrangea borders.

Alice hears a loud snap, like a dry stem breaking. She looks around her, but can't identify the sound.

'Alice,' Laura's eyes lock on to her sister's, 'let's not fall out. You've been amazing to me, I know that. I couldn't have done without you. It's just that—I just *wish* you could have *said*.'

'What could I have said? I don't have the thing with me, the thing Mr Brocklebank was worried about. I don't have funny specimens in my pockets.'

'You know what I mean. What you took from the lab has to do with this, hasn't it? Being here. Why Arnie's missing. Admit it.'

'The lab thing was a secret, a secret Arnie and I have been keeping. It wasn't right to tell you our secret.'

'Not even once he went missing? When I offered to help? Not even then? These weird events hang together, don't they? Remember, you mentioned a secret to me once before, on Thursday when I was ill. A surprise, you said, a secret. I can hardly bear to think what you were planning to do with it then. What you've gone and done with that specimen now I can't bear to think either. You and your knives.'

A shrug shifts through Alice's shoulders. Her arms describe an empty-set square in the air. She sees her sister pull her jacket more closely round her.

'What can I say, Laura? I can't hide that we've been hiding. But you've been having an upsetting time, you're forgetting. The last thing I wanted was to upset you more.'

'What do you mean *upset*?' Laura's indignation grows shrill. The wind blows her hair into her open mouth. 'I had a funny episode, is all. Pains, a bit of bloating and a bad period, is all. Things you don't know too much about yet anyway. I wasn't *upset*. Actually I was strong. I took myself to hospital. A story about a secret lab experiment might have distracted me in my hospital bed.'

Alice worries the toe of her trainer into a crack between the paving stones. She glances at her sister and swiftly away again. She doesn't want to be reminded of how Laura pinched and squeezed herself during those hours she felt poorly, all the messy events that separate her sister's body from her own. 'Look, let's just say that up until now it didn't feel like the right moment. And, no, I haven't been cutting the specimen into pieces.'

Huffing and blowing her lips Laura turns her back. Alice studies the skid-marks of the wind in the grey sky stretched over the roofs and chimneys. She sees a daylight moon shimmy sideways through the high clouds.

She draws herself up taller. 'You remember, Laura, you were always so cut up about that bit in *Wuthering Heights*. A few years ago when it was your best book. That bit where Cathy's ghost comes to the window. You used to read it aloud to me and cry. Where the ghost wails '*Let me in,*' and Mr Lockwood saws its wrist on the broken window pane to make it go away.'

'And so?' Laura says abruptly. 'What does that have to do with anything?'

'And there was the memorial garden. I wanted to talk there but couldn't. There were those girls in that ward with you. Flat on their backs.'

'Alice, stop it. This is past the point. You joking or what?'

Laura's hands rise jerkily, involuntarily, to her waist. Her thin fingers grip tightly.

Alice feels she is about to commit a horrible cruelty but that she cannot help it. The dye is cast, the blade will go in.

'See, Laura, the specimen we've been talking about is a little foetus.'

'A baby foetus?'

Alice pushes her toe into the crack between the paving stones.

Eventually Laura says slowly, 'That's what you took from the lab? A *human* foetus? Are you both off your heads, you and Arnie? You'll be arrested. There are stories about this kind of thing in the papers. Unlawful removal of body parts. Hospital fridges loaded with dead baby bits. You say Arnie's off on a journey with a baby foetus in a specimen jar?'

'A foetus, not a baby foetus. And I don't know if Arnie has it with him at this moment. I wish I did know.'

Alice holds Laura's gaze. She watches how her mask of shock breaks down into confused and baffled patches, then into a tired frown. She holds her sister's gaze steady a long time, till something clear and definite moves between them. Silently they agree to draw a line. They are sisters: at the end of the day there's a car to drive home, a mother to deal with, a very bothered mother...

It's Laura's turn to study the sky. Alice traces with her toe on the stone the shape of that concave cut, the cut she made into the baby corpse. All in all a neat cut, considering the time there was. And Arnie breathing down her neck. An experienced person might have done a lot worse.

There's a movement at Mrs Binn's window. They see her thin shape behind the net curtains, its whitish gradations as she moves, dipping from side to side. Alice waves and Laura waves. The white shape makes no sign of recognition.

'We should say goodbye,' Laura says without expression.

Alice is already on her way.

The front door doesn't give to her push. This explains the snapping noise she heard. It was the door clicking closed, either at the touch of the draught or on account of Mrs Binns's own pulling.

Alice knocks sharply. She steps back from the door to see whether Mrs Binns will react. She does not. The white figure at the window, swaying but rooted to the spot, faces Alice on the path.

Alice pushes her sister forwards to take her turn. Laura loses heart even as she raises her knuckle to the wood. The knock makes the softest pitter-patter. Mrs Binns keeps her post behind the net curtains. Laura warbles 'Goodbye Mrs Binns' at the keyhole. Alice is already halfway down the pebble pathway to the garden gate.

She throws over her shoulder, 'I think she's telling us something.'

'I'd have liked a glass of water.'

'No chance. See how pleased she is, rid of the both of us.'

'We'll have to stop at a service station. I fancy something wet, wet and bright. Bottle of sugar and invert syrup with cheerful colour added.'

Alice stands at the locked passenger door. Laura meets her eyes across the car roof.

She says, 'You'll have to return it, you know, your baby specimen.'

'Foetus specimen,' says Alice.

'Do as Brocklebank suggests. Leave it quietly at his classroom door. He'll forgive anyone who's as mad about science as you are. You can trust a man with a big minotaur face like his.'

She unlocks the Fiat but makes no move to get in.

Alice is shaking her head across the car roof.

She says, 'Even if I knew where the thing was, Laura, I wouldn't return it. We'd be accused whatever happens. They'd say it had been tampered with.'

'And has it? Is it as bad as that? "Woodpark pre-teen pair mutilates baby body"?'

'Nothing so bad,' says Alice lightly.

She forces herself to think of concrete things. She sees how the car roofline crops Laura at shoulder level, passport photo level. She wonders how she manages to get her hair to lie so soft and straight, just grazing her shoulders, when her wavy curls lift permanently to the sky. She registers how many rose bushes there are in Daphne Binns' garden, all along the back fence and here in the front. She sees how one of the high cirrus clouds runs at an exact tangent to the moon.

Finally she says, 'Formalin spilled out when we first examined it.'

'Examined it?' Laura gives a wince of distaste.

'Yes, formalin spilled. And now, who knows?' Saying even this much makes Alice feel queasy. 'I'll have to think of another way of sorting it. Getting rid of it, I mean. It can't go back.'

'There's burial,' Laura volunteers.

Alice frowns at her. This is not something you offer as if it were a mug of tea. You've got to plan ahead, weigh the options. Talk to Arnie, the main Foetus Minder. Above all, you need a full and occupied specimen jar in your hand.

'There's burial, but not in your memorial garden.'

'There's nothing wrong with the memorial garden.'

'You said it yourself, no burials. Babies aren't laid to rest there.'

'They are and they aren't. But I wasn't thinking of the memorial garden. I was thinking of, really, any bit of earth. Any spot, with a bit of a marker on it. That poor specimen is, like, so totally out of it. That's how I imagine it. Out of this world.'

'I thought you were talking about burying evidence, as in a murder.'

'Alice, I don't want to quarrel.'

'I wasn't...'

There's a noise like a dull explosion. Mrs Binns's front door has burst open. She has wrenched it in hard against the internal airlock of the house. Alice edges her way round the car, back towards the garden gate. Mrs Binns's swaying body stands in the doorway, her face full of blankness and insatiable blame.

Round her neck is wrapped a length of the sitting-room net curtain. She has plucked it down and dragged it with her, the material huge and stiff like a clown's collar.

Her arm flings out and an object hurtles through the air; Laura's mobile that she left lying on the sitting-room settee. As the phone clatters onto the pathway it begins to ring. Skittering over the pebbles and coming to rest at their feet it's still ringing. With a crunch of conviction the plastic backing bursts free but the phone doesn't stop ringing.

'Don't answer it,' Laura grabs Alice's descending wrist. 'It'll be Jilly, making sure we're on our way.'

The phone rings on.

'Jilly tried the landline earlier, remember?' says Alice. 'She won't be calling your mobile. Not yet.'

She squints to check the incoming number. The phone doesn't recognise it. It doesn't say *Home*.

The ringing ceases. Mrs Binns begins to drag her front door closed. The ringing resumes and she opens it again. They all three stand stock still, mesmerised. Laura, her face stained by the cold wind; scowling Alice, scrambled hair flying; Daphne Binns, a tangle of net curtain suspended in the doorway.

The ringing ceases for a second time, full-stopped by the bleep of a text message. Laura dives to the ground but Alice is faster. Her hands shoot forwards, her knees hit the ground. Daphne Binns gives a surly cackle.

The text is plain. Alice reads it first, with aching, disbelieving eyes.

This is 4 Alice.
Im OK. Im @ T4 Heathrow.
B home soon.
Dont call back.
Arnie.
PS Its OK

The sisters' arms go around each other's shoulders.

'He's OK,' Alice says.

They do not see the sunlight breaking over Mrs Binns's face, the tears glistening on her cheeks.

'He's on his way,' she says with grand resignation. 'After all. He's on his way and I knew it. After all these years.'

She steps back into her hallway and closes and locks the door behind her.

Laura and Alice grip arms; these arms they know so well, their exact roundness, their long wrists and bony elbows. They jump up and down, just as they did years ago when a younger Laura entertained small Alice by playing Ring-a-Roses, when they tried to signal reasons for uncontainable excitement to Jilly quietly groaning, '*Oh please pipe down.*'

There is something reassuring and wonderful about performing this little merry-go-round, so they jump and shriek longer than Arnie's brief message gives them cause to do. They are friends again; this is their firm and convinced feeling. Their troubles are nearly over and, if they stick together, everything will eventually be OK, everything. They have helped each other through and at the end of the day, at the very end of the day, as Leo diCaprio says, this is the most vital, most important thing.

210

Then, to mark that this has been a full moment that they cannot bear to leave behind, they sigh loudly and Laura gives a couple of after-shrieks, till Alice, suddenly impatient, says, 'So what do we do now?'

Laura looks at her blankly, her mouth flushed with unfinished laughter.

'Er... Em,' she says, mocking her own fazed look.

'*Er*, bloody, *em*,' says Alice. 'I mean, Arnie's alive; Laura, that's cool, that's very cool. Unless of course his abductor has managed to get your number and is tempting us to a meeting at Heathrow. But now what? Do we do a Mrs Binns, go home and pull the front door closed behind us? Or do we worry about Heathrow? Do we think he's leaving on a jetplane? Do we talk about going after him?'

She knows that, if she could drive, she'd be nosing the car down bare and wintry Beecroft Street and towards Heathrow this instant *right now*. She wants *right now* to regroup with Arnie. Two united feels a lot better than two divided. In the past couple of days this is what she's learned.

'Going after him means using Phoe's car,' Laura breaks into her thoughts. 'I'll have to follow up on his smiley and check that it's OK.'

Alice gives a bad-tempered grunt. Since this morning flaky Phoe has barely loomed any larger on the horizon than the famous but invisible Mr F. Khan himself.

Laura brandishes her mobile. 'Look here, Alice,' she blushes. 'A text from Phoe was waiting behind Arnie's. A proper text after all, not just a smiley. It says, oh this is lush, it says he loves me. He *loves* me! I've been away too long today, he misses me, he wants to catch up.'

To Alice's eye the text looks too short to say that much, but Laura has caught a powerful whiff of its fairy dust. Her thumb presses the arrow keys, scrolling and re-scrolling through Phoenix's lines.

Alice refuses to think about Phoenix. She walks round to the passenger side of the car. Her sister's boyfriend is always an interference. Arnie's the one she's sure of, Arnie her Friend who is Found. Who has gone out and had what looks to be such a very big adventure.

She puts her hand on the car door-handle, then has to grip tighter. To keep herself from falling over she has to plant her feet, brace herself, squeeze closed her eyes. For the second time today she is pouring sweat.

An image floats into her mind's eye, something from one of the hundred books on anatomy she has rifled through in the past few months: *Essential Physiology*, Richardson's *Dissection*, *The Pocket Atlas of the Moving Body*. She sees the photograph of the dim interior of an anatomical museum. The photograph, she remembers, was on the left-hand side of some illustrated page. She sees a room with foetal objects on display, each one looming bulbous and awry in its illuminated glass case. She feels she is inside this museum, walking in amongst specimens that look almost alive, the terratoma and dysplasias sprouting in all directions like exotic tree ferns. At the end of the walk, close to the exit door, she sees an exhibit that is only a face, a complete, fully formed face. The exhibit is at eye-level and the face is Arnie's. A severed-head Arnie. Her blood runs cold.

She shakes herself and wipes her arm over her eyes. Quickly she turns the door-handle and climbs into the car. She must escape these daylight visions of Arnie; she must try to imagine him differently. It is possible now. She must imagine him stepping out from the shadows, stepping away from the scary exhibits, his head ducked down, his skew-whiff chin. There he was, his familiar self, waiting for her all along, biding his time, even when she had given up on him.

Overhead the sky with its pale daylight moon whirls around in a lopsided circle.

Laura slides in behind the steering wheel, mobile gripped and held aloft.

'And?' Alice says. '@ *T4 Heathrow*,' she adds to herself. Wasn't that a clear-enough signal, an invitation even?

'We have to bring Phoenix on side, Alice.' Laura rests a furtive eye on her sister. 'We have to pick him up and bring him with us. I'd like to have him along.'

'Whatever it takes,' Alice silently replies. To Laura she says, 'As long as he doesn't have a go, start calling me Jack the Ripper, Jilly the Ripper, stuff like that.'

She tries to laugh but the laugh surfaces as a choking noise.

Laura leans her forehead on the steering wheel. Her face sets hard and her jaw locks. It's the same expression as when she quarrels with Jilly. She drops her mobile into her lap and shakes her stiffened fingers loose.

'There's just one more thing, Alice. In exchange for all this, you agree to do something for me.'

'Depends,' Alice mutters. She wonders about that *all this*.

'You agree that before the burial you dip the specimen's toes in henna, henna or something else red. If you do bury it.'

'Er—?'

But Alice can tell that Laura means it. Her face has turned dark. Her lips have disappeared into her mouth.

A long pause and she continues, 'Any red dye is, I guess, fine. It's what the old Pharaohs used to do with their dead . . . to speed them on their way. It's in my books about Ancient Africa, the ones I read while I was ill. As it's your foetus and kind of our responsibility, we can treat it as an African baby, don't you think? We can say it's our right.'

'It's not a flipping baby, African or not African,' Alice says grimly, but after an interval. 'I keep telling you it isn't a baby.'

She remembers the afternoon with Arnie and their Thing under the weeping willow tree, that jolting feeling when she looked into its face. 'Yes, I could belong to that somehow. It could be like me, yes. Stranger-than-fiction but true.'

Laura maintains a second silence, longer than the first. She turns the key in the ignition. Backing off the curb alongside Mrs Binns' gate she says, 'Well, there's no harm pretending. I'd like to give it an African link. Pretend it's an African foetus.'

She drives the Fiat a few car's lengths down Beecroft Road, then judders it to a halt. She grips Alice's shoulders with unusual gracelessness and speaks full into her face.

'It *is* possible, you know, that it's a black baby born here in England. I don't need to be totally making it up. There were plenty of Africans and Africa-connected people passing through when the school was founded. Students, soldiers—nurses, too, during the War. They'd have met white people, like Farouq met Jilly. I can imagine this distracted young mother abandoning it somewhere, on a shop doorstep maybe, in an office bike shed, only for some Brocklebank type eventually to come wandering along. "*Oh, what's this*" He says, "*Oh, the poor little dear, a little mixed-race thing.*" But it's too late. The baby's snuffed it. So he nabs it as a specimen for the future generations of Woodpark children to goggle at.'

'The foetus's too young to fit your story,' Alice says. 'I don't think it was ever born. It doesn't look like it to me.'

Laura doesn't seem to hear her. She gives a thoughtful sniff and once again starts the car. They resume their crawl down Beecroft Road and her jaw at last relaxes.

Laura's story has left Alice cold but in a position of advantage. If she agrees, that is, to grant her what she asks.

She says, 'If dipping's what you want, then I say we hurry.' She takes Laura's phone from her lap and without asking slides it into her combats pocket, beside her knives. Till she's face to face with Arnie she wants to keep this link to him close-at-hand. 'I say that right now we make tracks to Heathrow. We pick up Phoe and then speed down to pick up Arnie at the airport. Arnie and the foetus. I say we go and we bring them home.'

Chapter 13

Arnie

Jim Noelson dropped me off on a bit of covered road-way signposted for buses and taxis. There in front of me was the oblong Terminal building. I walked straight in, without a moment's hesitation. The sliding doors opened in front of my face even as he was smiling his stretchy smile and winking his round glasses and saying to take care.

Inside was a warehouse full of neon-lit instructions: *Queue Here*; *Passport Control*; *Boarding Passes Ready*. The left-hand wall was pasted with shops offering last-minute deals and 3-for-2 offers. There was an HMV, a Boots, a Café Select, pretty much like the High Street at home, so this was information I could blank. A public announcement told me not to leave my luggage and personal belongings unattended. *As if.* When my number one personal belonging was my Fish wrapped in his indigo-and-white cloth.

I dropped my empty plastic lunchbox with the suitcase fasteners in a rubbish bin beside the sliding doors. This way I was lighter. I could wedge Fish back inside the willow-pattern bag. I was chiselled down to the bare essentials of our journey.

With Fish in tow I made my way to the check-in desks.

It turned out that only a handful of airlines served this particular Terminal and that most of them were home-based or European, not African. It also turned out that I was, all the same, in luck. *Fish and I*, I mean, were all the same in luck. Things shaped up so as to fit our special destiny. It turned out that these same home airlines ran flights to Africa: West Africa, East Africa, Cape Town, you name it. To West Africa in particular, names I recognised from Year 7 geography: Lagos, Accra, Abidjan, the Gambia. Also Cairo. Not Khartoum. I remembered, *The Gambia is a country that lies entirely along the River Gambia.* I wondered whether Jim Noelson knew about the links between Africa and this Terminal when he dropped me at the sliding doors and left us to our fate.

I studied the Departures boards. More luck. I patted Katrina's whorly key-ring mask in the pocket of my tracksuit bottoms. Although it was past four o'clock, today's flight to Lagos, Nigeria, hadn't yet left: Lagos, Nigeria via Kano. People were beginning to queue at the check-in desks but in an ambling, unbothered kind of way. The queue of mainly black people, almost exclusively very black people, made three elongated loops along the blue Tensa Barriers at Desks 34-37.

The first person I approached was a woman at the very back of the queue. She was bareheaded, wearing a blue cotton dress that bagged round her body. From behind you could've mistaken her for a kid. She was skinny though tallish and she stood kicking the edge of her suitcase.

I sidled up gripping the willow-pattern bag. I was thinking of no particular thing. I had quit planning. I was empty of feelings. There was just the one fixed picture in my mind, the rough shape of Africa's bulge from the world map on my geography classroom wall. A bulge, a bit like the bumpy, lopsided back of Fish's unborn or newborn skull. A bit like the outer whorls of the pattern on Katrina's key-ring mask.

A shape that said: 'Bring me here and lay me down where I belong.'

I skirted around the woman-child and faced her. I saw she was a lot older than I'd bargained for. Her forehead was lined and her cheeks scarified with criss-cross razor marks.

'Ahm—Madam?' My opened mouth was already speaking. 'Madam, are you travelling on this flight to Kano and Lagos today?'

Before I had reached the end of my question she had stepped back and grabbed the tow handle of her case.

'None of your business.'

She jerked the case a couple of paces forward in the queue.

I followed after her. I circled around her again.

'Let me explain, please. My name's Arnie Binns. I'm a Year 7 at Woodpark Secondary. That's in South-East England. I have a bundle here, no monetary value. An item that needs to travel to Africa. I know it looks difficult but you kind of have to trust me. We'll be doing something very good if we get this bundle back to Africa where it belongs.'

She cut me dead so smartly that the breeze of the movement stirred my hair. To continue our conversation I had to pretend to join the line and shuffle in behind.

'See, I can't travel there myself,' I hurriedly added.

Speech broke from her suddenly, loudly, as if I was stone-deaf. As if she wanted to ignore how very close to her I was standing. The back of her neck was blank and unforgiving.

'When were you born, child? It's a non-starter, see? Asking a person to take a bundle. In this day and age! You could be arrested. Security will spot you. Or I should say, hopefully they've already spotted you. I can see three CCTV cameras just standing here and not even looking. You speak another word and I ask someone to come.'

I wasn't about to wait for the heavy hand of a security guard to tap me on my shoulder. I knew I had to move swiftly, pass Fish on quick as I could, so I at once ducked away under the blue cord barrier. But as I straightened up I heard one more thing from her. I could have sworn she spoke again.

'Don't quit trying,' she said, I'm sure she said. 'It's always worth trying. There're people who are suckers. And how.'

The second party I tackled was a big man with a gigantic woman beside him, both wearing large smock-shirts decorated with lace borders and standing at the very back of the queue. While I'd been talking, people had been steadily lining up. The woman-child in her blue dress had by now moved nearly half a queue-loop away but even so I felt hot and tense. I worried that someone who'd over-heard my plea the first time might overhear again and raise an alarm.

The man was nearest to me so I addressed myself to him. I followed with my eyes the pattern on his smock, green shields alternating with black spears. I kept a good, safe distance but even so the smock seemed to rise and flow all around me. I could've been wrapped inside a king-size sheet billowing on a laundry line.

Speaking more softly than to the woman-child I said, 'Excuse me, Sir, but are you travelling on this flight to Lagos and Kano today?'

The man looked down his hooked nose at me. He drew back his lips, revealing an upper row of pure gold teeth interrupted in the front by two ordinary teeth, which were stained orange and broken down. When he spoke his voice boomed so low that it resonated in my face-bones.

'Certainly we're off to Lagos, young gentleman. How about you?'

'No, Sir, no, unfortunately, I don't have a passport. I've never travelled in a plane before. That's why I'm asking.'

'What's that? Look up at me when you speak.'

'See, there's this parcel here ... '

'Pardon me, boy, pardon. Did you say parcel?'

'I have this parcel, Sir, that's extremely precious but very safe.' All I wanted was to cringe away and hide, but I threw my voice, even so, directly into his eyes. 'It needs to get to Africa, to where you're going. I've no way of getting it over there myself.'

The man looked like he didn't know whether to laugh at my stupidity or grin at this show of crazy ambition. He glanced over at his smocked companion but she was watching a moving billboard above the 34-37 check-in desks and took no notice of our conversation. He stooped down to my eye-level so that his face filled my whole field of vision. Neon reflections from the overhead lighting glittered off his gold teeth.

'Young gentleman, haven't you ever heard these words before? *Sir, have you packed your bags yourself? Sir, has anyone asked you to carry anything on their behalf?*'

I shook my head. 'Like I say, Sir, I'm not used to air-travel.'

By this stage my cheeks were aching from the effort of smiling nicely, putting off zealous security guards by making it look as if I was asking an everyday favour.

'Well, those words are the words that the check-in lady over there will shortly be putting to me. If I take your parcel, were I to take your parcel'—he waved breezily in the direction of the willow-pattern bag in my hand— 'what will I say to the lady?'

'I don't know, Sir.' Taking a breath so deep, quivering and rib-expanding, that even Fish in his jar could've sensed it. 'You could trust me and pretend it was your parcel.'

The big man reared back and roared, his body shaking under his smock, tears of laughter and surprise spilling over his face. His wife looked at him with round eyes, then down at me, in irritation. She tugged at his sleeve and together they took a giant stride forward in the queue. I had to shunt up against the Tensa Barrier to make room.

The big man considered the conversation over; this was clear; but, as I slipped under the barrier, I couldn't help my body grazing his floating garments. This nudged him to speak one last time.

He talked looking straight ahead of him, his mouth turned down.

'Son,' he said, 'you don't know what you're doing.' His voice somehow sounded even more echoey than before, breathy and echoey, as if blowing through bamboo. 'I'm not going to tell you to stop what you're doing because that's your business, but I am going to say to you, Sit Up and Think. When it comes to smuggling things, you name it—clothes, foodstuffs, body parts even—we Africans you'll find are on our guard. Don't you read the papers? Bad things have been done in our name. The world sends death to Africa, and we take death and brew some deadly concoctions of our own. We have our own medicines to cast out spirits. This is not the time or place to ask an African to carry a suspicious parcel home.'

'I see—' I began, and actually I did see. I'd seen Alice's Christmas present to Farouq Khan, a pinewood photo-frame she'd made in DT, arrive back in Albion Street in March, *Address Unknown: Return to Sender*. I had seen her swallow with disappointment as she tore open the plum pudding-decorated paper she'd wrapped up back in October.

I saw that Africa didn't want donations without proper destinations piling uselessly in a warehouse. I saw that nowhere in the world wanted gifts carrying blank gift-tags. As if under a laser light I saw that I had no plans for Fish beyond getting him to Lagos. Was I keen for some airport hangar to be his grave? Till now I hadn't confronted the smaller details of my Home-to-Nigeria plan.

I wanted to tell the large-voiced man that I understood what he meant, but when I tried *I see* out loud a second time a flight announcement wiped out the words.

I stepped away from him. The queue had grown a whole loop longer. The tribal-marked woman-child had shifted from view and seven or so people and all their suitcases were lined up behind where the big couple stood.

I took a look at the last person who had joined the queue, an aging white tourist with a flaming pink suntan, a wispy beard and an enormous rucksack. There was plenty of fight left in me but suddenly I wasn't sure how to set about using it. I shuffled a few paces in this man's direction. I stopped. I passed Fish's Past Times bag from hand to hand. I didn't know what to do. Cold calling like a double-glazing salesman wasn't exactly producing results. It was only a few months since our recent war and everywhere in the world people were still nasty and suspicious, mad as snakes. No matter how I put my story, the 'Security Issues' would trip people up.

Yes, could you carry my parcel with you and then, ahm, bury it also? Could you please be not only Fish's courier but his undertaker as well?

Standing there shuffling at the Tensa barrier, jiggling the bag like a hot potato, I gradually became aware of a presence hovering at my left shoulder. The presence or person was outside the edges of my vision though standing close. Close enough to make it uncomfortable to whip round and face them.

I thought vaguely of Jim Noelson. Had he popped in from Smith's in Duty Free to make sure I was OK? Not likely. His sister would've ended her shift by now. He'd be driving off with her somewhere in his white Toyota. Their heads would be turned towards one another as they chatted, both at the same time, I imagined, catching up.

The figure just outside the corner of my eye was in any case too small and skinny to be Jim. The person was about my height, no bigger. It could almost be, but couldn't, couldn't really...

But—

I felt the smile breaking out all over my face even before I properly realised it was her; even before she was grabbing my elbows and shaking me till my teeth clattered, like she often did.

'Talk about *sore thumb*, Arnie! Spotted you from the door with that crazy-looking bag and dirty hair sticking up all over your head. Told Laura it was you and she could hardly believe her eyes. Where the hell've you been?'

Alice, Alice. I couldn't reply. My mouth was locked in this grin that couldn't go wider. It was so *good* to see her! It felt like someone was suddenly holding me up where before I'd been stumbling and in danger of losing my balance. That stupid quarrel about Laura and Fish didn't count any more. Not now that she was here, grinning as wide as I was; not now that I could feel how amazing it was to have her standing right here in front of me. She kept looking away, and straightening her face, and looking back, and breaking out smiling again.

'Hey, Alice.' *There*, I'd said her name, Alice's name out loud. 'How did you find me?'

That way she put her head to one side considering.

'You sent a text, Barmy Arnie, *remember*? *T4*, you said. It didn't take *that* long to find you once we had that. The text was up on Laura's mobile the whole way here. We were worried sick actually. All of us, Evie included. And then when we got here, me, Laura, silly old Phoenix, like I said you stuck out in the crowd, you and that ridiculous bag and that *thing* poking out of it. I can hardly believe you've still got it, but, boy, am I *relieved* to see you. Both of you.'

She danced her knee against the willow-pattern bag. I pretended to ignore this.

'What about Laura? How's Laura?'

'Laura? She drove me here, her and Phoenix. She's OK, as things have turned out she's OK. They're both OK. And they've just left. They've gone to hear a band in a pub not far from here, Stones or Staines or something. A pub a mate of Phoe's manages. It's all Phoe's plan, killing several birds, though likely as not he'll sleep through the gig. Laura said she'll make sure to pick us up later. They'll come away before it gets late.'

Her eyes swept the people massing past. Then she cocked her head, looked at me sideways and said, 'Yes, she *is* better now, she's fine. Nothing to do with me. She always was pretty fine. It *was* a women's thing; I was right there, but not as bad as I suspected. Or anyway that's what Laura wants us to believe. I'll tell you about it. But first you should take a break from whatever you're up to, Sore Thumb. Let's get something to drink.'

We found a coffee stand at the top of the stairs leading down to the Arrivals hall. By now the queue for Kano and Lagos stretched beyond the blue barriers and curled up against the shop front of HMV.

Alice bought us orange juice in plastic coffee cups with lids. We sat in the only two free chairs standing together. The chairs were stainless steel and cold against my legs. I couldn't stop looking at her. She couldn't stop looking at the willow-pattern bag.

'So, what are you trying to tell me and the world, Arnie? I watched you working that queue. Trying to palm our Thing off on whoever, as long as they're African. Am I right? And so I'm wondering, what's up? Where've you been hanging out? Has Laura been talking to you privately or something? Have you and her got into some Back-to-Africa business while I was busy doing other things, like scoping out specimens, trying to work out how to make her better?'

'There's a lot to say,' I said, 'But later. Right now we've got to get a move on. The flight to Lagos leaves in about an hour-and-a-half.'

I sat stunned at the voice that came from my own mouth, so decided and steady. Alice watchfully pinched her lips.

I said, 'I'll explain everything. Just believe me and don't laugh. We've got to try to get Fish on that plane to Nigeria, that's the main thing. Your guess wasn't far off the mark. Our Thing, our Fish, ah, Foetus, he could be a magic baby. He could be African, part-African, about the same as you. And so he needs to go home. These folk I met up north where I went to see my dad; I'll do these folk a favour if I get him back to Africa. Dad's girlfriend mainly. Our baby will help tie up her loose ends, I know.'

A massive sign crept up from somewhere inside me.

'Look, basically he's a baby who's been too long in a bottle. Now everyone including him needs out.'

'Well, you can say that again,' Alice said. 'He's been out since we had him out, that's for sure. I can tell from the smell.'

This was how she was my true friend. She didn't bat an eyelid. She didn't make a fuss about the incredible announcement I'd just made. Right now she didn't even correct me when I used the danger word *baby*. She snatched a look inside the bag and did nothing but wrinkle her nose.

'*If* he's African what you say makes sense, yes,' she was saying. '*If* he is. *Obviously* I get that. It fits somehow. We could say he's an advance party. Wouldn't that be good?

225

An advance party for when me and Laura eventually go to meet Farouq. And sending him would erase all signs, definitely. Problem is whether there's a mad-enough person out there to buy the idea.'

Erase all signs? I frowned.

Leading the way back to the Kano-and-Lagos queue she cast a piercing whisper over her shoulder, '*Brocklebank knows.*'

I frowned harder but she didn't want to say more. At the Tensa barrier she stuck her elbow into my ribs and winked.

'Had you thought about the Royal Mail at all, Arnie Binns, as an alternative to a direct flight? It would be easier than this airport begging-deal.' She pulled at the stainless steel joint in the barrier, as if working out how to break through it. 'Then again,' she went on, talking to herself, 'Posting might be trickier. Think of your parcel jammed in amongst the mail, spreading a yellow stain. "Now, now," the Nigerian postman will say, "who put the Coronation Chicken sandwiches in with the air letters?" She snorted cheerfully. 'Messy to get rid of a body, isn't it, like all the crime stories say?'

A powerful feeling of relief now came over me, the relief of operating together again as a twosome. There was nothing to beat it. It was as if a pair of damaged hands had been restored to good order, as if the hands were once more moving in tandem. We were, I suddenly knew for certain, a good working pair—a great team. We stood shoulder to shoulder on this safe near-side of the adult world, the world where people had scary, cold hands and bottomless, nameless griefs. Even though we would join that world sooner than defeat it, we had this togetherness now, like an energy, a force field moving between us.

Please, kind energy, I prayed, ward off that other world for as long as can be allowed.

'*Fish*,' I said in her ear. 'He's managed to find a name. His name's Fish. He's a good friend. He stayed by me all the way on my journey.'

In reply Alice chucked her chin at the Lagos queue. She wanted to have her turn, make her move. She took the willow-pattern bag from me. She selected a woman along the middle of the line closest to us, a light-skinned African woman, lighter than Alice herself, wearing a blue-and-white batik headscarf that trailed down her back. You could tell this woman was travelling alone, that she was the kind of person who kept to herself. Stacked all around her was easily the largest stockpile of luggage in that queue, three bales of stuff tied up in hessian and string.

I poked Alice in the ribs and indicated a mountain with my hands. In her old, familiar way she didn't bother to notice.

She slid under the blue barrier and into the line. She planted herself beside the woman, blindsided and facing in the same direction.

'Excuse me,' she said and at the same moment lifted Fish in his jar clean out of the bag. He was mostly wrapped in his cloth but the bottom of the jar was exposed and you could see his feet poking down, his tiny globular toes pressed against the glass. Today like all days it was difficult seeing Fish's toes. It was difficult looking properly at them. They were a very human part of him, human, but behind glass. You could see clearly that it was a specimen jar in Alice's upheld hands.

I ducked under the Tensa barrier and slipped into the line beside her.

'Do you see what I see?' Alice asked the woman.

'I see a thing from my dreams,' she said in reply. 'I see what any woman would recognise and want to hold if alive. I see an indigo cloth exactly like the kind that is made in my home state, with the same white-leaf design.'

227

Alice lowered the jar and looked at her in blank surprise.

The queue moved forward and crowded the three of us close together. We were tented round by people, trolleys, baggage, coats. It was a case of safety in numbers. None but an extremely tall person would have been able to peer over our shoulders and see Alice, still goggling, unpeel the indigo cotton covers from Fish's jar.

When all was revealed the woman said, 'Well now, how could you have guessed?'

'Guessed?' said dumbstruck Alice.

'Guessed *things*,' said the woman. 'Things that hang about. Did you see as you approached, the things that live with me? Maybe you saw.'

I sensed Alice shaking her head though I kept my eyes on Fish's toes. The woman now bent her head and spoke with extreme rapidity.

'Maybe you saw my mother. My memories of my mother and my eldest brother stay close to me, just here.' She patted her left shoulder with her left hand. Alice and I looked carefully at the shoulder. It was as ordinary a shoulder as you could imagine. She dropped her voice to a whisper. 'When I say eldest brother I mean my mother's first-born, called Jesiah, her still-born son. She carried Jesiah's embalmed body with her till the day she died. Smaller than that one there. He lived in a casket, painted blue. He sat on her lap when she worked at her sewing. She said it was better so. Better than for him to go wandering the earth like a sad baby ghost.'

'My friend thinks this little one is from Africa,' said Alice.

The woman turned her eyes to me. Her eyes were strangely pale, light-green, without depth. She shuffled backwards in a kind of dance-step.

228

'So then. How does your little one get here to London, boy? My mother travelled nowhere she couldn't take her casket.'

There was nothing I could think of to respond with, here in this airport queue. The thought came to me of the Pampers boxes on Grange Terrace pulled together in a cosy circle, of Katrina pacing up-and-down in her back-to-back house and rattling her row of keys.

We moved forward in step.

The woman said at last, 'So you must know somehow. How many people's lives are filled with how many dead babies?'

I found myself saying yes. 'Yes-yes—*yes*.' I remembered what Katrina'd said about her babies-who-might-have-been. How they milled about in her memory and punched and pummelled their fists and wouldn't be budged.

'Why else show me it?' the woman said.

Alice looked from me to her and back again, her eyes shining. Our project, I could tell, was beginning to agree with her.

She said, 'We need to ask you to take it back. It needs to be housed wherever you're going, in Africa.'

At this the indigo woman drew herself up and stood with squared shoulders like a queen.

'It'll fit in some corner in all this luggage,' said Alice.

'Impossible,' the woman said. 'You have my sympathy, small sister, but no. I don't want the extra burden. Africa needs no more dead babies. As for you, you're a smart girl; African yourself by the look of it. You will know that someone needs to receive him over on the other side. You have family there to sort him out when he arrives? Or what must I do when I step down on the Lagos airport tarmac? Place the jar on the edge of the runway when no one is looking? Leave him out for the pariah dogs? That's

229

for you to work out, see, how to lose him properly. Put an end to his wandering about.'

We were looking through the portal of an incredible chance but already its shutters were closing. With an extra portion of luck Fish in his white-vinegar capsule would be receding before us even now, vanishing into the dark mouth of the x-ray machines down there just beyond the passport control. He had no knives on him, had he? No sharp implements that the machines would pick up? No drugs stashed inside his person? But the good fortune that Alice had mysteriously glimpsed in the shape of the indigo woman didn't stick around and wait.

The woman shot me a sudden, conspiratorial look. 'You shouldn't send him away,' she said, 'not yet in any case. He has the marks on the shoulders, as is right. But I wouldn't imagine you've yet made the ceremonies of departure. Laid ritual offerings to help the passage. As I say, you've got to lose him properly and work things out.'

I had to squeeze my eyes shut, then take a break. But when I opened my eyes again her unblinking gaze was still on me.

Beside me Alice jitterbugged on the spot. The conversation was going nowhere and she was ready to give up. The whole thing was now a drag. '*No-eye-deer*,' I could almost hear her say, like she and Yaz Yarnton used to chorus in class behind Mrs Humphrey's back. I felt the slew of her body against my arm.

Still the woman's green gaze wouldn't let me go.

'Follow your path back to your own house,' she said, 'where the whole world can be found. Don't send your creature away. Sing over it. Hollow a space in yourself and put the memory of it there. *Intussusscept . . .*'

I didn't get it. I thought she'd slipped into an African language. She saw that I hung confused on her lips.

'*Intussusscept it...*', she began again but a late boarding call for Cairo drowned her out.

She took the noise as a prompt to shrug us off. Using her shins and shoes as scoops she shoved her bales of luggage forward.

'*Yikes!*' Alice whistled as we stepped out of her way. 'What was all that about, Arnie? What *have* you been up to in your time away?'

Time away? That wasn't right, I thought. *Time away* made me imagine a pathway and me stepping off it, onto the grassy verge, the grass wet with dew. It made me think of lying down in the grass and cooling my burning head. I knew I would like to lie down and cool my burning head. I took the willow-pattern bag off Alice and then grabbed hold of Fish. I was feeling all of a sudden very bad. The bright neon lights planted whirling diamonds in front of my eyes. My whole skull ached. The crowd squeezed in on us from all sides, the faces in the crowd querying, perturbed, ready—I was sure—to eject loud sighs of rebuke and dismay.

'Let's get out of here,' I pulled Alice's sleeve.

Her voice came from a far distance, 'Arnie, actually— you don't look too great.'

At that moment a slim, long arm reached across her face. A finger tapped her on the shoulder.

'Sorry. Do you mind? Could I have a moment of your time?'

No, I signalled urgently, windmilling my hands, but Alice had already turned. By now she'd got the hang of this 'Back-to-Africa' game. She wanted more opportunities, more time to play. She always was a sucker for a second chance.

'Geetha Hathaway, freelance journalist,' this person said.

Alice's hand was clasped by the interloper's two.

We were invited over to the Café Select. My muttered protests, lagging feet, were briskly brushed away.

'Alice, we're busy, remember? We've had juice. I've got a headache.'

In reply Alice put her finger to her lips. I could tell what she was thinking. *The newspapers, Arnie, you never know. It's an opening. Could be our one last chance.*

At the café we sat down. Ms Hathaway offered us glasses of Coke with ice and lemon, a massive chocolate-chip muffin each. I refused on behalf of us both. She smiled upon us with her big, sparkly smile. No, it wasn't a smile—it was more like gawping, like gloating with amazement attached. She pored over us gloating. In minutes she'd extracted our names and written them on a notepad bound in a two-tone elastic band.

'You kids,' she gushed, 'I *had* to meet you! Have you any idea how incredibly stunning and impressive you are?'

She said she'd been watching us ages, from this same table, having a coffee before meeting a colleague in Arrivals. 'That's a journalist for you, eyes always open. More vigilant than the security guards I've seen prowling, I must say. I spotted you lot working that queue, first you, ah—Arnie, and then the two of you.' She checked our names in her notebook and twinkled at Alice. 'Handling that bag of yours like it was some sacred relic, Alice. The looks you were getting! The awe. I'm *fascinated*. What could your curious secret be? I feel there's something in it. I'd like you to tell me about it. I could try to take it further for you.'

Take it further? What did that mean? It looked ominous. It looked like grown-up business come to bother us, to throw obstacles in our path. I had to be rude. I had to be very offhand.

The journalist lady was saying, '... especially if this has an international remit. If you're looking for someone abroad, even in a place like Africa, a well-placed or eye-catching article . . . '

Under the table I shuffled Fish still half out of his covers back into the willow-pattern bag. I grabbed hold of the handle and stood up. I took two steps backwards. My hand was soldered onto Alice's arm, '*Let's go*.' She jerked into vertical like a puppet.

'God, Arnie, wait a minute, not so fast.'

She made apologetic eyebrow expressions in the journalist's direction.

Geetha Hathaway stood up in time with us, as if an invisible rope connecting her waist to Alice's body had dragged her upright.

'You never know how far a newspaper story can reach, Alice, Arnie,' she said, the light in her eyes fading. 'If I wrote up your mission, you never know who might read about it, who might get in touch. A positive story about children on a big adventure, people would love it. There are so many negative stories. It could be your mission accomplished, goal achieved. Think of it. Both of you transformed into Household Names.'

We made our escape, but not before the journalist had handed over her business card. Not before Alice had foolishly released her telephone number and promised to ring at some point soon, it would be great to be in touch. Yes, she said, there probably *was* a rich and wonderful story to tell: a wonderful story but at the same time, Geetha should know, a quite ordinary story. A story about, you know, life and death, just that: life, death, and remains.

'And survival,' I silently added, tugging at her, but wasn't going to give a thing away. By now the whirling neon diamonds were going like Catherine wheels in my eyes.

We left Geetha Hathaway sitting in front of her empty coffee cup, her surprise freeze-dried onto her face.

As we skidded across the polished Terminal floor, Alice turned on me exasperated. 'So much for that, Arnie Binns. I mean, do you totally want to raise suspicion? Ruin our big chance of success in the process? What's with you, rushing off like this? That journalist was a lifeline. Her idea about using the newspapers was spot-on. I thought you wanted your big plan to succeed.'

We were dodging through streaming masses of passengers, around legs, pushchairs, trolleys, trailing skirts, all in movement. A purple passport slapped to the ground beside me and I picked it up, placed it back in a cupped hand. I heard in the distance the first boarding call for the flight to Kano and Lagos.

'You don't know anything about my big plan,' I yelled. 'Look, let's go somewhere. Home. Anywhere. Get out of here.'

'But *how*, Arnie? You thought of that? The small but important question of *wheels*.'

'You said Laura—?'

'Phoe's friend's gig won't have started yet. Yes, Laura has her mobile, the one you texted, and I've borrowed Phoe's, so we could call them, yes. Then again, no, Laura won't be impressed if we call so soon.'

But the solution to the wheels question was staring us in the face. The yellow Bus Station sign stood overhead, the black arrow pointing. We turned to follow the arrow. A revolving door spun in front of us. A single bus stood waiting in the nearby bay, its engine ticking over.

Still clutching Alice's arm, her feet stumbling behind her up the steps, I led the way into the local bus, marked for Richmond and Twickenham.

* * *

By the time the bus reached Richmond it was pitch-black night with low clouds chasing across the sky. We could have been anywhere that had winking streetlights and blowing trees, Leeds or London or Nairobi or Lagos, I didn't much care. I could feel the tail-end of my headache still twitching behind my eyes.

On the journey Alice had filled me in about *all signs erased* and Mr Brocklebank's *no questions asked*. I'd kept my arms folded around Fish's jar sitting squat and safe on my lap. When she'd fallen silent I'd found myself humming Jim Noelson's funny tuneless tune: *Where are you keeping?*—hum, hum—*why you so long?* I told her I couldn't help it. I must've heard that tune from my taxi-driver friend about a hundred-and-nineteen times today.

At Richmond the bus looped us over the longest river-bridge I'd ever seen. On either side, the dark river rolled and churned and the lights of the traffic and the town looked like tinsel scattered on the moving water. It was Alice's turn to pluck hard at my sleeve. At the first stop beyond the bridge we climbed down. The bus doors unfolded and closed behind us and we glanced at one another. Then we turned in unison and headed straight back to the river.

The town's contrasts were sharp. Immediately behind the brightly-lit shop fronts and neat, new townhouses lay the muddy stretch of the river's edge. There was no grey zone in between. At every point you knew exactly where you were, either on the bright street or by the dark, rushing river.

We made our way down a narrow lane between two shops that, though we couldn't be sure, felt muddy underfoot, and then over a bumpy area where an upended boat was parked. After the brightness of the street we crept slowly, groping. By the time we clambered onto the rocking landing stage I was holding onto Alice's wrist. It was very dark here and slick-wet underfoot. A single long barge carrying a load of something like creosoted planks lay moored to the downstream end of the landing stage.

We hunkered down facing each other with Fish planted in between our feet.

One of us had to speak. Someone *had* to say it.

It was Alice: 'We could let him slip away right here.'

Already I was uh-huh-ing.

'We could, uh-huh, we could. There's been a lot of rain, uh-huh. The river's running high.'

Together we looked downstream, to where the dark waters charged fiercely at the long bridge and whirled away through its stone arches.

Alice, graphic as usual, said, 'The fish won't get him. Imagine chewing on that formalin-soaked *hide*.'

The skin on my neck contracted at the thought.

'On the other hand,' she said, 'maybe it would be best for the fish to wolf him. So no one's any the wiser.'

'We keep our hands clean,' I said. '*All signs erased.*'

She stood up suddenly and walked to the edge of the landing stage. She peered upstream, took a few steps backwards, then forwards, peered again, as if measuring something. She spoke into the empty air that swept across the racing water and carved out its high waves. For Alice she spoke slowly. If I hadn't known her voice so well, I'd have missed most of what she said.

'You know, Arnie, it's got a hold on me now, I've got to tell you, this Africa thing. I keep bumping into it and it's grabbed me. Now, even your Fish—I mean, think about it. There's Laura and her issues about our African Dad or Dads. And then that woman at Heathrow, speaking to me almost as if she was related to me somehow.'

'I saw that,' I said. I'd noted it of course.

'And then there's what Laura said when we were on our mission to find you today. I haven't told you this, this very

236

weird thing. Laura said she wanted to pretend our Fish was an African baby.'

'So I didn't say it first?'

'No. You could say it was Laura sensing something. She said she's been doing all this thinking and reading; she has the time this year; but still, how did she know? Like I said, she found out about the specimen from Brocklebank and Jilly, not from me. We were talking about getting rid of it; I mean trying to bury it or whatever. And then suddenly she made me promise to colour its toes red like the Ancient Egyptians used to do with their dead.'

I tried to make out Alice's face, or, no, the back of her head, a vague outline against the shadowy water. I guessed that her peering and pacing meant she was trying to steady herself, get her bearings. There were these Amazing New Things to think about, after all.

And she didn't even yet know the Most Amazing Thing of all, the one perched at the very top of the Amazing Things pile.

I'd not yet said a word about Katrina, or special cuts, or the little house in Harehills, or Fish tied like a tiny baby, a baby brother, to Katrina's back.

Alice turned to look at me. Her eyes contained small golden stars, reflections of the streetlights. My friend and crying didn't usually go together, but I was almost sure her eyes were wet.

I collected myself to say, 'Well, you *are* part African so maybe it's not so weird to *feel* excited. It's like when you hear a new song you enjoy, you keep hearing it played, wherever you go.'

Alice lowered her head at me.

'This is different, Barmy Arnie. This obviously isn't the first time I'm finding out about being African. It's just that this time I'm discovering echoes everywhere, wherever I turn. You won't believe this but even when we first got Fish out of the jar, even then, I felt something; I don't know, as if I could belong to him, as if he was African himself. I thought I was seeing things so I didn't say. But I felt something, like I knew where he was coming from somehow.'

'There's a lot of Africa about,' I said stupidly. 'If you think about it Africa's not so far away.'

Alice's head shot up. 'That's exactly it,' she almost crowed. 'The same moment you said that I was thinking— I was thinking that if we let Fish go right here and if there were no predators, if we set him on his way from this landing stage, you could imagine him drifting to Africa. I mean, if we let him slide down into the river and out to sea, there's no barrier anywhere, not really. Dolphins come up the Thames all the time. You could imagine him drifting all the way across the Mediterranean, and up the Nile past Cairo even, fetching up in old Khartoum . . .'

I poured cold water only because I was getting spooked. 'Not counting for a minute the Aswan Dam in the way,' I said.

Immediately I wished I could bite back the silly-ass remark. *Why* did I say that? It was *so* bad. The problem for me was how strangely things were working out. How our ideas were moving together in a dance. I thought air, she thought water, we both thought journeys along to Africa.

'You'll know what I mean, Arnie, if you think about it,' Alice said.

She walked back over and squatted opposite. There was a long pause. We sensed this feeling in the air, a kind of expectation. We were waiting for a right moment to arrive, whatever it was. We knew we'd wait as long as it took. The whole weekend had been building up to this instant, this *thing*, this Weird Event. I put both hands on

238

the lid of Fish's jar. Was it time to open his fishbowl and let him flow free? A quick goodbye, a pat on the head, a tiny turbulence in the racing black water—

Jarless and fleeceless, my fellow traveller, our four-limbed fish.

Naked as the day he wasn't born.

I looked at Alice; she looked away.

The frantic scurrying took us both by surprise. It came from under the landing stage, then moved to the water's edge. The sound concentrated around a post on the river-bank next to the landing stage. A wooden box like a large mailbox was mounted on this post. We hadn't noticed it before. From where we were squatted it blended in with the row of hip-high bollards lined along the quayside.

The scurrying and the scratching now came mainly from the mailbox. In the murky grey light we saw how the top of the post seemed to heave and billow. An elongated snout reared itself against the grainy grey of the bank.

The same moment I saw a hefty, cat-size body swarm up the post after its mates. Alice craning forwards spat out, 'Rats, Arnie, rats!'

It was a whole nest of them, their wet coats making porcupine spikes. The rats had converged on a daily delivery of milk and bread that some local barge-dweller had failed to collect. They had retreated at the moment of our arrival but now their swarming and agitated screech-ing broke out with new force. Eight or so rat rumps bulged out of the wooden box.

We stood leeched to the spot. The landing stage moved ever so slightly underfoot and I could sense Fish rock in his Past Times cradle.

When one of the smaller rats fell shrieking off the post, Alice turned to me. I saw the whites of her eyes. This time her eyes weren't swimming.

'Are you thinking what I'm thinking, Arnie?'

'Maybe. I'm thinking hunger. Rats are always hungry.'

'I'm thinking that if the fish don't want our Fish the rats probably will. Rats eat everything.'

In their turn a cluster of three squabbling rats tumbled off the post and immediately scrambled up again. The second or third in line must have grabbed its leader's leg between its teeth. A bitten rat screamed like a hurt child.

Again Alice spoke my thoughts.

'Looks like we'll have to leave our river plan for now. We can't set Fish afloat here. He won't reach Tower Bridge, let alone Africa.'

'But what if those rats turn on us? Imagine they sense Fish through his formalin and turn on us.'

'Arnie,' said Alice, 'Fish *is* mainly formalin. And rats aren't dogs.'

She sidled to the end of the landing stage that was farthest from the post.

'No they aren't,' I said creeping after her, 'they're hungrier.'

I held Fish in his bag high over my head. Alice jumped; I jumped. The rats never noticed. I kept my eyes fixed on them but they gorged on nonplussed. The riverbank was good and solid underfoot. It was the kind of surface you could sprint on.

* * *

We found a place to sit up against the warm window of the Boots Chemist on Richmond High Street. Alice spread her raincoat to make a seat. We unwound Katrina's indigo cloth from Fish's jar, still dampish, and pulled it over our shoulders. The jar stood behind us in the crook made between our backs and the plate-glass frontage. I could feel the cold of the jar at my elbow and the warmth of Alice's arm against my arm.

I almost asked, 'So what do we do now...?' Except that the self who liked to put Alice those questions seemed to have been left somewhere back on the M1.

Instead I patted the pocket of my tracksuit bottoms and said, 'We have some money to get home with. I took my savings with me on my journey but there's a bit left over.'

Alice studied the side of my face.

'You were well set on running away weren't you, Quiet Arnie? Taking your life's earnings and all.'

'I wanted to get away, not run away,' I corrected, avoiding her gaze. 'And only for a while to have some time out. Right now I've enough to get us both a coach home. If we can find our way back to Heathrow, I mean.'

'We don't need to worry. Laura really is expecting to take us home, Arnie. She'll call to find out where we are. It feels late but actually we've not been here long and we've not come that far. What I say is, let's sit and wait and work out what to do.'

The thought of a wait there on the pavement with the river at our backs rushing away into the darkness made the night feel suddenly colder. Bed was a better place to be by far, I reckoned. It was three nights since I'd last laid myself down flat in bed. For all that Richmond High Street might look prosperous and well-kept it felt abandoned, emptied-out, not exactly a place to relax. The occasional passerby here hurried more than strolled, the cars hummed smartly by. The glossy posters of rosy lipsticks hanging suspended in the Boots window looked a huge, warm world away.

I shoved myself up against Alice's warmth. She didn't mind, I didn't think, not as she used to mind. She didn't shift away in any case.

I wanted to tell her things, stuff, what I'd been up to, everything. It seemed like the right time. To begin where on Thursday night we'd broken off.

I said, 'I was angry with you the other day when you wanted to give your wake-up-call biology lesson to Laura, when I made off with my friend our Fish. But now I'm really glad you're here.'

In reply she shifted the tiniest bit closer.

I said, 'I'm glad he means something to you, too.'

'I don't know about that, Arnie. I wouldn't go as far as that. I will say I'm over the moon to have found you. What you'd have done tonight on your own, God knows. You could have been arrested. You'd have been bloody cold, that's for sure, and maybe lost.'

I said, 'It's weird, I know it sounds stupid but this weekend while I was travelling, now and then it felt like there was someone with me, almost helping me, standing by me. Once when these boys were threatening me, then especially. It was then that for me he grew his name, Fish, like I said. For me it was as if his name might help him get a life, become alive, or at least not dead, less dead. Everyone I met wanted a look at him, as if he really was someone.'

I felt my monkey-bone grind against the paving stones lying hard and flat under Alice's thin raincoat.

'People are just curious; that's what I've discovered,' Alice said tartly. 'They like to stare. They're all just stupid and curious.'

A threesome of teenage girls on white espadrilles came tottering along the row of clothes shops opposite. The one nearest paused to gawp at these two kids in the street, sitting on a raincoat. Alice stared defiantly back.

'*That's* what I mean,' said Alice. 'Stupid and curious. People look just to look. They don't *do* anything with their surprise. As for me, when we last saw each other, when you ran off and vanished Fish away, what I wanted was to help Laura; that was all, to help put a smile back on her face. That's why I planned what I planned. *Everyone happy*, remember?'

She waggled her head mockingly at the backs of the three retreating girls.

I said, 'Everyone happy, everything clean, I remember. Except I don't know about all that any more. Everything *clean*? How can I say that when I've stuck my hands so often in Fish's jar? When my skin's soaked with him?'

'But he's dead, Arnie, and always will be. He didn't come alive for you on your travels, not really. Even if you were some higher Force and managed to raise him up; well, what's the point? What would he do with his second wind? Think how he's been caught in-between the living and the dead for all these years. He couldn't settle to anything else. So the best thing, I say, is set him free. Let his spirit go free.'

'You said *spirit*, Alice?'

'I think I did.'

Alice looked almost bashful. I must've gaped like a loon.

She said, 'While you were away everything you said about that flipping specimen fixed itself in my head, including the spirit stuff, I was that bothered. There was Laura disappearing to hospital with her bleeding thing, and then going on about burial and reddened toes. And now there's you and your Africa lark. Why wouldn't I say spirit?'

I said, 'He has African marks on him, maybe, if you look closely. Special lines on his shoulders.'

It was Alice's turn to shiver. Her shoulder knocked against mine. At the same moment, as if on call, Fish pressed a freezing boulder into my back.

I thought, 'These are our final hours together, the three of us, Fish and Alice and Arnie. Which means we don't have much longer. We may as well have him out of his boulder-cold jar one last time.'

So I set to work on him. I unscrewed the jar lid. The thread of the lid seemed smoother now, less grainy. I dug my hands in without a second thought. I couldn't believe I'd ever baulked at this. But I had to reach down deep, so deep that the vinegar covered me up to the wrists. There was something about him tonight that was different from before. I felt it at once. Something odd. Was he suddenly smaller, infinitesimally smaller? Was it that? He seemed to escape my hands. For the first time I had to stab for him, poke around the jar, walk my fingers through the liquid. When I managed to get my hands on him he felt looser somehow, floppier, kind of *slack*. When I lifted him into the air he drooped where before he'd stayed compact.

I dried him off on Alice's coat, lying him first on one side, then on the other. I thought of how Evie covered the fresh pork chops she so liked in breadcrumbs and flour before frying them, lying them first on the one side, then on the other, till they were coated. Under the orange streetlights Fish looked very *un*coated, very naked and bare. The coarse hair sprouting at the back of his head made a funny, puffy tuft.

The sight of him was too much for Alice. She stood up and began walking the pavement, blowing on her hands and beating them together. The rosy light coming off the lipstick display in the Boots window up-flushed her cheeks.

'Hurry, Arnie,' she said. 'Do your worst.'

I tucked Fish into the crook between my legs and my body, where he'd sat once before, back on my bed at home, in his jar. I drew my top down over him. He wasn't quite pressed against my skin but still I felt his dampness, this extreme, moist cold that was soaking off him. Most of all though I felt his floppiness. He was like a fragmenting jelly draped across my waist.

Alice quit pacing and slouched, one foot drooped in the gutter, her head firmly turned away. Eventually she sat back down on the raincoat though farther off than before, hugging herself. I shoved the indigo cloth in her direction but she ignored it. She began speaking in a wandering, drifting way, as if we were having a conversation before sleep, in the dark.

She'd been thinking, she said, that if we couldn't give Fish a proper water-burial, an earth burial might be the thing; in some green spot. We could hang paper streamers in the trees and paper lanterns and invite our families. Bury him crouched like a Celt, an African-Celt. Remember that Roman legionary guy Laura's dig-team had found? He had lain easily in English soil. If I thought about it, she felt, I could get to like the idea.

This wasn't a question so I didn't reply. I noticed that she was rocking herself as she spoke.

What was for sure, she went on, was that we had to disappear him. If Brocklebank came searching, we had to be stripped of suspicious signs.

'*Erase all signs,*' I whispered.

'Mind you,' said Alice slowly, 'I do keep wondering what our school's doing with an African embryo in its store cupboard at all, if that's what it is? One human embryo in the collection and it's an African? An African or half-African, shut up in a bottle? Could we say this to Brocklebank? Isn't this a bit suspicious? What gives you the right? How is it yours to own?'

She lent way forward as she pondered this; way forward, her nose almost touching her knees. Then she jolted back and her shoulder blades made a dull thud against the window of Boots.

'What had that GP in World War I been thinking?' she said even more slowly. The one who collected the mammalian embryos in the first place? Had I, Arnie, wondered about that? It had been one of Laura's questions. Had our Fish belonged to a student from Africa, lost and wandering the streets, missing their home? Or was he a Nigerian soldier's child, born during the War, the child of a man on leave in England? Or maybe an interpreter, some-one over in London for a few months' training, hanging out in pubs, hoping to talk to the natives?

Or was Fish's mother the African? Was she a nurse or a performer, a singer even?

Had the doctor, she asked, leaning over to me, *lent his quizzy hand* to some poor girl in trouble? Some young unmarried English Mum? Some unmarried young African Mum? If so, how long had our Fish been stranded in indignity in his Kerr jar, his burial delayed by decades?

But I was stuck in an earlier groove, an anxious one. I wanted to shrug off her thing about Fish's Mums and Dads, and family links. I didn't want to think about wombs. Wombs looped together with wombs.

'See, Alice,' I said, and had to cough to speak, 'about disappearing him and erasing all signs, I'm thinking how we can really? I mean, I stink of Fish. There are formalin stains on my clothes. Even before I left home on Thursday, Evie said I smelled of something strange.'

A sudden fit of yawning gripped Alice. She squinted at me between yawns.

'Laura always carries perfumed wet-wipes in her bag,' she mumbled optimistically. 'Though, yes definitely, Arnie Binns, there might be a bit of a whiff about you.'

I could have kicked her for saying this, except that the yawning made her face go blotchy, and the blotches gave her a defenceless, beaten look.

By now Fish had soaked me to the skin. The wet patch of him was creeping up my chest. The longer we sat the more he seemed to loosen and stretch thin and flounder about.

'Here's a thought,' Alice at last said fuzzily, sounding like she was sitting at a far off distance. 'Maybe we could leave a note for Brocklebank in the place where the jar used to stand on the storeroom shelf? A computer print-out, blunt, to-the-point. *Who said you could?* the note could read.

Or just the one word, *FREE!* In capital letters.

Or even, *Gone Home*. And then, *Anon*.

Telling everyone that the people who took him meant to do right by Fish.'

Still mumbling, Alice said Brocklebank told Jilly the lab embryo collection was to be sent to some anatomy museum in London. It was a convenient story, of course, a convenient plan. A nudge for us and, if true, a money-spinner for the school. The afternoons she'd worked in the lab no one'd ever said a thing about museums and special collections. No one'd breathed a word about the embryos under their coats of dust.

Well, we'd show the grown-ups how to do right by our foetus.

'But who has the right?' I said to myself. 'Who has the right to do right?' I thought of the journey south with Jim, my desperate boast about setting Fish free. Who could say *FREE!* with respect to our dead bottled baby? Or even *Gone Home*?

'The note could say nothing,' I said. 'It could be just a blank sheet. A sign that someone tried to explain.'

Alice rolled her shoulders impatiently and blew on her hands.

'This earth burial,' she said, catching my eye to check she still had my attention, 'you should give it a think.' It could be the way to go. Burial would show everyone that England—like Nigeria, like the Sudan—England, too, has been a place for Africans. The Winborne Clumps, for example, wouldn't they make a good airy place for Fish to lie, nested inside the roots of some tufty tree? And he'd have good company. Ancient people, after all, had prepared the way. People like Laura's tall Nubian officer with his long, bronzed bones.'

'We could all gather round in a circle,' Alice said. Evie could bring her special oils and beauty lotions to sweeten his limbs. Jilly, well, Jilly could bring a photo of Farouq, to represent the African side of things. And she could tell her stories, about how she, the Thames Valley tree-climber met the resident of the Nile's blue-green banks.

'And you could invite your humming taxi-driver friend,' Alice said pointedly, giving my arm a sudden jab with her finger. Was he the one who noticed the African marks on Fish's shoulders?

As for Laura, Laura could dig the hole. She'd had good training as a digger. She'd get stuck in and go deep.

And Alice herself, she'd do the dipping of the feet that Laura had asked for. Red food colour would do the trick just fine. She'd be happy to make her sister happy. To claim Fish for Africa, a Nile baby no matter what.

And finally, Alice said, 'You, Arnie—it will be your job to place Fish in his resting-place and pad his grave with one of your fleeces.'

Again she bent double like she was reading an invisible text off the top of her trainers.

And me finally; and me. But no, it didn't work for me. It didn't feel real somehow. I could have repeated word-for-word everything Alice was saying but I couldn't *see* the scene she drew. It felt very far distant from this street gleaming with rosy posters, and the ancient river racing blindly past our backs.

A white man walking a black dog approached on our side of the street. The man's nose jutted and his mouth was bitter, but it was his bounding, eager-to-please dog that bothered me. Frolicsome dogs like to sniff out new friends. From as far back as Thursday I'd worried about sniffing dogs.

I put my hand under my top to check on Fish. My finger made contact with some part of him, ribcage or back.

Whatever it was felt like moist cheddar, just about crumbling under my touch.

The man flashed us a glance, as we might have expected. We were after all sitting in his path. In return Alice gave an ear-to-ear smile. 'Parents!' she said with a silly, fed-up look, as if a delayed and apologetic Jilly was about to drive into view and offer a lift home.

But the man wasn't bothered. He sidestepped us with quick legs. The dog managed a nuzzle at the raincoat in the area of my feet. For a moment his leash stood taut and dangerous, then the man dragged him on.

The pair vanished around a bend in the street, in the direction we had come earlier, towards the bus stop. Not long after a woman in heavy boots and a black coat with a feathery trim followed in their path. She passed us with her chin tucked down and her eyes trained on the paving stones in front of her. I waited till her steps, too, had died away. From a distance now came a low, thudding, Saturday-night sound.

At last I lifted Fish up and pulled him from under my top. Alice had to turn her head away. I couldn't blame her. The truth was he wasn't looking good, not very good at all. In fact, there's no other way of putting it, Fish was coming apart. Breaking up. His limbs were fraying at the edges, all over, at his elbows, ankles, wrists. The gashes on his shoulders that Jim had called "sick-a-tricks" looked more like cracks, the skin splitting and bursting open like drying mud.

'Was any of this Katrina's doing?' I wondered; tried to stop myself but couldn't. Had she dried him out in that graveyard and speeded his decay? Or, worse, had she done something directly to him, something hard and wrong, to create these furrows in his skin?

No-no-*no*! I sat up straight to keep my head clear. Fish had carried just the one special incision, even this morning, and that was the razor-cut that Alice had made.

Her cut was still there, though pretty well camouflaged by the hundred splits and cracks that ran criss-cross all over Fish's body.

I pressed my finger into what had been his belly and felt it give way. I withdrew my finger and he gave a popping sound, as if he was already semi-liquid. I couldn't stand holding him but I knew I couldn't lay him down. On the ground he might spread like a blob of toothpaste and I'd have to scrape him off the stones.

Alice kept her head trained in the opposite direction. I had to say the obvious.

'Alice,' I said, my heart in my mouth, my mouth dry as dust, 'Fish is kind of melting. If we don't do something fast he'll vanish.'

'Poor thing,' she said through tense lips. Then after a pause, she said again. 'Poor thing.'

I wanted her to see him while he still looked a bit like himself. So she'd be able to see that her cut by now was the very least of Fish's troubles.

I touched her elbow but she didn't budge. She had not the least desire to turn around. By the time she spoke again she sounded less mournful.

'It was to be expected, Arnie, he's so old. He's been preserved in liquid a long time. He's been trawled around so much.'

Her hand tried to make contact with my arm, my shoulder, but didn't quite stretch the distance.

'What can we do?' I pleaded. 'If we put him back in his jar he might dissolve completely.'

'Then don't put him in the jar. Bundle him in your cloth here.'

As I made moves to wrap Fish she turned at last. She watched me pulling the edges of the indigo fabric tight together. When I tied the corners, his swaddling bands of Nigerian cotton, she lent a finger to hold the knot. I left the top of his head exposed. It was the only part of him still solid. Then I laid him down on the raincoat between us.

'It gives us something to tell Brocklebank, I suppose,' she said with a sigh. 'Yes, Mr Brocklebank, we can say, we *did* unfortunately take the human specimen, the *African* specimen, from your valuable collection; we're so very sorry. We were curious, you see. Curiosity with intent is good. But, ever so sorry; we can't return him; there's no way. The anatomical museum will have to miss him. Here's the empty jar to prove it. Thing is, he began to disappear. We couldn't help it. We were keen for him not to but in the end he did. In the end there was nothing left of him. Nothing but a bit of spine like a fish bone on a plate.'

'I can't imagine saying that,' I said. 'It sounds like a lie.'

'We might have to lie,' said Alice. 'Look, do you mind if I put my head on your shoulder? Don't know about you but I'm tired. Tired, and really sick of waiting, too.'

* * *

A chunk of vacant time then faced us. When it began it was about ten. When it ended it must have been long past midnight. During this time Alice slept and I kept watch. That's to say, I had my eyes half-open, on guard for dogs, but wasn't fully conscious. I didn't want to be conscious. I didn't want to think of Fish breaking up and disappearing. Our gentle creature, my fellow traveller, lying here on the ground beside us like a sleeping baby but all the while splitting, cracking and going to seed.

Somewhere around one o'clock it seemed to grow warmer. Alice stretched and made narrow slits of her eyes. Small sounds came from the back of her throat. I lent my head against hers.

251

Somewhere around half-past-one or close to two Laura rang Alice on Phoenix's mobile. Alice had the phone stashed in her raincoat pocket, which turned out to be just beside Fish's sleeping head.

Laura sounded loud and apologetic. I could hear her clearly from my place beside Alice. It had been a *brilliant* gig though it had *gone on*, she shouted. As it was Phoe's friends they couldn't really *leave*. *Where* were we anyway? Still Heathrow? *What*, where was that?

Minutes later she called again. She'd meant to say that there were important messages on her voicemail for Arnie. Two of them. He should listen to them in full, soon as possible. The messages were both from Evie. One was an oh-my-darling and why-didn't-you-say-you missed-your-father and I'd-have-tried-to-understand-and-done-something-about-it; *et cetera* . . . you can imagine.

The second message was sharper, Laura said, a lot sharper. Evie made it sound like an afterthought but actually it was as important. Evie wanted to report that Arnie's dad had called. He'd called to ask if Arnie was home yet. He'd said, Next time you visit we'll do better. And Katrina sends her best. His exact words: "Katrina hopes Arnie Binns is as well as he can be."

You could hear Evie curling her lips on the voicemail, Laura said.

Though Alice didn't have to, she repeated Laura's information virtually word-for-word.

She was still mid-flow when I pulled Katrina's carved key-ring out of my pocket and began to trace my finger around its carved lines. Almost as familiar to me as the cursive *Kerr* on Fish's jar. Katrina hoped I was as well as I could be. Why did that make me feel so let down, so weirdly *flat*?

Alice shot me a puzzled look. Then she dragged herself up-right, yawned, stretched, began again to pace the pavement.

'What's the matter? You went all the way north to see your dad? You missed him but you met the girlfriend? At least there was someone there for you.'

'I liked her, Katrina, the girlfriend. She's the one who thought—'

'Yes, I wondered.'

'I didn't mention her name before.'

'She's the person who gave you the idea Fish belongs to Africa. Didn't take a genius to work that one out.'

Although it took a while I now managed it, to give Alice the Harehills story. Putting my secret mask into my pocket, I began to tell her almost everything about last night, including about Katrina's broken weeping and her beautiful wrapper dress. I told her how she'd swaddled Fish and pressed him to her like a real child and how she'd arranged the photographs of the babies on the stone in the graveyard. How I'd left her on her own with Fish. How Fish was the witness to whatever she'd asked the powers and energies she believed in to give her.

And I told Alice not to worry about the cut that she, Alice, had given Fish: the sick-a-tricks. All babies who insist on dying must bear cuts, I said, to mark them on the rebound. Katrina, without herself fully realising, had taught me this.

'As if I was worrying,' Alice glowered, but I didn't let this faze me.

I put my hand on the bundle that was Fish, his exposed skull gleaming like a fading light bulb. There seemed almost nothing left inside his parcel of cloth.

Suddenly I couldn't stand it any longer, sitting helpless as Fish melted, so I joined Alice in her pacing of the Boots frontage. We began to walk in opposite directions along the same stretch of the pavement and to turn at the same instant. At each halfway point, at the shop entrance, we bumped shoulders. The bumping gradually grew harder and stronger, till we were knocking each other off course. We made each other stagger and stumble about, and chased after one another, and bumped again for good measure, beginning to *ouf* and then to giggle.

When Laura and Phoenix at last arrived we were standing leant over, catching our breath, the backs of our legs against the warm Boots' window. Laura was at the wheel of the Fiat, her mobile clamped to her ear. She veered the car abruptly in our direction and stalled it to a halt in front of our encampment. She flung open her door.

'Hello, you two,' she gave a bright smile, 'you look like you've been out all night.'

I saw Phoe on the backseat of the car, fast asleep.

'Flipping heck, Laura, did you want us to die of exposure? What took you so long?'

'Steady,' said Laura, 'You merry wanderers are hardly the people to ask that. I've spent ages looking for this place. It's too late at night to read maps properly. As in, I'm too exhausted and the car light doesn't work and we don't have a torch. And Phoe wasn't much help, as you can see.'

She raised her voice when she said his name but he didn't stir.

'Anyhow, before I forget, this bloke called Jim phoned for Arnie, just this minute. Jim Noelson. *Late as it is*, his words. He sounded funky and very nice. He wanted to check you were safe home, Arnie. His phone remembered the number you called earlier, when you reached Alice. I told him you were fine, you were nearly home, you were cool.'

'As cool as cool,' said Alice. 'In fact, freezing.'

'Alice, I tried my best.' Laura stepped on to the pavement. 'Arnie, Jim said to let him know about developments. He's in London all weekend.'

And then Laura screamed—a strangulated sound, like a wild animal's cry.

Her foot had made contact with my bundle. Her footprint had noticeably changed the look of my bundle, had pancaked it down.

Her mouth was a distorted shape.

'Oh God, oh my God, that thing—it *squelched*.'

She hopped about, curling her instep around her knee.

Alice pulled her close. She stage-whispered, 'The thing you know about.'

Laura fell immediately silent. She came over and hung an arm across my shoulders, a too-warm arm.

'I'm sorry, Arnie,' she said, 'I'm really sorry. God, it felt like only liquid inside that bundle. It could be that your specimen body isn't keeping. It does look a lot like it. We'll have to act fast to find it a place to lie.'

To Phoenix the word *body* must've worked as a prompt. He sat up suddenly, blinked hard, looked out.

'We tried to find it a resting place,' said Alice. 'But there was nowhere here. Nowhere without rats.'

Phoenix opened the back car-door and uncoiled his long legs.

'Alternatively,' he said slowly, in a sleepy, slightly trembling voice , like some meditating holy man who'd not used his vocal cords for months, 'you could alternatively commit a body, any body, to flame.'

Alice gave a sniff and ignored him. Laura walked over to the car, leaned up against the boot beside him and rubbed her legs against his legs.

'Whatever we do,' she said, 'there's red nail polish here in my bag. That we could use for the toes. It would do the job just fine.'

My skin was crawling.

But once Phoe had grasped hold of an idea, we discovered, he wasn't one to let it go in a hurry.

'If water won't work for you and earth doesn't grab you,' he said to me, holding up his cigarette lighter, 'try fire, like I said. Refining fire.'

He clicked the lighter and blue flame danced in the air.

Laura's boyfriend, I then realised, might have more going for him than Alice had let on till now.

When no one responded, he went on, 'Make it a water-and-fire burial. Seeing as there's the river, we build a raft, we bind the body onto it. We light our pyre and it drifts away. The flames get it before any predator can.'

'A burial fit for a Viking prince,' Laura said loyally.

'Or an African princeling,' said Alice, her sudden involvement taking me by surprise.

She was pinching her eyes in my direction as if to point to a secret message I should be picking up.

'Gets rid of all signs, doesn't it, Arnie?' she said softly. 'And sends him in the direction of Africa. And we leave a note for Brocklebank just the same. A blank note even, if you like, put in the place where the jar used to stand.'

Laura said, 'There'll be packing cases piled around somewhere that we can use to make the raft. Here behind Boots or one of the other shops. We need cardboard packaging. And that tough plastic banding, to tie him on with.'

'I don't want his toes done red,' I said, talking to Phoenix.

Laura didn't look as crestfallen as I'd expected.

I drove my message home, 'We don't know that he has toes, not to mention feet, left.'

'In that case,' said Laura, 'We could maybe try a different Egyptian touch.'

I felt myself go cold, colder even than in the graveyard in Harehills.

Laura pressed on. 'In ancient Egypt they loosened the mouth of the corpse with a blade or a pen to set its soul free. So it could join the after-life without any obstacle in its way.' Like Phoenix she now talked directly at me. 'What do you think, Arnie? Before we put this thing of yours on its raft, I say we open its mouth and release its soul.'

To this day I don't know from what deep place my courage erupted.

I said, 'OK, let's do that. Let's claim him for Africa any way possible. There's just one thing I want to ask. It means a lot to me.' I hardly paused before adding, 'I want Alice to do the job.'

'You've got to be joking,' said Alice, but she knew I wasn't.

I saw her hand move down to her pocket and check for her blades. But I already knew they were there because I'd heard them chink.

She spoke under her breath. 'Arnie, not a second time.'

'It's not cutting,' I said quietly. 'Not this time. It's *uncutting*. You use the flat of one of your knives. Fish's lips are open already. All you do is open them wider.'

'How do I know I can? I'm bloody cold and my hands aren't steady. What if my blade misses? What if I give him a new cut in spite of myself?'

I tried to make my thoughts clean and plain enough to say this most important thing.

'Alice,' I said, 'if you believe that Fish belongs even a bit to Africa, then let this happen. You said it yourself. Let's try to set him free.'

Her expression was closed. Reaching into her pocket she threw a look in her sister and Phoenix's direction. 'You turn your backs,' she said. 'This is total bar—barbarism as it is.'

There was the bell-like sound of her blades moving against one another in her pocket. In this way the matter was decided between us.

Alice hunkered down beside Fish. But what she drew from her trousers pocket was not the velvet pouch of knives as I'd anticipated. What slid into the chilly, early morning Richmond air was her grandad's cut-throat razor; the one I'd last seen on that unhappy, rainy day when we, I mean she, dissected the dog's eye.

It was hard for me to imagine what Alice was feeling as she crouched over Fish with the sharp silver blade held out in front of her like a lance. The first time she put a knife to Fish's body it had almost been an accident. Now it was different: it was an act with intent. With intent I saw her pull back the patterned cotton cloth and lay bare Fish's pale skull. With intent, but gently, she cupped his jaw and brought his head round to face her. There was the crumpled stare I now knew so well, the squashed nose and grey mouth. She jutted her blade forward.

It was only later she told me how Fish's dead lips resisted her as if he were *some stiff rubber doll. Or better, an empty Coke bottle, a bit of rubbish.* The body's lips might have been pursed slightly open but even so she'd had to prod and to yank. She'd had to imagine that Fish was a vessel, a balloon literally filled with spirit and ready to be popped.

'*And pop the balloon I did,*' she said.

As for me, even at the time I felt what it took. I felt the fear that poured off my friend in a stream thick and black as crude oil. I was the only one there to feel it. By then Phoenix had led Laura, dry-retching, around the side of Boots.

I was proud of Alice that day. She did what she did with care. And she put her grandad's blade to good use.

Then she stood up and looked me straight in the eye, long and hard. She wiped the tip of the blade on the soft cloth it came wrapped in. She wiped it a long time.

Phoenix called from around the corner of Boots. He and Laura, he said, were off in search of cardboard packaging for our funeral raft.

Alice wound the soft cloth around the cut-throat blade and slid the blade-and-cloth back into her pocket.

Then she walked off down the street with her arms held high over her head and her fingers splayed like wings.

And me, I turned my back on Fish's body for just a moment. I wanted only to catch my breath. Within seconds I'd be turning to deal with what was left of him; I'd be back there for him. So I did not blank out. Time did not stop. Nothing out of the ordinary appeared to happen. Though I was exhausted I remember I felt calm and almost relieved. I walked just a few paces in the opposite direction to Alice to catch my breath.

I will never stop puzzling about what happened next. I have thought about it till my head hurts and my heart races and jumps in my chest. I have told this story to myself over and over, like I'm doing now, and I get to this particular point and pause; I cannot explain.

I may be a believer in spirit and silver-skinned Elves and other invisible beings who drift about in a world parallel to this one. But what spirit was it that broke Fish's jar into a hundred pieces? This I cannot tell. What spirit atomised Katrina's indigo cloth and vanished it away, thick and robust as it was?

No ghost dog or man could have whooshed down that street at the speed of light and done these things.

So I looked down the brightly lit, deserted street. I breathed hard. I remember thinking what a waste it was to burn so much light for so few passersby. Far off I heard a dog barking in a lost, uncertain way, as if his owner wasn't home. Then I turned; swivelled on one heel. I saw clearly that in the other direction, too, the street was empty. Alice like Laura and Phoenix had disappeared around the corner of some building. There wasn't a soul about, if soul is the right word. There wasn't a person or a cat or a rat to be seen. There was no sound. And there was no Fish. No bundle, no cloth, no Fish. Only his jar broken into a hundred tiny fragments and a few dark, oily blobs left on the paving.

I shouted out then, shouted and shouted, '*Alice! Phoe! Alice!*' whirling about like a mad thing. I darted in one direction; I darted in the other. Alice burst out of the lane that led down to the river. Laura and Phoenix emerged from a side road opposite. Phoenix threw the squashed cardboard box he was carrying into the street.

At once they saw what the matter was. '*Whaaat?*' whistled Phoenix on a long in-breath. It was the only thing anyone said. For a moment he put his arm around my neck. Then he took Laura's hand and set off down the street. They peered into a rubbish bin, and then another, their heads close together, Laura shooting me furtive backward glances over her shoulder.

If they suspected I was the perpetrator of whatever had happened I didn't blame them. I could see how much it looked that way.

Alice didn't say a thing. I saw she was still shivering. I also saw that she knew what I knew. That we wouldn't be seeing Fish's body again in a hurry.

For about an hour we fine-combed every nook and alley that we could find up and down that High Street but it was from the start a half-hearted, foot-dragging sort of search. When, around four in the morning, a newspaper truck came grinding down through its gears and drew up at a newsagent across the way, we took it as our signal to call it a day. Laura marched wordlessly over to Phoenix's Fiat and unlocked the doors. Alice handed me my willow-pattern bag. I picked up the glass-and-copper top of Fish's jar where it lay beside Alice's raincoat. It was, unlike the jar itself, cracked but not broken. I picked up Alice's raincoat, too.

260

Phoenix was the last to get into the car. He scoured the street for a few minutes longer. Then he took his flattened cardboard box and made an attempt to sweep pieces of Fish's broken jar into the gutter.

'Leave it, Phoe,' said Laura.

She shifted herself from the driver's seat into the passenger seat and handed him his car-keys through the window.

Ending...

A quotation on pink card, carefully printed in Laura's neat hand, lies on her desk, waiting to be blu-tacked to her computer.

> *Now if this text be recited over him, he shall come forth and thrive.*
> *He shall escape from every fire and none of the foul things shall encompass him.*

* * *

I, Arnie, now woke from a dreamless sleep. Alice was beside me, her eyes open and staring. Behind her head towered a grey dawn sky. A lopsided moon was setting over the hazy buildings and trees and yet more buildings of London. A continuous ribbon of motorway stretched in front of Phoenix's skimming car. The tiny lights of the city twinkled all around us. If you watched them closely you saw that they were one by one going out.

Seeing me awake, Alice said, 'We were lost for a while back there in Richmond, but Phoenix got us out. We're on the road home now, Arnie. And Evie knows you're coming. I called her for you. Jilly has hot chocolate waiting. She just called us. The phone must have woken you.'

I reached for her hand, I don't know why, and fastened on two fingers.

Without pulling away she whispered, 'I've been thinking, there are other things we can do. We could find a dead frog or something and bury that in place of Fish, along with his jar lid, if it makes you feel better. If it gives us a grave we can go visit.'

'We don't have to go to that kind of trouble,' I said. 'I'm all right without doing all that. I don't know why but for me it's OK that Fish went off, disappeared himself, whatever. It was somewhere by the rushing Thames after all. You could imagine him drifting downstream, making his way home.'

I shifted my position so I could lean my head against her headrest, close to her shoulder, a bit like we were before, outside the Richmond Boots, except that then I had been her pillow. I wondered how I could feel so peaceful, empty but quiet and peaceful. By rights I should feel cheated, hard done by, obstructed, but I didn't.

I tried to imagine that Fish had found his watery bed somehow and come to rest.

I leant back still half-asleep and looked out at the long, streaky clouds and thought about that *somehow*, about Fish somehow coming to rest.

Maybe, I thought to myself, it was Alice's doing. It was Alice who, driven crazy by her job of freeing Fish's lips, had rushed back into the street at that moment when none of us was looking. Maybe she'd grabbed dissolving Fish in his cloth and run him to the river after all, crashing into his jar on her way. Maybe she'd slung him in with a straight lob of her arm so that for a moment he and his cloth were spread-eagled in the air, and then she'd heard him go plop. For the time being she couldn't say anything but one day, one day I knew she would.

Or maybe Fish really did collapse in on himself, I thought, just as he'd threatened to do. He'd been breaking up for days; he'd lived in his Kerr jar many long years. At the end of the day he'd fallen in on himself and left those oily marks on the paving as his signature.

And one of us, Alice or Phoe, had stumbled over his jar by accident, and broken it into hundreds of pieces.

Or maybe, again, miracles happen. Maybe a silver-suited spirit did visit us. Maybe an angel came flying down that blank street and, when Fish's ghost was freed at last, cradled him away, wrapped in his midnight-blue swaddling bands.

So, at the end of the day, Fish had wound his way home, trailing no light, no clouds, nothing to mark him.

There was a plane overhead, stacked high in the London sky and preparing to land. I followed it with my eyes. It was full of people buckling their seatbelts and stretching their swollen legs, I imagined, but for us it was just a circling light, hardly bigger than a fading star. I thought about how huge the sky was and how huge the world, and how full the world was of lives as well as of dead things and how incredible many of these lives were and how short. And I thought about how life catches you unawares. How, while you're looking the other way, a whole chapter in your life has been noiselessly winding itself down—a chapter about being twelve-and-a-half and searching for your Dad and minding an alien visitor and finding out at the end of your journey that your place is with your friend...or friends. There's a ton of things difficult to explain unless you live through them.

I watched the plane for sometime till, suddenly, the light of the rising sun caught its windows and it flared for a moment like an orange comet and then disappeared behind the high, blue-grey cloud.

'Like a supernova,' said Alice, her eyes on the plane just the same as me.

'Like *this*,' I said. I don't know why, and squeezed her hand hard.